DISCONTENTS
THE DISAPPEARANCE OF A YOUNG RADICAL

Published After the Disappearance of Emory Walden

By James Wallace Birch

ISBN: 9781976800436

Imprint: Independently published

This is a second edition, first print publication (2018). The first edition of this book was published as an e-book in 2011.
pb3.2

This book is dedicated to a long lost friend.

As the publisher, I do not know where Emory Walden is.
So please stop harassing me.
- James Wallace Birch

Take an absolute. Draw it out to its logical extreme.
Take a look at it again.
You will find it has turned into its opposite.
- Unknown

FOREWORD

Summer, 2011

To the Reader,

It all started because of a letter I received.

I'd just lost my job, and the girl, Janessa. And who knew where the mortgage payments were going to come from? After the layoff I stopped at a gas station on my way home and bought a pack of cigarettes. My first in years.

For some time before, I'd been all around feeling terrible and sad as though maybe I was making big mistakes with my life that I didn't understand. Things that'd once seemed harmless now kept me from sleeping, or going into restaurants to have a meal. Then, I was jobless and alone.

When I got home Janessa was gone and so was Max, our dog, along with the food and water bowls and the bag of dog chow. A few orange and brown kibbles were left scattered on the floor by the refrigerator. There wasn't a note.

I sat on the loveseat facing the blank TV I was still paying off and smoked another cigarette (who cared about whether the place stunk of smoke when the bank reclaimed it?). That's when I saw the envelope in a stack of mail. The envelope looked like it'd been used as a doormat. The letter inside looked as though it'd been typewritten and a good bit of dirt had seeped into the envelope and it got all over the floor (who cared? Have another drag).

The letter began like this "*James, it's Emory from high school. Don't throw this letter away. Please read it.*"

Emory. I had not seen or heard from him in maybe

eight years. And I had been glad it was that way. In the last few years when he was a renegade idol the police were looking for, I'd hear him talked about on the news and I'd felt nothing but hate for him. I felt no sympathy when I heard he'd vanished and everyone began speculating that he was dead. I crumbled the paper in my hand, threw it against the wall and cursed his name, and my life, and the wall that would soon belong to some bank.

A few days later I picked the letter up. I guess I was lonely and thought maybe I'd get some nostalgia from reading Emory's words. Even if it was hateful nostalgia, it was better than feeling nothing at all.

The letter read "*I need your help. This is serious. You're the only one I can go to. I'd like to think you're over all that. I hope you've forgiven me. I've forgiven you. So much has changed. Please do this for me as I know you would've done before all that happened.*"

"*If all cannot be forgiven then here is a tangible incentive: there's money. It's enough to make it worth it. Trust me. When you've done what I'm asking for in this letter, the location of the cash will be clear to you. This is no joke. I promise you that. If you're still reading – thank you, thank you!*"

I'm not sure why I continued reading after that. Had I seen him on the streets begging for a dollar the week before, I'd have gladly pushed him away. So why care to know what he wanted help with? Maybe it was the promise of money – if only some small amount. Maybe it was the ambivalence I now felt toward everything in my life, as though helping him or not helping him didn't matter the way nothing you can do really affects big things like the moon and tide or the process of birth and death. Or maybe it was want for the memory of the days when the streets of our neighborhood were newly paved; like I could do something for the friend I had then and that friend would somehow be able to appreciate it, rather than the

Emory who I'd grown to hate since all that had happened between us. I'm not sure if any of that makes sense.

At any rate, I kept on reading. "*There's something I want you to publish for me*," he wrote. "*It's to clear up what happened to me. The only way people know things is through the slanted news reports and a corrupt half picture. I wrote my story out – just as it happened. By now it's been months. I want whoever will listen to know about some people and things that happened. Then, maybe they'll think differently about me and know the truth about what became of me. I hope you understand. Please read it. Another envelope will arrive in about a week with further instructions."*

"*There's something called a data drop. Have you heard of this?"* I hadn't. *"It's these flash drives in public places plastered in the wall or under a chair. You can plug in your computer and add and copy files. Do you remember the bar we'd get served at in high school and SHE threw up in the men's bathroom stall while you held her hair? And do you remember under the bench where Reed used to hide cigars by the lake? Go to those places. Take your laptop and there's going to be a file on each flash drive named JAMES.emy. When you have both files on your computer in the same folder you can click on one and it'll open with the password. The password is the title of her favorite song (no spaces, no caps). That's my story. That's what really happened. People need to know."*

"*I don't know how to say thanks. But I know I'll never see you again. – Emory Walden*"

I went. But first I vacillated about it for a while. I'd like to be able to say that just like that I went, straight over to those places that day and all with the letter in my pocket. But that's not true. It wasn't that simple for me. After all, Emory had stolen the first girl I'd ever loved.

Eventually I did go and when I got the files in the folder and entered the password, which I struggled with the most, I opened the file. I printed it and drove to the lake with a flashlight and stayed up all night smoking and reading, finishing as the sun reached about a quarter of the way into the sky the next morning.

I could not believe it. I sat in my car and cried for some time. Then I went home and slept, and when I woke up late that evening I checked the mail. There was an envelope just as before.

The second letter began with a brief and general apology. Then there was a thank you note for reading the book and the instructions. He figured I'd gone and gotten the money already. I hadn't.

There is one thing I'd like you to know. I had thought the story would be about me and what'd happened years ago between me, Emory, and the girl who came between us before he went in the direction he did, way before Europe. But it wasn't. I guess that was a bit self-centered for me to think but it made sense because I was the one Emory contacted. But the story was about things that'd happened in the years after I, and the people we grew up with, had last seen or spoken to Emory. But although it's not about what happened between us, I think in a way it is. At any rate, it affected me deeply because I think I understand what Emory meant by the whole thing. I've since quit smoking. Again.

I began the process of bringing his story to light. For sake of brevity I'll summarize the instructions:

1. Editing: Emory asked me to read it through and edit it the best I could. He didn't care that I wasn't a professional and all that. What was important to him was, he didn't want what he called "*captains of industry*" "*co-opting*" the story and turning it into a mainstream fake "*based on a true story* [thing] *with predictable characters and plot lines and a market-researched, crowd-pleasing ending.*" He wanted it to be authentic. The story exactly as it'd happened. So I'm sorry it isn't perfect in terms of

editing. But I did the best I could. If you find any mistakes, please take it in stride, and send them my way.

2. Publishing: I had to self-publish because no publishing house was going to accept abdicating control over the content, editorial process, etc. I figured an e-book was best because I don't have money to pay for print copies.

3. Promoting: He wanted people to know – that was the whole point. Maybe I struggle with promotion the most. I'm still trying to figure things out and would appreciate any help.

In closing, I've done everything he asked me to do to try to get the story out. I hope you'll read it. And I hope you'll get others to read it. I'm sure he'd thank you if he could. He wasn't perfect. And some say he deserved what happened. But he was my friend once. And I miss him. And no, I didn't bother to go find the money. I don't care to. I'm doing alright.

What follows is his story.

- James Wallace Birch

PART ONE

EXIGENCIES

Sometime in 2010

1

TOMORROW THEY COME. They come and put me to sleep. There will be a tube placed in the vein in my wrist, I am told, and I will drift off to sleep in no time. I don't even have to leave my bed. They can just put me under right here in my room and wheel me over to the operating chamber. I don't even have to see the room where they'll cut me open in my brain or something and stand over me in masks speaking hospital jargon. I don't have to see the room that I might die in.

At times like these. That's what they say. "At times like these." At times like these, I always hear that. I hate that phrase. "At times like these you've got to think positively." Truth is, there probably won't ever be more times like these. You face down death maybe twice if you're lucky. And at this time, this one time, this very likely only ever one time, I don't want to spend it staring at this ceiling lying to myself that I'll see the sky again. And I certainly don't want to think about her. I want to think about Fletcher Spivey and how he ever found me. Without him, I'd be nothing.

Think positively?

Everything's been compromised. Infiltrated. I just know it.

For all the nights I've been in here, something on this ceiling hasn't looked right. I stare. I toss it around in my head and get nowhere. And I hear people out in the hall, see the light under the door. I just wish I could hear what they were saying.

We all want to live. But somebody wants me dead. If I can figure out why, maybe I can save the movement. There will be new leadership. Ideas don't die with people. It must go on, with or without me. We've come too far.

Think back. Figure it out. It's my last chance.

Think positively.

* * * * *

It was New Year's Day 2009 and there I was standing in the rain holding the January edition of an airline magazine staring at a picture of a restaurant, the paper swelling in blotches. A bored man, somewhat older than I, pointed me down the street as he poked at his cigarette beneath an overhang. He grunted when I asked how far and steered around my rucksack perched high on my back. In seconds he was landscape, just part of the painting, wandering with raindrops.

The effeminate steward on the airline from New York told me he knew a guy who was a waiter, or a bartender, or a chef. I couldn't remember. I'd just returned from Ireland via Dublin through a New York connecting flight and was back in D.C.

The rain bled through my windbreaker and I was starting to wonder how much further this restaurant was. I pushed on unsure of any long-term intentions. Five minutes down the street, clinging to the buildings for shield from the lonely sky. I started to wonder if I was lost. Then, there across the street, the blue neon of human progress glowed through the downpour and that sense of warmth that only an advertisement can give you had me pacing towards the light.

"The Ritchfield Steakhouse"

I was in the door and out the rain and the hostess, young

and listless, had never seen a half-sober backpacker in puddles before. If I stood here long enough I may disappear, she told herself. But I was heading in her direction and she gave me her disappointment with a shift of her weight. "Table for one?"

"No, thanks." I ate on the plane.

So where's this Peter guy? I hung around by the hostess who was pretending she was alone while a waiter went looking for Peter, the flight attendant's pal. I compared the picture in the magazine to the real thing, glancing down then up and around, and back down to the swollen magazine paper. Reality and advertisements. The same. Different. The glossiness of fantasy and rows of smiling faces versus finished mahogany wood in faded light and relative emptiness. Aside from this high school girl hostess fiddling with her cell phone and a few servers and bus boys, two customers in suits sat in a corner eating under the dim light.

The waiter stuck his head out of the kitchen door as light beamed out over his shoulders. He called me "you", which may as well have been my name. "You, come on back," he said. So I weaved through the maze of empty tables with lights hung low, rows of silverware wrapped neatly in cloth, past all of everything I was not at this moment, and towards the light. The two dining men ceased talking and glanced up at me. No one in America had ever seen a wet backpacker before. I shuffled past, clothes sopping. Slosh, slosh, slosh on dark wood flooring. People in posh restaurants need to get to know more people like me, I thought.

This guy Peter stood in the kitchen, propping himself with a hand, fingers folded over the edge of a steel table when I walked through the door. The steel shined, Peter shined, his teeth shined, his belt buckle shined, his shoes shined. Everything shined. When we shook hands it was almost as if he was expecting me.

I told him about the steward, Roberto, and the conversation we had. He gave me his interest with a slight tilt of the head and a prolonged stare into my eyes. I told him the basics of my situation: I'd just got back into town and this was my first stop. I needed a job.

He started asking about Roberto. How *isss* he? Peter hadn't seen him in half a year. Is his hair still long? Does he look like he's doing well? Peter missed him, hoped to see him soon. I told Peter that Roberto and I were good friends and I used some made-up anecdote I used to tell people over in Europe in situations like this.

Peter smiled. He missed Roberto. In the back of his mind he was picturing Roberto right here in front of him. But it was me and I needed a job. I needed some money to put food in my stomach. But I played along. How do you know Roberto? I asked. They saw each other for a while. Then Roberto got the airline job. With a sudden dab of jealousy on his tongue, were Roberto and I a *thing*? No, no. I'm not… well, it's better to leave things ambiguous with people like Peter. I needed a job.

"He's a great looking guy, but I'm involved," I said.

By the end of it I had a job as a busboy. Peter was reminiscing with a smile and smoothing out the wrinkles in his pants with his hands as if Roberto just might walk through the door any minute.

Exit bound, I ducked out the kitchen into the dark cave of the restaurant. I felt Peter's eyes pressed against my backside. The customers had resumed their meal and their conversation. Shadowy facades exchanging words. Of course, I didn't know it then, but I would meet the older of the two men some months later at that very same table.

2

I KNOCKED. BANGED. NO ANSWER. Nothing. I rattled the knob. Unlocked. Inside and glancing around. There, on the couch.

"Yo."

There was a bong on the table and a jar of weed. He was passed out with a lighter on his lap, head on the armrest, the lamplight on the end table illuminating stubs of hair on his shaven head. The TV blaring. African leopards hunting zebra.

I set my bag down and fed myself peanut butter on crackers from the cabinet. From the fridge, a glass of expired milk. I stood and watched him sleep as I ate at the sink. Were I back in Europe I'd have robbed this place. Sold the weed. Sold the bong. Taken the food. The clothes. Raided the drawers for valuables. Maybe I'd find a laptop and selling that would've bought me a plane ticket. How the hell do you think I had gotten back here to the States?

I finished up, wiped the crumbs with a sponge and quaffed the rest of the milk before washing out the glass. Then I pulled out a travel bottle of mouthwash that I kept in my pocket and rinsed. I walked over towards him lying there and he hadn't so much as changed his breathing pattern. So I got undressed, took off the sopping windbreaker, the soaked sweatshirt and undershirt, wet shoes, soggy socks blue with ink bled from shoes, pants heavy and dark with rain. I stripped down to my underwear with the wet cotton papier-mâchéd to my sack, found a place on the floor and called it a night.

I awoke to the sun burning through clasped eyelids and there was that moment of fear where you've forgotten where you are, that childhood vulnerability of waking from a nightmare into the darkness. You sleep in so many new places and still you never get used to it. Then my eyes focused in on the bong and I was right back in the room. Pat Drassell was stuffing a wad of hamburger into his mouth with a fork. The meat was just sitting there on a plate, no bun. He cut off a piece, dipped it into sauce, then took another bite before noticing I'd awoken.

Pat was in his boxers with no shirt on, the dough of his belly patched with hair. He was glad to see me and we shook hands and he offered me a bong load but I quit that trash when I graduated college. Pat never did. Pat barely graduated just a few months prior, two years behind schedule, and I had no idea what he was doing these days or how he afforded this apartment. He probably was doing just this: smoking weed, watching the Animal Channel and eating an assortment of meats in his underwear on his couch. His daddy was probably fronting the bill for this flat and the nice furnishings and I doubted he had a job. But he was glad to see me and I'd neither an apartment nor a job worth a damn. Years before we were great friends. The kind you have in high school. The kind you get into trouble with. The kind you'd lie and break curfew for. The kind you'll never have again.

"I've read about you," he chewed. "Wondered where you were. I mean I've heard things, on the Internet. Read them. It's weird you know, your way over there in Britain and Ireland and all that doing your thing and we learn about you second hand." To hear someone you know tell you they've read about you makes your actions feel criminal. Like your mother saying, 'I heard what you did.' No matter what it was you did, it was judged only through her eyes.

From time to time life gets like that for all of us. You push, you kick and scream, you slam your fist and dive deeper into the opaque. There exists a sense within telling us that what we believe in, our goals, our focus, and conviction is right - that if we simply persist through adversity we will succeed. For a moment you almost have a Voice. And then there comes the deluge, the time where the mothers of the world see all the muscle you put into something as bad, wrong, deplorable. Every action was a mistake. The flame subsides, the wick trails off into smoke, and what was once a fiery passion is now a hangover.

That kind of thing happened to me once, years ago, before Europe. But not anymore. Now, there was a moment where I heard the intonation in a person's voice and saw the discontent in their brow. And that's as far as it got. I had no lapse, no second-guess dissonance. I acknowledged presence and wrote it off. Second-guessing is for people buying cars and considering marriage. Conviction is righteous. Dedication is relegated to the minds of the extreme.

Lying on the couch gazing up at this grown man in plaid underwear reaching for his bong, his little safety net, I opened my eyes wide.

"Everyone's been wondering if we'd see you again. I knew I would. It's good, you back and all."

I smiled, "It's good to see you too, man."

"You're somebody to some certain kind of people, I can't explain it. There are people around here, so says my girlfriend. Oh- oh - I'm dating this girl now, Lilleth, she works for a company that does those standardized test prep courses."

"You got a girl?"

"She's hella hot, man. She's always at the Mezzanine, you know, that club where all the DJs play?"

I nodded.

"Man. Listen to me. I've been following everything you've done," he said. "Read every word you wrote. Tons have. I mean, I mean, there were people at school talkin' in muffled voices between classes. You see?"

I leaned forward as Pat continued.

"I told Lilleth about you. Said she'd heard your name before and then she remembered that she overheard kids in a prep courses talking during break and saw something with your name on it some kid left behind in class. She brought it over here and turns out it was from that website you write. We kept it and she has it at her place." Pat boy laughed. He took a bite and chewed. "My boy's this big time writer now. This thought leader."

I smiled. "It's kind of surreal, isn't it?"

Pat grabbed a lighter, lit the fire and pulled himself into the bong. Poison pocketed into the cavity of his chest where it settled in silence before streaming out through his nostrils.

"So what can we expect now?" he asked with smoke amid his words. "What's your next move? What next for Emory Walden?"

Emory Walden.

I had not heard my name come from the lips of a friend in too long to remember. Without a name you can become anything. Names ground you. They remind you who you are, who you once were. These days names are Brands. They're selling points. They're letters with marketing power. Companies call it "good will" in their balance sheets. It's an asset. If This Company gets bought out by That Company, This Company pays a premium for That Company's brand name. There's nothing tangible behind it. Just a name. And it can be worth hundreds of millions of dollars. And I had a name again and a name can be or a name can be leveraged.

It had always been my job to synthesize information. I took what's out there en masse and wrote a synopsis for other people. That was the objective in grade school tests and papers. That's what got me an honors degree in college. That's what churned in the change at my job after college.

And since that's all I knew, that's what became my obligation during my emancipation.

The company I performed office labor for was - well, honestly? They had some euphemism they used to market it to the very people they were laying off. I conjured it up: "streamlining resources." Nice, isn't it?

But the blunt reality was that they were in the midst of a layoff because they were shipping jobs overseas; I think to India or maybe it was China. So right, the need for a crafted lot of officespeak emerged. The people will always prefer the euphonious over the obvious and that's where I came in. Fresh, young, driven. A talent to be tapped. A pen for a chisel. I hacked away at the facts until they hacked away my soul and I could no longer see the words from the page.

In my emancipation I renounced the blood of my former pen. I think somebody famous said that once. Anyways, I would live only for freedom and thus I would write only for freedom. People can say college or this or that teaches a person a lot about freedom. Parents tremble as their kids walk out from under the family awning in fear of what freedoms their kids might find. But it was not so much these things because in life there are a number of fences set up by culture that we're simply too afraid to leap over.

People spend their lives talking about freedom, making laws and fighting wars over it, selling cars and cell phones that are supposed to grant it and buying albums, clothes, and addictive products that rape the word and spawn a commodity. I've met less than a handful of people in my life who've ever truly experienced freedom, who are actually free. And when I found it and I quaffed it and danced entranced to it as a possessed man does to a fire I made a vow that I would clench my chisel between my fingers and hack away at anything and everything like a caged lunatic until the bars bent and snapped and the people spilled free, wild-eyed into the night.

3

I THOUGHT, WHERE DO I know this guy from? His bowl-shaped head, his bowl-shaped haircut, a post-teen trapped in the 1990s was glancing at me from time to time as I shuffled back and forth between the kitchen and the tables. He was a waiter, and I – the bottom-feeding busboy - knew him from somewhere.

I expected him to approach me, a flannel shirt wrapped around his waist in some grunge bar 15 years ago, and try to start a mosh pit. I suspected he was like those disco queens of years past who couldn't swallow the stale fact that times had changed, that everything they'd believed in was just a fad.

I scooped up tables of dirty dishes, half-eaten steaks, licked spoons, snotty cloth napkins and hustled to the kitchen. The heat poured over me as I rushed through the doors nearly knocking into 90s Boy carrying a tray of lobster.

"Watch out, stain," he grunted.

First day on the job with a pair of black pants borrowed from Pat draped from the bones of my hips, and I started to remember every job I'd had before and why I never had any money. Because each job was the same and they all boiled down to guys like 90s Boy getting power trips off their little sliver of authority and passive-aggressively flexing it like it's Big Throbbing Life. I know where I knew this guy from. He was all over the place.

Break time found me bursting through the back door, gasping for fresh air. I leaned against alleyway brick with its soft layer of years rubbed off by the backs of break time employees. Closed my eyes. Ten minutes. Gasped for every breath. Live it. Suck at the timed freedom, the calculated peace.

"Out of breath?"

"Just trying to get as much as I can get," I said.

"As much what?"

"Air," I said, "untainted air."

"Got a jack?"

"No, I haven't any jacks."

The voice wanted to know why.

"Because I don't smoke," I blurted, "therefore why would I carry jacks? Does a man carry a maxi pad?" I asked. "I want air, fresh, unadulterated air."

Laughter shot skyward. "Just air, huh?"

"Yep, you got it." I opened my eyes and 90s Boy was sipping a soda and cradling a lit jack in the same hand. He had that same look as always and just as he was about to say something, I turned and headed back inside.

* * * * *

Something about a uniquely beautiful girl had me feeling as though I was a child again and everything was soft and simple as mud. As I stood there in the violence of a restaurant kitchen, the shouts, the frying slabs of dead flesh, the heat and odor, the sizzling of burning fat, I ceased to battle the suffocation around me. Unique beauty stood by the counter with a tray full of plates as the chaos careened around and by, just barely missing her. Unique beauty, the desire of all that have become the droning masses. The objects of our affection are those who have held onto youth, who have defied the odds and somehow, mystically, won the heart of a god too in love to let time change them. We want them. We want to swallow them. We want to pack them up, take them home. We want to own them.

I was in the way of everyone. It meant nothing. Clinging to her was the light as she swallowed the energy of the room with every breath. Everyone fed off her but, in some Newtonian way, she fed off them. Off us. Off me. I struggle now even to encapsulate her within the imperfections of description. I saw only unique beauty. I can say only that she was lithe with eyes that seemed to give away nothing of her intentions and a smile like the light that passes through the tree's leaves of adolescence. She was the reason for all those dreams you wake up from struggling to remember.

* * * * *

Her name was Carolyn.

I threw my bag over my shoulder and headed out the door. In the alleyway, I stopped where the dumpster leaned open against the brick near where I stood earlier. I glanced around. No one. I listened, hearing only the sound of garbage water trickling down asphalt. Above the dumpster was a low ledge maybe two feet wide and a foot or so deep. I could reach it if I could just get balance on the dumpster's edge. Above that, maybe four or five feet, the rooftop. Upon that? Opportunity.

I wedged my foot onto the dumpster's side and pulled myself up. The door swung open just a few feet away. Get down, walk away. I headed for the main street. I don't think they saw.

"Carolyn, what are you doing this weekend?"

I glanced over my shoulder. 90s Boy was walking backwards a few steps ahead of Unique Beauty, facing her and wanting to know about her captured youth and what it all meant. He was asking trivial questions. What has she been up to? Is she free this weekend? But I know what he really wanted to know. He was wondering about the youth and the beauty and those dreams he'd been having.

This is how I learned her name, from hearing 90s Boy asking her out in an alleyway behind a restaurant where I worked.

On the surface is the persuasive element. We need only glance at something to make swift judgments. 90s Boy was bowlish and attractive in a common way. He was determined and assured in the ritual of persistence. I don't want to sound vain to you, but I've always had the advantage of a distinct look. I am safe and harmless yet intriguingly distant and amorphous. I'm verisimilitude. Or, so I liked to project myself. I am confident, but never in the face of true beauty.

At the corner I paused and sifted through my pockets. Carolyn and 90s Boy caught up. "Listen, I've got these tickets to a grunge concert at the Mezzanine," 90s Boy said, teetering on desperation. "Would you like to go?"

Carolyn lied, said she's busy.

This is where I chimed in, "Hey." Acting harmless. "Hey, do either of you know where the bus stop is for Dash 7?"

90s Boy was about to speak. Carolyn cut him off, "Sure. Yes. I'm off that way now actually. You're the new guy, right? Come on, I'll show you."

Carolyn led. 90's Boy sulked behind. He called, "When you figure it out, give me a call. Tickets were hard to come by."

Carolyn kind of grunted, then whispered to me, "I doubt that."

I laughed. She laughed too.

"Who cares about grunge music anymore, anyways?"

"Seriously," I said. I thanked her for showing me to the bus stop.

"Anything to get away from him," she says.

"It's that bad?"

"Yeah."

So, where am I from?

I told her I wasn't really sure how an answer would find that question. "I just got back from Europe," I said.

She'd always wanted to go but couldn't afford it.

It's not so expensive, it just depends on your standards of living, I told her, to which she responded, "that's an interesting perspective."

She wanted to know, what's my name?

I told her and she'd never met a person named Emory before.

Neither had I.

We walked and worked our jaws and it turned out that she was paying her way through college waiting tables, had plans to get her Master's degree and work for a non-profit. I was detail digging. But she wanted to know about me.

"I grew up in the suburban sprawl, just west of here," I told her. "I've got a degree."

"What kind?"

"Double major in sociology and communication."

"You graduated college?" She laughed, doubtful.

"Magna Cum Laude," I said.

She smiled, then what am I doing working as a bus boy?

If I told her, she wouldn't understand.

"Sociological experiment," I said. "I am a writer too," I added, "and I'm working on a novel."

To intelligent, educated girls, there is nothing more intriguing, more romantic, than a novelist. Carolyn reached out, her hand touching my shoulder.

"Thanks for saving me back there from Mr. Mosquito."

"Mr. Mosquito?"

"Yeah, that's my little nickname for Brock. I've got secret nicknames for everyone. He's always, 'hey wanna do this? Hey Carolyn, wanna do that? Hey, hey, hey.'"

I laughed.

"I'm not kidding, that pestering, that incessant buzz in your ear. I'm always swatting him off, and he keeps coming back." she laughed. "I gotta hand it to him. He'll make a great cop with his disposition."

"Cop?"

"Yeah. He's taking classes. Training to be a D.C. police officer. He's always macho-ing it up trying to impress us girls with it."

"A cop. I can't see that," I said.

"You can't? The hunger for authority? The way he's always in your business?"

"He just – yeah. I guess when you look at it that way. But the rest of him. I don't know."

She shrugged and I could tell that she couldn't see my point. I smiled because I didn't know what else to do.

"Anyhow. I love nicknames. Real names are blah. Nobody earns real names, they don't mean anything. It's the names you earn that capture who you are. That's what counts."

"That's funny 'cause I've been calling him 90s Boy."

"90s Boy?"

"Oh you know, his haircut, the way he dresses, the music he likes. Everything. I think we went to school together, except it was 1993 and I was in the 5th grade. Guess he never made it out the other end."

She laughed as people and cars blazed our peripherals. Horns. The drum of the city. Carolyn and I stood face to face, focus locked on the moment, her head high, her eyes not looking into mine, but rather, examining my face. Examining what I was, what I was doing here. Trying to fill in the gaps. I saw in her eyes that she saw something in me. The sky never seemed so far away.

"Let me ask you this, Emory. You're smart. You've got your degree."

"I'm not smart," I cut in. "I'm educated."

She laughed, "Well, Emory. You're educated. You've seen the world. You chose to come back here and clean up the leftovers of these rich people. You've seen me. You saw me working today, you saw me in the kitchen. I know you saw me because I looked your way and you looked lost. That's the look guys always give me. Well, but now, you don't look lost and maybe I was wrong. Anyways, you're the novelist. You saw me for one day. Right now, after one day, if you had to give me a nickname, what would it be?"

4

LUCK WOULD HAVE IT I grew up the follower of boys who were the brightest in the Northern Virginia region; boys whose parents worked for the United States government and, by will of their dollar, had sent these boys to Montessori schools and the like. These were the types of parents that ensured that little Charles and Betsy or whoever were placed in the gifted and talented programs in such cultural milieus as art, music, and English.

As a consequence of my intellectual infancy in comparison with my friends, as the fissure was quite obvious between the status of their education and that of mine upon my family's arrival in Virginia from a small town in Vermont, I came to suffer steadily from an inferiority complex. I struggled for years with this disease, often manifesting itself in bouts of late-night reading frenzies in my bedroom. I would hide under the covers with a flashlight and read the great American novels on into the morning hours, like some teenagers sneak their father's dirty magazines. I got really into Fitzgerald. Read all of them. *This Side of Paradise* was my favorite. I got into Salinger, of course too. I didn't care for Hemingway. Then I got on the Beats, then Kesey, then Hubert Selby, Jr., and somewhere in there I read *A Separate Peace* three times. Keeping scraps of notebook paper for bookmarks, I wrote on each all the definitions of words I did not know or could not pronounce. Ineffectual. Supercilious. Atavistic. I studied them at breakfast, my father down the hall in the bathroom shaving to the hum of the electric. I never let him or anyone else see me. God forbid. It was an endeavor I understood for only myself and I would have been mortified had my parents caught me. Nobody ever knew what was going on with me. I don't see how a teen's idiosyncrasies can ever be fully explained.

Years passed. I established a sophisticated vocabulary that I rarely spoke. The "project," as I came to refer to it, was not an endeavor I undertook for any present reward. The person I was then, I declared to myself in those late nights, was nothing of the person I would become. My middle school and high school years were in preparation for some great Emory Walden that was to emerge a polished, learned, and reputable man; like that of Pip. I had witnessed the gap between the opportunities afforded the parents of my friends, Dr. Thomas Carothers, Mrs. Rebecca Smoot, Esquire, and so on, and the opportunities which had befallen my parents, two bright Americans who established themselves only from the tires of self-sacrifice and who had seen nothing of privilege. It was my obsession to transcend that gap – to become more educated than any of my friends, or friend's siblings; to surpass everyone I knew and grab hold the opportunity my parents had worked so assiduously to afford me.

I scored my high school education with a library card, a flashlight and some pencils, and a few notebooks of paper squared into bookmarks. I earned a near perfect score on the Verbal section of the SAT. I went on to attend Devon University free of charge, all expenses paid courtesy of some sad, endowed old lady who set up a scholarship in obeisance to her late husband. It was a strong school, not quite there, but the scholarship was key. To score it all, I had to simply shake her quivering hand at a banquet dinner and give a little thank you speech about how humbling it was for the rich to help out the deserving but otherwise incapable dependant class.

Privileged kids, as any reader of this who is one will attest, are some of the most despondent people in the world. Let's not get into it now, but I assure you. Only privileged kids, or people who waste their youth aspiring to emulate them, such as myself, can be entering high school and have the time and character to be invested in the hope of a world-wide exigency on January 1, 2000.

Can you believe it? Most of the kids at my high school, the ones I knew at least, had entered high school hoping, praying for societal meltdown. Y2K. They saw the world their parents inhabited and wanted nothing of it. There had to be a better way to live. And yet I worked hard anyway. So, when the scholarship was won, I went to Devon. As for the Charles' and Betsy's? They hung around the suburbs and leeched off their parents.

If there is anything that ravages the rich and privileged more than their disdain for the world at large, it is their envy of their peers. Maybe it affects you even more if you're the one who doesn't come from much, like me. Our friends become our greatest competition. We take what the other has. And what we cannot take from him for our own, we see that he too cannot have it. Accolades. Riches. Women.

I heard it said best once when I had a falling out over a girl with my closest friend in the summer before college. He said to me, "Your success is my failure." Then he turned and walked away. I never saw him again.

That was the thing about Pat Drassell, though. Things had never been like that between us. He had always been like the naïve kid brother who looked up to me wide-eyed, asking questions and giving these reassuring pats on the back as if no matter what I did it made him swell fat with pride. In the feebleness of his heart he had always felt that he could never quite get over that lump that would make him the success he saw in me. And knowing this and the failures his parents projected onto him, Pat invested himself in the torments of the flaccid youth. I was confident Pat could've been more.

But on this night Pat wanted to celebrate my return.

"Wanna head over to the Mezzanine? Lilleth can get us in for free."

"Nah," I paused between changing out of the work pants he had lent me, "I think I'm going to take it easy tonight."

"Beat?"

I nodded.

"Garbage. Come on. It'll be straight. Just need a little pick-me-up is all. Lilleth will take care of that. We need to get you some strange, anyways. This man is somebody! The gazelles at the Mezz will fawn over you. Once they catch the name, I mean. How couldn't they?"

I told Pat I wasn't too sure about that last part and really to go on ahead. He persisted no further, although I could see his dejection. I lay down on the couch and closed my eyes. Soon he was gone. In an hour's time I was rooftop a few blocks from Adams Morgan, the sound of the youth wasting away below, ambling around the streets, stumbling, pissing in alleyways, hollering obscenities to the steel castles towering over them. They wanted only to be who they could not be by day.

My face was swollen from the gusts cutting above buildings, my cap pulled low. It reminded me of those November days on the school bus way back when. I used to lean my head up against the piss-thin glass, the window fogged up, and I'd just try and fall asleep. More than anything, I hated the bus rides home in autumn and winter. The smell of it all and the feeling of being dirty and wet with these dozens of kids cramped on top of one another breathing sultry and yelling their heads off, having to be the loudest kid in the whole racket, and the feeling of that cold glass and metal pressed up against my coat and hat made me want to go home and sit by the electric fire.

Once, when I was in second or third grade, during the first Gulf War, I tried to write the word 'peace' with my finger in the window fog. Some girl a grade younger laughed, pointing to the letters. "Can't you spell, ditzoid?" she buzzed, "P-E-A-C-E, P-E-A-C-E, P-E-A-C-E. Not P-I-E-C-E." I tried to play like it was intentional and wrote beneath the words "of cake" but she just laughed, her friend joining her.

Finishing up, there they were all below. I packed my stencil and spray cans and then was off back the way I came, over a few rooftops. Here it was, the way down. I descended the fire exit and hopped down onto the street, standing in an alleyway maybe two school bus lengths from the looming streetlights and the ambling drunkards passing underneath them. I was not far from the Mezzanine and I needed to be real sly-like and make sure I didn't happen across Pat as he stumbled home. I pulled my cap down low and threw the hood of my sweatshirt over my head. Just then, these two lushes about my age stumbled into the alley. The one pressed the other against the alley wall.

For a moment it looked like things were going to erupt into fists. I crept closer as water dripped from a rail with a ting-ting-ting; about 30 feet now. I crept ever so slowly until I could almost see their faces in the shadow. I stopped, ducking low behind some crates or something. The man was about my age or so and a bit taller than me. The woman had short amber hair all done up and the highlights of her hair gleamed in the streetlight that leaned into the alley. Just as I suspected, they were arguing about something but it was muffled like they were hiding.

I could see them from my vantage and it was an odd feeling to be so intimate with people and at the same time so unknown and hidden away. Just as I thought he was going to haul off and strike her, she dropped down into the light where I could see her better. She grabbing at his pants frantically. She got a hand on the belt and then the thing was on its way out. She took it whole into her mouth. His hand met hers on his chest, his other finding its way to the top of her head where he ran his fingers through her hair and pushed her head forward and back. It was lit just well enough that I could see the face of the girl as she fiddled with his thing slow and careful. But he was pushing forward and back, forward and back. He wanted it faster and faster. And then he was done.

Real romantic.

She stood up and they kissed a bit. I wanted to see this guy's face so I crept slowly around the crates until I was maybe 15 feet. A crash erupted from behind me, ricocheting off the alley walls. The two quit kissing. Shit, did something just fall out my backpack? I froze there in the middle of the alley hidden in the depths. The guy took a few steps toward me, and just as the girl grabbed his sleeve to pull him back, I saw his face and the fear and confusion that sculpted it. It was him. I am sure of it. It was only a moment, but I am sure of it. It was 90s Boy. Brock. Not the arrogant veneer I'd seen earlier that day but a scared, anxious countenance. She pulled at him, motioning toward the streets. She got him by the hand and the two scurried off.

*****

I found Pat passed out, tossed like broken glass across the floor tiles. I filled a cup of water at the sink and placed it beside him. I couldn't help but sigh.

5

A MONTH OR TWO FLICKERED PAST and I kept myself busy with my online publication. I'd also been out painting graffiti. An ounce of theory or a ton of action? As most things in life, one has value only so much as the other influences it.

On this particular night I had a date with Carolyn. It took me a while to build up the courage. Something in my gut told me she said yes out of pity and this was all some kind of joke that girls play. It'd been since before my trip to Europe that I'd opened up my heart to any possibility of love. You see, love itself is inherently buttoned-down.

I needed to get out of work by 9pm to get home and dressed to meet her by 9:45. The clock on the wall read 8:39. The restaurant was mostly empty, looking much like it did the first day I came in a month or two before, sopping wet, desperate for a job. In the low light, I rushed around trying to close out all my tabs. I was promoted from busboy to server a couple weeks before when one of the servers quit during a busy holiday shift and the manager, Peter, promoted me on the spot. Peter was still asking me about Roberto, the flight attendant, and I'd kept the story going any which way I could. I needed this job.

One of the last two tables paid and left. All in all I had $142.23 in tips, a total killing. I was standing in the kitchen having just counted my money and waiting for the last customer to finish up so that I could bring him his bill. He'd been at his table at least an hour and now it was 8:47 and I was anxious to get going.

The door swung open and Brock called, "Hey, stain, your customer at Table 9 says he wants to talk to you."

What now? I thought. I ignored Brock's cut down and the intonation in his voice, wanting to boast to him about who I was going out with tonight. I remembered the expression on his face when we were back in that alley and I sort of laughed to myself and called back, "yeah, sure thing."

I approached the table.

"Sir?"

The man glanced up at me and all night I'd been thinking he looked familiar. His face was hugged by a white beard and his white hair, what little he had, had been dragged atop his head with a comb. He was a groomed and handsome man in a tan sports jacket, but a bit fragile in his motions.

"I just wanted to comment on your work tonight," he nodded. "Very fine job. I remember when you first served me, oh, a few weeks ago, and you weren't so polished. You dropped that tray of food and, quite so, I thought for certain you'd be fired. But here you are this very day. You've filled out the role here, quite so. Finely done."

I thanked him, and yes, I somewhat remembered he'd been in here a few times.

"I must say, it's arduous, being a server," he continued. "Why don't you take a load off? I'm an aging man who could use some company."

I wanted to keep my job and knew enough about these people to not say no, and so reluctantly I slid into the booth across from him. The restaurant was practically empty save that young hostess, a busboy or two, and Brock – who was closing tonight. We were over in a corner near the window and I could see the cold air was holding the street light's bright for me and Carolyn.

"You've seen me in here before, you recall?"

I nodded. "Yes, I believe I've served you before, sir."

"Yes, and do you know who you were serving?"

No, I didn't, I apologized.

"You make a man humble," he said reaching into his breast pocket. He slid a business card across the table which I turned over and read: "Fletcher Spivey, CEO Spivey & Frettington, LLC."

"You were in the airport magazine, the one I got off the plane! I remember! Largest marketing firm on the East Coast. Fortune 500, just had sold the business or something?"

"It was my father's, I inherited it. But, quite true. The business card is old news since I've retired."

Then I remembered. It was the man from the night months before when I'd come in from the rain with my rucksack on my back and gotten the busboy job from Peter. This man Fletcher Spivey had been sitting in the corner eating a late meal with another man whose face I couldn't quite see in my mind. I wondered if this rich old bastard recognized me as the same man who strolled in here sopping wet in need of a job, a shower and a shave.

"Well, congrats," I said. "You must be living the dream."

"You must be," he replied.

It's not a bad gig, I told him.

"Which, a writer? Or an artist?"

He stared at me a bit, removed his glasses and cleaned them with a cloth from his pocket. The streetlights outside. The big restaurant, all wood and dark and the rich smell of mahogany. This man here in the dim light, an empty plate, an empty glass of wine to his left. Perhaps he was drunk.

"I think I'd like to be one of those things one day. Wouldn't we all? But no sir, I'm not working here for that reason. I mean, I'm not a struggl- aspiring artist, sir"

"You're certainly not struggling," he nodded, rotating the ring on his right hand with his thumb and pinky.

"This job is profitable, very true," I said.

He gazed out the window. "This is a strange city isn't it?"

"None like it."

"Full of strange people."

Uh-huh, I nodded.

"Strange things happen here."

I nodded again.

Turning back toward me he asked, "Does that bother you?"

I shook my head. "It is what it is, I guess. All you can do is embrace it."

"A fine perspective," he nodded.

I stared at him a moment, growing tired of the chit-chat. I wanted to leave so I wouldn't be late for my date but was unable to think of a way to exit the conversation.

"Emory," he said after a moment, "Emory, I'd like to be of help to you." I glanced down at the name pin on my shirt. I thanked him, "but sir, I'm not looking for a handout. Really, I'm doing quite well at this job, and really it's the best I've been doing in a long while, sir."

Well then, perhaps I can help him, he said.

Another glass of wine? Maybe a bottle? But no, he didn't want these things.

He took the card from me, scribbled something down, and slid it back across the table. It was an address handwritten in shaky blue letters. He pulled his wallet from under the table, producing two one-hundred dollar bills. An empty plate, a wine glass, and two one-hundred dollar bills. A forty-dollar meal.

He stood with fragility and looked down at me, the card with blue ink propped between my fingers. He placed his napkin on the table and said "I've read your work, Emory. It's fresh, impressive. It's inspiring, and to a lot of people." Then, with a nod towards the card I held, "I'll count on seeing you there soon." And with that he walked out.

6

I WAS PANICKED THE WHOLE WAY, at times running, at times walking, until I rounded the corner and slowed to a normal pace. It was ten o'clock and Carolyn was sitting on a bench just where she said she'd be. She was still here, I sighed. She gave me a drop of a smile and even less of a nod. I tried to start things out positive with: "I got held up at work and I'm really sorry."

She said it's okay but in an upside down sort of way and I could tell we were off to a piss-poor start.

We walked and talked awhile but it was mostly surface stuff. Why did she even bother to come? How many other guys asked her for this night?

She stopped by a window, glancing in. I felt she wishes the glass was between her and I - that she was the mannequin living a different life, unacquainted, and looking out at me standing alone in the street. And then maybe she'd laugh at this figure staring in at her. In there she would always be in season, always be in fashion; in there, where it was warm and welcoming for all the mannequins.

In her reflection I watched the way she adjusted her glasses. "Have you ever been in love before?" She said to the window.

"Yeah. Or, I thought I was. Years ago. It didn't end well. I guess it didn't start well either. Before me, she'd been with

– and so it was complicated. Anyways," I sputtered. "I mean it's hard to say what love is, you know? It's just one of those sorts, well it's kind of that –"

"I was in love once," she blurted, turning to me. "He was a lot like you, except a bit taller maybe and with blonde hair. But your sort of type, do you know what I mean?"

I nodded.

"Do you know what happens to love?"

I shook my head, "I can't remember." I didn't want to.

"Me neither," she frowned. And we walked on as couples passed us holding hands. I kept mine tucked in my pockets as I glanced down at her fingers poking out from her jacket.

Was she with someone now?

She shook her head. "Oh, no. I haven't had any serious relationships other than him. That was years ago. Now, I guess I'm – you know - you meet some guys sometimes and it's fun. I spend a lot of time eluding stalkers and losers, like Mr. Mosquito. I'm a big piece of metal, like a refrigerator, and all the wrong magnets keep trying to stick to me." She laughed at this, and then her eyes fell to the sidewalk. "It's that my parents are getting divorced, you see. Twenty-five years together. Their anniversary is next week, next Tuesday. But that sort of thing is never enough."

"I'm not sure if love itself is enough," I said. The look on her face had me regretting ever having words.

"Oh, no." she said, "I'm not upset they are getting divorced. In a lot of ways I'm happy for them. It's freedom, really. Especially for my Mom. She loved my Dad. She did. But you can't change other people."

"If you can't change others, what can you change?"

She shrugged, the frown seemed only to deepen. She told me a bit more about it and how she was happy for them - that both will be better off on their own, and maybe they can find new love. Then why was she upset? But she wasn't upset, she said. She was contemplative.

"I've been cogitating love, and why my Mom's love wasn't enough. I just wanted to know what you thought about the topic is all."

Cogitate. I complimented the word choice. And we laughed. I could love you. A dangerous thought. "I don't know anyone whose parents aren't divorced," I told her. "Mine are. I haven't seen either of them in maybe two years."

She asked me why not.

I told her "I think they split up because of me," to which she nodded, whether or not she understood.

We spent the rest of the night walking around down by the museums and the monuments and it was real comfortable now the way we talked and things. At about one in the morning we caught the Metro back up towards where she lived to drop her off. I gazed at her fingers dangling there on her lap as the Metro rushed us closer and closer to the end of the night. Reach out and touch them, I thought. Feel the skin and maybe her fingers will slide right into place with yours.

7

ANOTHER MONTH. ANOTHER FLICKER. I finished another job, my fifth that month, and was back down over the buildings the way I had before and down the same fire escape. I had to crouch down again behind the crates because right then a stout man was imposing himself on a dumpster in the alley. I've got to find a better place to descend, I thought.

He pulled something out, and after looking it over, tossed it back in the dumpster, repeating this behavior over and again before I heard: "So how about ya tell me what the fuck you're doin' way back there, bro-minnne?"

His wide back was steeped over now in the dumpster and I figured if I've got a chance this was it. So I stepped to, making my way towards the edge of the alley when he jumped down and turned towards me, bulging in the tight alley, looming down over me, blocking the way.

"Somethin' for the road?"

His hand clutched a sandwich, the wrapper half-torn with a bite missing on the side.

I shook my head, no, no, I'm good. I was queasy just looking at the bread, mustard, stale lettuce and folds of reddish-brown meat that were mashed together and squeezing out from between his hand.

"Too bad. It's *really* good," he said.

He wanted to know if I was sure. And when I showed him I was confident, he shrugged, then husked a big mouthful of it, and chewed contemplatively. This mass in the shadow gulped it down and said, "So if you're not hungry, what ya doin' back here in an alley this time on a Sunday night? Sleepin'? Suckin'? Shootin' up?"

"One of them."

"What ya got in the bag?"

I told him it was my personals knowing that, as a breed, street people are very respectful of each other's personals.

Grabbed another bite, "You camped out here?" He tossed the wrapper over his shoulder and it spun and flipped, falling listlessly and disappearing behind him. I shook my head.

"You need a place to crash?" And I might as well have because I didn't feel like going back to Pat's to sleep on that couch.

"I've got nowhere to go," I told him.

He went back to the dumpster, grabbed something and shoved it into his pants pocket.

Street people always go by one name like a first name but it's never an ordinary first name like a Christian name. I picked this knowledge up in Europe where, for some time, I was of the breed. This one went by "Renton." And he shook my hand when he told me this, and his head jerked up and down and I could see now that he was wearing circular glasses with tiny frames propped on his bulbous head and a thick, knotty, red beard protruded from his face. It all made him look like Santa Claus's reject of a child, the one he had illegitimately with Mom like in that old song; the one Santa and Mom gave away to an orphanage and Dad was none the wiser.

Renton was a good foot or so taller and one-hundred pounds heavier than me and smelled of rotten vegetables and grass stains. His voice was powerful yet humble with a Midwest pull to it. When the two of us spilled out of the alleyway into the street I could see his clothes were stained all over and his skin was dark with earth and grime. In his right hand, which bore three scars in concentric circles, he clutched a plastic grocery bag in which he carried his personals.

"Whatta they call ya, bromine?" he asked giving me a stiff pat on shoulder.

I couldn't remember the last time I'd met someone so genuinely interested. I gazed back on old early-teen reveries and told him I go by Pip, and he laughed at this and said, "Well, I didn't realize I was in company with a young bromine of great expectations."

I laughed.

"Sir, I seek not to disappoint," he said in his best old English accent, "but accommodations in this town are splendidly raucous. *Har har har.*"

And again he laughed and then I did too.

It turned out, as I learned over a night sitting up on a park bench in Dupont Circle chewing air, that Renton had lived in just about every place I could imagine, had held just about every dead-end job a man could hope to avoid, and lived just about as hard a life over the past eight years or so as any poser, trust-fund Rasta, or wannabe thug from my high school days could possibly have a wet dream about.

Suffering always looks a lot better when it's stylish and that's the appeal with the middle-class community. Were any of those kids to show up here in Dupont Circle at this time of late-late night and see the truth of what they coveted, the doped-up apparitions sleeping on the sidewalk, the man getting arrested by the police just across the way outside a drugstore, the ambulance screaming by in the night rushing a stab victim to the hospital, the teenage, hollow-faced drug dealers on bicycles tooling around the streets, the hookers ambling around in the night itching for a score? Yes. I could just see it now. They'd give up their imitation style, hard talk and music and go hump a mortgage for a suburban home with a white picket fence and a security system.

A sickened soul strolled up to us and asks for "a lil'

sometin to calm un upset stomach, brothas." So Renton reached into his pocket and produced a tear of bread. The man bowed and ambled off.

"I been out here on the D.C. streets two years. And let me tell you bromine," Renton said, "It's sad. You see the same people with the same habits, same problems. Nothin' ever gets better for them."

Renton had mostly been active in the anti-war movement and a number of humanitarian causes like African aid and worker's rights in Asia. He had spent a lot of time at peacetests and peace-ins, these civil disobedience type deals on the Mall, at the Capitol, the White House. He had spent a lot of time in churches working in soup kitchens for a few days or weeks at a time here and there but never anything that broke a month. He had spent a lot of time at night salvaging for food. And, he had spent a lot of time scouring for safe places to sleep to avoid trouble from what the city became after the people who ran it left for the suburbs of Maryland or Virginia.

I asked him if he was an anarchist and he said he was not really sure, but he didn't think so because he used to live on an anarchist collective compound in Montana and he decided that way just didn't seem to be a viable way for life. He was a religious man, he said, but not of a religion per se. He was driven not by economic or political philosophy, but by what was moral and just. He abstained from just about everything; getting employment, finding a place to live, paying for food, and on and on as well as drugs and alcohol. All for moral reasons. He pronounced with his Midwestern humility and happiness that, by choice, he truly was living off the surpluses of society.

"Freeganism," is what he called it.

He grabbed a gulp of tea from a can I bought us and a bit trickled down into his shabby beard.

"How are ya?" he said, which I took to mean 'what's my story?'

So I pulled for a deep breath and for the first time in a

long time I shared myself with another person: A homeless guy, maybe five, six years older than me with nothing, not one thing, to hold dear in this world but the confines of a plastic bag.

"It's hard to know who you are nowadays. I know what I stand for and I think that's more important than trying to be something you're not. I used to do that. I've lost a lot of friends who are trying to do that. I just want to affect this upside down world and make a change."

I looked over at Renton who was watching me intently as if what I had to say was the most genuine thing he'd ever heard. Looking at his condition, I felt guilty to complain about anything so I told him never mind. He shook his head and waved his hand urging me on. In his Midwestern way he said "staawwppp it." So I went on and told him a little bit about my upbringing and how I used to have great desires of joining the ranks of the well-educated and powerful.

He found this amusing, saying the Dickens reference made more sense now and he told me that at least I'm a lot further along in these sorts of plans than he was. We both shared a laugh and then I told him that I was naïve then to want those things. I wanted now to have influence of a whole other breed. To hell with establishing a personage.

I wanted to be the match. But I didn't want to be the fire. I wanted the fire to be everywhere, of everyone, all around me at once. I wanted it to sweep through the land smothering the old and clearing the way.

"That sounds *really* good. You and I, we aren't so different, bromine. Except for the fact that I'm fat as shit and you're not ugly. You know there's people like you. Some people like me. And a lot in between. Yup, I've met 'em. Iconoclasts of all different colors shapes and sizes. There's so much motivating people. There's a youth movement, actually, in D.C. Bunch of high school teens advocating for some local graffiti artist got busted 'bout a year ago, thrown in jail. I think he was a Situationist. Wasn't older'n seventeen I don't think. They're pretty active round here, toolin' with the metro lines and fightin' gentrification and corporations and all that shitarsky. They put out a communiqué one night and so my homeless chub figured I'd go check it out. They paraded through the streets with music a blastin' and they were dancin' and yellin' and blocking intersections. And there were kids on bikes in black masks and they were putting down cinderblocks in the road to stop traffic and disrupted all sorts of shitarsky. It was *really* interesting. And they even got into it a bit with the Pigs. The youth are *real* motivated these days."

I hadn't heard about any of this.

"Yeah, the graffiti artist that got busted's tag name was Animus. He was a kind of porky little half Irish half Hispanic dude that went to a nearby prep school. A rich kid. But even them don't get along too well nowadays." Renton laughed his *har har*. "His whole thing had an air of tomfoolery to it."

I acted disinterested in graffiti.

"The problem for guys like us is that you got to be careful out here," he began again, "because the shitarsky with the Pigs. Sometimes they come give me trouble. Takin' a look at me, they get the impression I'm out bringin' the destruction. But I tell 'em I'm for construction, that I'm for buildin' things up and makin' a positive change. I'm not the one causin' the trouble. I'm the one out fixin' it. But they don't get that through their knobs. The Power is leanin' on them from above so they lean down on guys like me. Be careful out here. It's no pleasantry to be a street person in D.C. at this juncture, not when things are stirrin' up like they are now."

"But I'm for change - for the cause. I'm of the struggle. You understand." I pleaded.

He gulped some tea, this time wiping the slop from his beard with the back of his hand, "I *over*stand. I'm just sayin' you can't do any good mired in the judiciary system. These Pigs are a headache for me now whereas just a year ago? Nothing. Maybe they just get bored and it's some obligatory game we play with each other – the street people and the

Pigs. Maybe that's what the movements are, a game, a dance between the powers that be and the change that would be."

"Who knows?" I shrugged.

"I'll be your friend," he said wholeheartedly. I asked him what he meant and he told me that earlier I'd mentioned that I'd lost my friends. I sighed, thanking him and he said "no I'm sincere. You need anythin' bromine, you come to fat ol' Renton and I'll help ya. There's nothin' more important than havin' some friends, someone a man can rely on. Heck, I ain't got nothin' but friends," he said, nodding down towards his plastic bag.

I told him I felt the same way, just substitute 'ideas' for 'friends.'

"That's sad, bromine," he said. "It's a lonely world. Ain't you got some friend, someone?"

The image of Carolyn sitting next to me in a park as we ate our lunches during break the week before popped into my head: the cute way she nibbled her sandwich like a child at summer camp, the way her green eyes grew big when she smiled, how animated she was when she talked.

"There's someone," I nodded, "someone new."

He smiled "that's *really* good" and said that he was getting tired and ready for sleep. The sun was just beginning to break the horizon so I got up to give him his space.

"Goodnight, Pip," he said as he leaned back into the park bench and rolled to his side.

I rinsed with anticavity and spit into the grass, looked around, found a comfortable spot on the lawn across from him, locked my arms around my backpack and called it a night. When I awoke Renton was gone and the people from the suburbs had returned to reclaim the city, if only for the day.

8

506301. THAT WAS THE NUMBER perched above the doorway. I stepped under the awning onto a carpet. There, a man held the door for me, but I paid him no attention. Another man wearing the same costume with the same little hat pressed the elevator buttons and up we went. The hallway where I found number 4700 was the same color scheme as those men's costumes. I couldn't help but laugh.

It'd been over a month since I sat down with the man in the restaurant and I had not seen him there since. I don't know why I'd waited so long to come here, just as I wasn't sure why I now stood at his door. I gave it a knock just the same. And here I was wearing a collared shirt and khakis borrowed from Pat. I'm not sure why I decided to tuck my shirt into my pants because I can't remember the last time I'd tucked a shirt into pants. For some reason, it felt like the thing to do. And now I felt uncomfortable and a bit stupid about it.

He answered the door, looked me up and down and smiled.

"I've come to talk," I said as assertively as possible. Was that effective or was it overdone and transparent?

"Indeed," he nodded, still smiling.

He motioned me inside. I'm not sure what I was expecting the apartment to look like, but it was not whatever that expectation was. It was spacious, modern, immaculate. The furniture was old, but not antique furniture store stuff. Rather, it was of a bright stylish plastic era. The place smelled of Formica and vinegar. Without a word, he led me down a short hall with high ceilings and into a study - a sort of library. He motioned to a chair and I sat, falling deep into the chair as he walked around a desk to sit.

He looked at me again as if he didn't remember how I got in here a moment ago and asked, "What are your thoughts on despair? Do you find it tart?"

"It stands the test of time," I shrugged in the big chair.

"Few things do."

Uh-huh.

"Often I wonder, is despair just a bad name for a keen sense? Give me a man with a sunny disposition and I'm suspicious. That is a fledging man, a man with no worldview. So little are most men, anyhow. So little in resilience, so heavy in temptation."

"I could agree," I said.

This seemed to please him, and so he asked "What are your thoughts on conversationalists?"

"Not too sure," I said, somewhat amused by all of this. "I find they make for good businessmen and politicians. But never for good friends."

He chuckled, "you're mind is ten years ahead of your body."

"My body is not the problem," I replied. "My mind is."

"Oh?" He pondered this a moment and said, "We have each the opposite dilemma. And, soon I shall regale you with why. But first, regale me. What do you mean your mind is your problem?"

"Well, I'm not sure why I'm here." There were many earnest ways I could have answered this question. This was no problem, he said, standing from his chair behind the desk. He clicked a button on a desk phone and in a moment a voice came on, "Yes, Mr. Spivey?"

"He's finally come," he called into the phone. "Can you

come down to the Georgetown condo?"

The woman on the phone said, of course, and the man clicked the button.

"Ms. Alice is on her way," he affirmed.

Now, the man didn't look so fragile. He sat back down deep into his chair, throwing his feet upon the desk. Was this the same man from the restaurant? Was this the same man who answered the door a few minutes before?

He crossed his hands behind his head and said to me, "Now to get back to it. Emory, I'm not sure why you are here, because you cannot know why I have asked you here, and thus you cannot have a motivation for coming and this is why I am not sure why you *think* you are here. But I can tell you why I have brought you here, and I can tell you very simply, and very straightforward, as I can only be this way with you from hereto forward. What I can tell you is that your coming here bears indication that you are seeking something more from life than the drudgery of work. Say, in your case, of waiting tables."

Uh-huh, I nodded suspiciously.

"And I will tell you that there is something worth seeking," he continued. "That you believe there is, is something I can see in your face, that every man, woman and child worth their salt who catches your veneer sees. And, I'd like to think, they hope. Oh God, deep down inside they hope, that what is deep down within you is right – that there is more. And so there *is more.* And this is why I brought you here today. Because there is more. And I would like to introduce you to it. I would like to show you what has been behind every righteous thing you've felt since you were a young man, behind every word you've written on your blog, every stencil you've decorated the walls of this city with," he threw his arms out in a V when he said this last part as if to indicate the city all around us.

At this I knew not what to say or think. How is it that this man knew who I was, and knew my writing? This old, rich man in a cardigan and loafers knew nothing of me and my struggle and my company. How had this man connected me to the street art I create on the walls above the city? He was just one of the droning masses, who, when he glanced up, he failed to see the cover peeled back on the spectacle.

"You're wondering how I know of your work, both your writing and your - what the authorities call," he made quotes with his fingers "graffiti?"

I nodded.

"Does it suffice for me to tell you that your writing has inspired an amalgam of people and I just happen to be one of them and that, concurrently, I love your witty art?"

I shook my head. Just then, I heard the front door open down the hall, followed by the clicking of heels on the wooden floor. That was quick.

"I know that at this moment everything seems very strange to you. Quite so? I imagine you're pondering this perplexing scene. I imagine you are thinking what interest does this wealthy old, former CEO have with the likes of me, Emory Walden, who stands as the supreme antithesis – perhaps nemesis - to what Fletcher Spivey stands for?"

I nodded, feeling very small in the chair and in these strange clothes in this strange scene.

"Before we go any further," I said trying to reassert myself in the conversation, "I'll admit I'm the writer you think I am, and that I believe all of those things I've written about the bloated, unchecked global capitalist system that's rendered our democracy – and all democracies at that - anemic, impotent, a joke. I don't know why you said there is something," with this I made finger quotes myself, "behind every righteous thing I've felt," un-quoting now. "Because I know what's behind it. It's education, experience and exposure to the logic of this high-jacked world." With a sort of nervous laugh, "There is nothing more and nothing less, and certainly not you behind the wheel. It's me. I am behind the wheel. But tell me this, Mr. Spivey why is it that you think I am - what was it that you said - a graffiti artist?"

Before he could say anything I heard a woman's voice

behind me, "Mr. Spivey, you can't forget to take your medicine every time I have a day off. Surely, you have got to remember?"

But Spivey hated those damn things, he complained. She walked around to my side and placed a glass of water and a small metal tray of pills on the desk. I glanced up at her. "Emory Walden," she said politely with a slight foothills twang in her voice, "it's a pleasure to finally meet you."

"Emory, this is Ella Alice, the young woman who keeps everything running around here." He motioned to the pills when he said this, but I was glancing into her eyes and shaking her outstretched hand from where I sat.

Ella Alice was an Arlington woman, dressed like they do on a weekday in that town; as if she were at work at a job at Spivey & Frettington and not in the home of the retired ex-executive officer. She had an Arlington beauty about her - face made up, eyes lined, cheeks powdered, the whole impeccable presentation. It was like talking with a magazine cover.

"Oh, don't listen to Fletcher," she said with an office meeting laugh, "I'm just doing my job." And at this she smiled a proud, confident smile as if there was a mutual understanding achieved between her and I in this handshake greeting. When her eyes came together with her smile I could see, and yes, it was all very clear to me. She may look very prim and prep, but there was no mistaking it. It was the girl who I saw drop down on her knees and take Brock into her mouth back in that alley all those many months ago. I was, for a brief moment that lasted the expanse of a loss of breath, unable to move, let alone retract my hand.

"Look," I said, feeling it all spiraling out of control. Breathe. Get a hold of this, this sick and twisted foray. "Look, I'm sorry, but this is all far too creepy for me," I said pulling my hand back and turning to Mr. Spivey. "Before I stand up and walk out of here and erase this day and place from my life," I was now desperate to grab hold of any control I had of this moment and speaking very loudly as I placed my hands on the arms of the chair, "I'd – I'd like, I'd like to know what game it is you psychos are trying to play here?"

"Glasses don't fix your vision," said Mr. Spivey in an insouciant tone.

I stood. "What the hell does that even mean?"

"It means you only see it from your perspective. But before you go, if you will be so kind as to take off your precepts and let your eyes adjust. Then perhaps you can, at very least, make some sense of this day before you go?"

I looked at Spivey and at Ms. Alice and said I'd like some understanding, warning that, once obtained, I would go.

"Quite well," Spivey said.

And so I sat.

"A minute ago," he began, "you said it is you behind yourself." Before I could answer he continued on so I nodded while he spoke, "The verity of that statement could be no greater. I agree, and entertain no intention of giving you the impression that anything but yourself, your mind, and your experiences have given you the impetus for the great works you have engendered. Very well done. Quite so. I was letting my zeal, my excitement get the better of me. There is no conspiracy, no force manipulating you without your knowledge; nothing so outlandish. Such would be merely the fantasy of science fiction writers, so beguiled are they by unrealities; Manchurian Candidates and the like."

With this he chuckled briefly before taking a sip of his water. "What I am speaking of, is the realm of the feasible. It is not the past, but the future we are here discussing. Of course, the future is born of the past. And the past can be either a site of hope or despair when one cogitates the future. Earlier I misspoke. Earlier, when I said behind, I should have said in front of, ahead of, in the grand future of. For what I am here to offer you today is to help you move forward with your work. Do not look at me, my title, my past, as it exists on the surface and see this opportunity through such a lens as it will stand between you and the reality of *who* I truly am and what it is I truly *want* with my expiring life."

His use of the term 'cogitate' had me thinking of Carolyn and a part of me would've liked to be off with her at that moment, safe from this strangeness. But I was here and the part of me, the loud majority, the momentum, wanted to know more. So, what is it that he wanted?

He turned to Ms. Alice and said he was getting hungry and asked her to prepare us each some lunch. She smiled, asking me if I ate vegetarian and when I told her sure, she exited the room behind me and her heels clicked off down the hallway.

Spivey turned to me. "As I told you in the restaurant, my father was the original Spivey in Spivey & Frettington. In the early 1980s, my father began his great plan to groom me to take over the family business and his then-waning fortune. This great plan, of course, was only implemented after my brother Charley, the rightful heir, was killed in the Air Florida 737 plane crash just over on the 14th Street Bridge. It was so abrupt! So tragic! Truth is, my brother and I hated each other because I never much agreed with my father. Thus, I refer to my father's plan for me as The Great Plan B. I have no intention of wasting your time with family matters, and apologize for what you may perceive as my musings."

He cleared his throat, sipped, and let off a bit of a cough before continuing. "My point is to demonstrate that I never wanted to become who you see before you now. I reluctantly took the position as my father grew sick, as I am now. I worked hard, rebuilt the company and abdicated much of whom I was, my morals, my convictions. See, I came into myself during a special time and mindset in the sixties and early seventies where the zeitgeist was the necessity of radical change. Where one could take action with the earnest belief that one may engender great change, may foster a more egalitarian world. One free of hypocrisy, of the evils of the system."

By this point he was leaning forward across the desk,

consuming much of the leather chair. He brushed his hand across the strands of hair on his head and patted his forehead with a handkerchief. His blue eyes glared into me and in them I could see the wideness of his vision and the depth of his past. His blue collared shirt had wrinkled from the excitement with which he spoke. He sipped water, returned his handkerchief to his pocket, and continued.

"Oh, I'm sure you've heard of such a time and have known it as one supplanted with something unsuitably described as idealist naivety. It was not so as termed. It was truly a possibility, but one undermined as most great possibilities are. Yet, years later, in that awful time and place that was the eighties, you must understand, I was without much choice. I had to take after my father. The Great Morty Spivey who was losing in a time where so many were winning, where there was an unprecedented affluence, a burgeoning yuppie-class. They were catching up with him. Morty Spivey was becoming common. Oh, be glad you vaguely remember such a time! I won't bore you with the great expanse between then and now, the terrible life I endured as an imposter, and worst of all, a sell-out. I had all but given up hope, you understand? This you must understand to some degree? And then came these terrible years of recent. This unrest I felt swelling around me precipitated by each exigency, and I knew there must be those out there like that which I once was so long ago in a more real, more hopeful time. I felt the swelling. The newscasters and politicians downplayed it, tried to suppress it after every crisis."

His fist slammed the table and I leaned back in my chair, startled. Fletcher Spivey didn't seem to notice, the passion in his voice rising, "Enron. Worldcom. Katrina and a government with no infrastructure to support its people. Abu Ghraib. Guantanamo and the endless hypocrisy. The selling of the wars and the questionable intelligence. Scooter Libby. The iceberg of politics and greed that trumps science and logic in this country! I watched and it hit me, a groundswell was forthcoming. And after realizing this, about two years ago or so, I began looking for what would come to be you who sits here with me now. Yes, I had sensed it right! Soon thereafter, the economy crashed and I knew, I felt it, the ice thinning. The public's knees began to wobble. Oh, you cannot imagine the potential of this day we share. It, so long awaited, feels so surreal as always do those days when a setting sun seems suddenly not to dissipate, but to brighten the sky."

Spivey, sweat on his brow and light in his eyes, wore the grin of an old man sublimely indulged in ruminations of all that seemed right in his life. I had heard much of the sixties and early seventies and admit that I had held a fair dose of contempt for what became of them. But those were the old days. And to those who came of them you can never say anything bad about the old days. Everyone who was there then remembers it and says it was good. To them, it only gets better with time. Then things were. Now things imitate. Then things were possible, then they were authentic and it was nothing like now when everything is… well, whatever it wasn't then. And only the people who were there can ever really understand.

Spivey was there and he understood well. But unlike the rest of those there, who abandoned the idea and sold the farm just as quick as something new and more profitable came on the scene, Spivey assumed his sell-out role only out of loyalty. His loyalty to his family came above all. Despite his misgivings, and his reluctance, he did what he had to do, playing the other side's game but never letting it sink in deep. I did, and still do give him nothing less than respect for both his resiliency and determination, despite its being suppressed for those many years. It was out of loyalty that he acted. And here he was now, with charity in his heart, a resurgent determination, ready to take advantage of the chaos of the time.

In a dining room just down the hall, the two of us ate the sandwiches that Ms. Alice prepared. It was here that I noticed the apartment was a small museum of Fletcher Spivey's long-gone era of the sixties and early seventies. Thinking about it now, the furniture seemed frozen in the era, an ongoing live-in display to museum visitors of the 'modern living' of those times.

On the otherwise empty wall aside the Formica dining table, there was a huge black and white blow-up of a photograph of a young Howard Zinn and some other guy being arrested. The two men were being escorted off by police officers in riot gear. The poster must've been five feet high and eight feet wide.

Spivey caught me glancing up at it while we ate and said, "You see that?"

I looked at him there smiling.

"That was me, that was me right there off to the side when this photo was taken. I was there man," he said, sounding suddenly like yesterday's hippy and not the polished, well-spoken man known publically as the former-CEO.

I asked him to point himself out, and he said, "No, no. I'm not in the photo. As I said, I was right off to the side." He pointed into space off to the right of the photo as if the camera lens could pan and we'd see him frozen in time, standing just right there. "But I watched him get pulled away that day."

I nodded, grabbed another bite and he began telling me about a few of the other decorations. The opposite wall was decorated by a series of simple black frames with enlarged photographs in them, I imagined eight-by-tens. An amateur photograph of Dr. Martin Luther King speaking in front of the Lincoln Memorial. Spivey was there. Another photo in D.C. that Spivey said was from a war protest. He was there. One of a bloodied youth, taken at the DNC convention of '68 in Chicago. He was there - the photo was a picture he took of a friend. A photo from the protests at the edge of Oakland where the Hell's Angels beat up some Berkley students. He was a student at the campus then, and was there. And then there, behind me on the wall hung an original Woodstock '69 poster. He was there, although he doesn't remember it.

Ms. Alice joined us at the dining table. She set down a bowl of grapes and began picking through them and I stared at her, figuring she was about my age. She remarked to me that it was all very fascinating, the photos and the life Fletcher Spivey has lived. I remember wondering then if I'd ever be sitting down somewhere, showing someone pictures I took years before, during the first decade of the twenty-first century. I wondered what stories I would tell, and if the photos I had would all be part of great, historic events that the people of the future would look back on in amazement, awing me, that I was there, a participant, then, way back during an almost magical time that changed the course of the world as we know it.

9

WE FINISHED LUNCH and Spivey asked me to join him back in the library. Ms. Alice stayed behind saying she didn't want to bother us, and besides, she had some work to do in the other room. I excused myself to the bathroom. Rinsed and spat.

Back in the library, I noticed for the first time some of the books in the built-in book shelf. Books by Alinsky, Chomsky, Zinn, William S. Burroughs, Abbie Hoffman, Alan Ginsburg, and on and on.

"So you're still here," he said as we each found our seats.

He looked tired again and I saw very clearly then the business side of the man. I saw that same paying customer that I served back at the Ritchfield Steakhouse.

"This is positive news for both of us. I see that something has changed in you from earlier today when it was your prerogative to excuse yourself from the company of Fletcher Spivey, from the memory thereof. You stuck it through, my good boy. Is it true that something has changed? Would you, at last, like to hear my proposal to you? The reason I have summoned you?"

"I've got only my mind to lose."

"Oh yes," he recalled. Earlier I'd said my mind was my problem, hadn't I? Yes. Yes I had. "Well then," he said, "shall we begin with what's failing me? Yes, it seems to be the very first thing so far as creating understanding goes. Let me put this very simple and very straightforward. I can only be."

I nodded, encouraging him on.

"You see, I'm dying Emory. I've got a disease. I won't say what. It's a bit embarrassing, I suppose. It's hard for a man to speak specifically about a function of his body which has betrayed him. You understand?"

"Sure," I told him.

"Suffice it to say that this betrayal will kill me. It is attacking me with no end in sight other than at the expiration of the man you see here before you. This is known for certain, the question only of the order of things we call time. And what does a dying man – any dying man, oh maybe women too, but these things of pride are always characteristic of men, so yes, we shall stick with men for present purposes – what does any and every dying man want?"

"A legacy."

"Indeed! My legacy though," he continued on, "is not to be of the turnaround I did with Spivey & Frettington – making some shareholders exorbitantly rich. No! My legacy will be the realization of my generation's dreams as they were then, in their purity and authenticity. Not what you see now on television! Not that portrayal; that co-optation of the possibility for truly radical change, that earnest hope my generation offered the world. Nowadays they're convincing you that you can buy dissent, you can buy a revolution – just consume, consume, consume and you're an authentic threat. To whom?"

"Nobody."

"Exactly! You're threatening your own vitality if anything – you're rebelling against yourself and your better senses, throwing away your hard earned piece of the world to line some executive's pockets. Somebody just like me. I sold that fake lot to my generation and those generations since. That was my genius, the seed of the turnaround for an outmoded marketing firm. My company pioneered that marketing scheme that has become the standard practice of the day."

"I know those ads."

"Yes! And now I seek to turn it all around. To undo the betrayals to my ideals. Just like my body has betrayed itself, I had betrayed myself and exploited what I knew and what I stood for. So now I rescind on the Fletcher Spivey that existed from the 1980s on to the cusp of the twenty-first century. You see, a dying man does not need nor want money. Nor does he want possession. There are no such things for such a man. He does not want security. And when a dying man has no family – no children, no wife, no siblings - that dying man has no one to want security for. A dying man wants to look back on his life and see that he has no regrets, no shame, no bitterness lingering in his gut like an ulcer. He wants to see that he was true to himself and, most of all, that he was true to the young man he once was!"

Fletcher Spivey looked a man on the verge of exhaustion and tears. Yet, part of that man looked determined, poised for a tirade the way he clutched his right hand with the little silver ring that seemed to be the only thing keeping his fist from bursting under the force of blood-swollen veins; that little silver ring, the one he was twisting ever-so slyly that night in the restaurant. He noticed me staring at his hand and eased off, letting go of the fist. And now he just looked the part of the pathetic dying man, exhausted and self-aware.

It took him a moment to recover. I watched this patiently. With a hold on himself now, he got back to it. "Enough about all that. What matter is it to you? What concern have you with the fate of the fading past? You're interest is in the here and now. Why are you here? What does this have to do with you? Stall no further, you're thinking, let's get to it."

And that was true. I had sat and listened to this old man go on for some time in his strange way of speaking. He had coaxed me back into my chair what seemed like hours ago. Someone else might've sat and heard him say all this and thought he was just a lonely, impotent old man. Half delusional. But that wasn't me. I wanted to know more. I wanted to know where I fit in.

He watched me a moment, his eyes seeming to take up the half of his face, and before I could say anything he asked, "But first, let me ask you, do you have regret in your life?"

I did, I told him. "A good bit of it."

"Then you understand. It weighs you down, doesn't it?"

I nodded.

"I feel shame. I feel sadness, Emory."

I stared at him uncomfortably, not knowing what to say.

"Oh I have such regret," he confessed. "Your work is important to me, Emory. It is why I've sought you out. Both you're writing and your art, but primarily your writing. Your blog has achieved a cult-like following in the movement. And with this you've established yourself a brand of credibility, of authenticity. A person whose name is used with admiration and awe, a name that conjures passion, dedication in the hearts of the loyalist. An identity that catalyzes commitment in the minds of the emerging ones who'd otherwise be vacillating on the fence of indecision - those who could choose the path to radical change or the path to stagnation. You are countrywide here in the states, you are worldwide. I assume you are aware of this?"

I was. Except, not in as a direct sense as Fletcher articulated it. But as I sat there, I thought back over it all and how it'd all started. It'd begun some time in Europe, after I started writing, of course. I guess I just needed to say some things – well, no, it was more a way of thinking things through. I'd been reading a lot then and developing my philosophy; you know the old writers who had ideas before all this commercial crap you read nowadays. Sinclair. Orwell. Conrad. Steinbeck. Then someone gave me Zinn's *A People's History of the United States*. And that led me to Chomsky and others. I guess I figured if people with ideas could write, I could write. So I started a simple blog and went from there. I told all the underground networks about it, and people at protests, and the indie publications, and all of that.

Of course, it did nothing. I was writing in a relative vacuum. I was preaching to the choir of activists and radicals. But the vast lemmings of the world were busy rotting on their couches sucking calories, gaping into the flashing worm hole in the box, buying up the culture industry with their week's worth of office labor. Numb. Vacuous. Driving SUVs off the edge of the world, useless plastic piled in their lap, their debt in their back pocket. Stagnant.

No one really had cared about the wars. No one was really all that upset at being lied to by the President. So they didn't have WMD? So what? Saddam was a bad guy anyways. Plus, the oil made for a nice spoil. No one felt too bad about civil liberties and whateveritwas with habeas corpus. What'd that mean anyways and why should they care? It wasn't them being tortured. What's torture was not finding the color towels you wanted to match the bathroom rug when you drove all the way across town and the customer service woman on the phone said they were in stock. Human rights? Yes, they had those – the right to buy affordable plastic-encased silicon chips and new sneakers. They wanted their towels to match the bathroom rug, anyhow. The global economy meant growth. No one was all that worried about the national debt then, either. We'll bomb our way out of it. Take your family to an amusement park. And why do you hate America, anyways? Relax. Turn your TV on, play your videogame, buy upscale jeans at the mall. Eat. Eat something. A gourmet cookie break would be nice. You've been shopping all day. Buy a home. Buy two. Flip it. Get rich. The water is rising, the rainforests are gone, but your car is getting old. You really should do something. Leasing is always an option.

And that's how it was. But in 2008 the pies in the sky fell back to Earth. The economy crashed. Fear set in. Everything changed. And things changed for me, too. More visitors to my site reading my work. More reader emails. More and more people, "everyday people," were interested in what I had to say. They felt how I did. They'd been taken advantage of and lied to. They'd been used up for all they had to give and thrown aside when they weren't needed. Their life boiled down to one thing. They were here on this planet to work so that others could grow rich. People saw that the governments were looking out for the big businesses who were, and always had been, looking out for no one but themselves. A crime had been committed right before the eyes of every citizen of the global economy and the criminals had prospered in a historic fashion. It was the crime of the century. People were afraid.

Thinking about it as I sat there across from Fletcher, I realized it was an email while in Dublin that opened my eyes to the power of one man sharing ideas. The email came from a woman from Louisiana who described herself as a divorced mother of 3 in her mid-forties who had recently lost her job, her house, and was seeking to file for bankruptcy. "I am probably not your typical reader," she wrote. "But I surely do know I am not the only person in my situation who reads you. You give me hope. I wish there was something common people like me could do to stand up to these big corporations and all this fraud. You just say it so well. You are a hero to those of us who feel powerless."

Soon there were protests across Europe. I was no fool. They'd be coming to America shortly. I realized then that sparks could ignite dead leaves causing entire forests to burn. I was on the verge of something.

By the time I'd gotten back the U.S. in January 2009 I had this heavy following and it was a good thing my face couldn't be matched with my name. It kept me out of trouble with the pigs and from any bugging on the street from those who followed my company. I'd get emails from this group or that wanting me to do things like come give a talk at their meeting or endorse some logic or plan. There was even this article in the *Post* about me.

WHO IS 'EMORY WALDEN'?

It was the kind of article that raised more questions than it answered: Is Emory his real name? What is his influence among the younger generation? What threat does he pose and should the police be trying to locate this man and speak with him? How come they don't know where he is?

Pat Drassell had clipped the article and kept it. As for me, I'd avoided any invitation by any group, any affiliation or endorsement. I'd kept my face and my person, as it existed in the everyday sense of the world, apart from an identity I had created for myself online and with my graffiti. Nothing about that other me was shared with that person that waited tables, that rode the public transport, that existed in the world you then traversed day in and day out.

So I was blown away that this man Fletcher Spivey could have found me. But I was glad he did. I began again to wonder how, but he interjected and my train of thought derailed.

"You are here today, Emory, because I want your help. Your status is important. You have the ability to help achieve the dreams averted so many years ago in the era of my youth. We two, the young Fletcher Spivey and the young Emory Walden, are of the same mind. I want to take you aboard, I want to help you get to the next level. I want to assist you, financially and otherwise, so that together we two can overcome any obstacle, such obstacles as those that stood in the way of my generation. You see, I've garnered my status, a status far beyond that which any of my then-contemporaries held. I am of the business world. I have influence, I have connections, friends in places that the public aren't even aware exist. There are people who owe me favors, if you follow. I am wealthy with the means to independently sustain the revolution. Yes, revolution. It's a term we fancied back in my era. It's a term that seems now antiquated, outmoded, forgotten, most of all impossible."

Mr. Spivey smiled like I'd never seen a businessman

smile. But was businessman the correct moniker? No. He was not the businessman. He was the man enwrapped in the businessman's outer skin. Was he not the catalyst? The expiring flame unwilling to smolder and trail off in smoke?

Enter Emory Walden.

Right place, right time? Maybe. It was just like Spivey said. No one really cared until the economy crashed. Why not take advantage of it? Isn't that what the politicians, and the corporations, and the rest of the power hungry do? So why not use it to bring real change that'd help with all the other problems plaguing this corrupt world?

I cannot explain to you how I felt. If you've ever wanted to be a part of something, then you understand. If you've ever felt let down by the world, then you understand. And if you've ever been to a party the night before a hurricane or a blizzard was supposed to arrive, where you've celebrated the prospect of the monotonous cycle of our everyday society being disrupted if only for a day, then you understand, though you may not have realized it before now. If Fletcher Spivey wanted to change the world, I was his man.

"Where do I sign?" I asked.

"There's no paper to sign," he chuckled. "But your word, your loyalty is vital. The procedures done with Ms. Alice must be done with you – for security reasons, you understand. Collateral so to speak, to ensure you're serious. Ms. Alice will deal with that process. What will be necessary between us this evening before I must retire for the night is a briefing." I realized then that the sun was fading and I must have been there for hours.

"You should return next week so that we may begin our work, but in the interim a few things must be taken care of. Most importantly, you must quit your job. It is a surprise to me that you have been able to keep your head in public this long. But, I suppose your employers have little choice in who they employ – more preoccupied with avoiding hiring illegals than with keeping their ear to the street – and this is why they've yet to let you go, not turn you in."

Good old Peter, I thought. Good old Peter clinging desperately to a false hope that one day I would serve as the conduit back to Roberto.

"Indeed you must quit your job imminently. You must not cause a scene. Do not draw any attention to your departure. Put in your two-weeks notice and if anyone asks tell them you're heading back to Europe, for work or travel. It doesn't matter. You will be afforded a stipend on which to live in order to take care of your personal needs. It will be comparable to your wages, as I am certain you've not a great deal of needs."

I nodded.

He asked me about my living arrangements and I told him I was a long-term squatter on a friend's couch. So I wasn't in a lease, didn't have my name on a lease agreement? No. Did I have credit cards? I had one, near expiration that I used only in severe emergency during my travels. Spivey instructed me to quit using it and to let it expire.

"Pay for everything with cash," he said.

I told him that all my transportation was via public transit so I didn't own a car, have insurance, nor did I have a cell phone, pay bills, or any other legal ties other than my passport, birth certificate, social security card, driver's license, a library card and the one credit card.

He asked whether my friend, the one I was staying with, knew about my work and that aspect of my life?

The truth is, I prevaricated when Spivey asked me that. I'm not sure why. I guess I wanted to protect Pat.

Then, Spivey said he'd set up an apartment under his own name for me to live in. It would be modest and appropriately furnished. From there, I could operate in private. I would be given a laptop to help keep the cover on my point of entry to the Internet. But I had a laptop that I operate from, a stolen one I took from a girl's flat back when I was in Munich. He smiled. He'd have some kind of 'Internet connection encryptor and scrambler' set up in the new apartment. We should never be too cautious, he said.

*****

I laid on the couch unable to sleep. Pat's snore traveled through the wall. I didn't know why Fletcher Spivey was dying, nor did I care. He was my benefactor, a willful and determined man. One who shared the vision, one who had identified and harnessed the current zeitgeist, and one who, despite the roles he had played for the still waters, in his fading life, had done the right thing. This old man had embraced the indefatigable young Fletcher Spivey. And I. I was just like Pip. I was just like the character from a Dickens novel, read under cover of blanket by flashlight when I was that teen boy back then all those years ago. What happened to that boy? I suppose he read so much that the stories came to life.

PART TWO

SIMILITUDE

10

SO I HAD LET THE WEEK PUTTER ON BY. Since I met with Spivey I hadn't been able to get any writing done, although I'd sat down to try, and not one good idea had come to me for street art. I gave Peter my two-week notice. It was a Tuesday and I did it when the restaurant was busy during a lunch shift so he wouldn't have time to express anything to me about Roberto or start asking a bunch of questions.

I was happy to be quitting my job and all and to be moving off Pat's couch. I told Pat about the move the same day I put my two-weeks in, and that I wasn't sure when I'd be moving but that I just knew it was soon. He thought I was leaving the city and seemed hurt when I told him I wasn't. I didn't say anything about quitting my job and not a peep about the auspices of Fletcher Spivey. I just explained to him that I'd saved up enough money now to rent my own place and that I couldn't bring myself to keep squatting at his apartment if it wasn't necessary. I thanked him a good deal for letting me stay there all the while and promised to go out with him and Lilleth to the Mezzanine that upcoming weekend as a sort of gesture of gratitude. He was excited about this and, despite my reluctance to go, it felt good to be doing something to make him happy. Finally, I'd meet Lilleth, he said.

Carolyn and I spent every evening together that week after work. She nibbled the fudge I bought her, got me to try on a hat in a store, and giggled at how it fit on my head. She rested her head on my shoulder as we watched the bundled people scurry by.

She radiated the streetlight. She left a trail everywhere she went. She did most of the talking. I was happy to move alongside her like a river to a city.

As instructed, I returned one week later to the condominium in 506301. This time I wore a pair of jeans and a t-shirt. Who did I have to impress? I had impressed. And the clothes on my back had nothing to do with that. I arrived, passed the costumed man at the door and shared the elevator ride up with the costumed man who pushed the buttons. At 4700 I gave a rap on the door and waited for Spivey to greet me with his 'indeed's' and 'quite so's' and his usual long-winded chatter. But when the door opened it was Ms. Alice who stood before me with her Arlington smile.

"Hello, Ms. Alice. I'm back, back to see Mr. Spivey."

"Yes," she smiled, "Please call me Ella."

I followed her down the long hallway, her heels clicking, and when we got to the library she motioned for me to have a seat. Sitting, I gazed around the room. In the corner hung a small window that looked out onto the city street and I could see the side of a gray building and a woman talking on a cell phone in one of the windows across the way. The woman, staring out into the streets of Georgetown, twisted her finger around a pearl necklace a few times before she caught me gazing at her. I glanced away.

The books in the built-in book shelf stood handsomely erect. On the desk before me sat a pile of colored folders. Next to them, a book of Gramsci's prison writings lay atop Alinsky's "Rules for Radicals," which was propped up by a book with the spine that read simply "Chomsky." Atop the stack sat a wide, clay-red mug. Soon I heard heels clicking their way back to me.

"Some tea?" Ms. Alice entered the study and she placed a

mug on the desk before me. "It's chai, with a hint of lemongrass."

I took the mug and smiled a thank you as she clicked around me to the desk. As she sat, she tucked a lock of hair behind her ear then reached for her mug.

"Familiar with these theorists?" She asked tapping her painted fingernail atop the book stack.

Yes. I'd read them. Herself?

"I'm in the process. Yes, I've always been an avid reader. And, Fletcher's collection is just – well I'm trying to get through his library of books here. Some of them I understand better than others." This last sentence was given to me with a kind of ditzy inflection that girls employ upon catching themselves coming across as too smart to a man, and so too threatening.

How long had she been working for Spivey?

"Five years. But it wasn't until about two years or so ago, I guess, that I came to work for him in this capacity. Before, I worked as his personal assistant. That was my job right out of college. Then, about two years ago, he took me in so-to-speak. Just as he has taken you in now."

And where was Mr. Spivey?

"As we speak, he's out closing the deal on your new apartment, actually. We're not expecting him here today for our meeting. His presence isn't necessary."

"Oh. Well, what is it that you do for him? I mean, why did he take you in – as you put it – for what purpose? I understand why I'm here, I just am not quite sure I understand -"

"My responsibilities run the gamut, you might say. But, in the basic sense, I work as his personal, trusted assistant. Someone with the ambitions of Fletcher Spivey could not possibly effectively perform all of the tasks necessary to realize those ambitions. Don't you agree? No, especially not in his state of health. There is simply too much work to be done. Fletcher needed assistance, someone he could trust. Someone who has been faithful to him. This is where I entered the picture."

I sipped the tea not wanting to interrupt or give her pause to halt her disclosure.

"This is why I read. There is a vast knowledge gap between persons such as yourself and Fletcher, and a woman such as myself who has known only the structured education system. Business and the overall logic that I ascribed to growing up was presented to me as an inevitability, a fact of the human condition, the simple, unquestionable reality of the organization of the world. And here now I have this wonderful opportunity to read and learn and understand that that configuration was not an inevitability but a social construction."

Ella Alice reflected on these words a moment, her eyes trailing off to the edge of the room. And then, as if cold, she picked up the mug and cupped it in both hands near her mouth.

"Last question," I said.

"Shoot."

"What's up with your hand?"

"Excuse me?"

"Your hand. Your rubber hand."

She labored to laugh.

"Your left hand. It's rubber isn't it? It hasn't moved," I pointed. "You hide it well."

"This meeting is about *your* appendages," she retorted.

I nodded. I sipped. Trying not to stare at her paperweight hand, I told her how I'd put in my two-week notice at my job, told my roommate I was moving out, and cut up my credit card and trashed it, finishing with "So that's not too many tied up ends, but it's a start."

Ella agreed. "Yes, yes. I was hoping to have the apartment all worked out today but sometimes these things get delayed. Fletcher had to go there in person and sign the deed. That business will be done by E.O.B. - that is, end of business today. And, with that taken care of, you'll be set to move in in just a few days. First, we'll get you some furniture shipped over and have the Internet set up. That'll be taken care of tomorrow. Wednesday, Fletcher's encryption people will come by. It's just a little box that scrambles the IP. Once those things are all taken care of, you are free to move in Wednesday night. We thought it best that no one sees you, not the furniture people, the cable people, or even the encryption guy. I will be at the apartment for the next few days signing for the bills and taking care of everything."

"Ok," I told her, "sounds great." I sipped the tea and Ella Alice followed suit.

"So, that leaves the identification to be dealt with," she said. "Your new identity is Liam Logan and the address on your ID will be a P.O. Box where you can receive mail. This is one of the means through which we will contact you, as continued visits back here is out of the question. You will receive your cash stipend in an unmarked envelope at this post office address as well."

Ella Alice reached for a colored folder on the desk, this one being green, and slid it across the desk to me with her paperweight hand.

"Inside you will find a social security card. You will also find a birth certificate. Neither are copies. Nor are they fakes, or forgeries. They are real, official United States Government documents. The only thing fake about them is the identity behind them. Your driver's license will also be an official government certified license. To get your license you could take these documents down to the DMV, present them, and you could acquire a real Washington, D.C. driver's license."

"I thought I was supposed to get a license from Spivey? And who said anything about a birth certificate?"

"The birth certificate was no harder to come by than the social security card, so we just assume get you one of each. It does no harm and solidifies you as Liam Logan just that extra bit. As far as the license goes, I said you *could* go down and do those things. It is not necessary that you do."

She grabbed the other folder off the desk, this one

yellow, and said "If you don't mind, follow me." Ella Alice led me to a bathroom with blue walls and a row of bright lights above the sink. She stood me against the wall, put some gel in my hair to smooth out the neglected mop atop my head, and snapped a few photos of me.

Afterwards, she handed me the yellow envelope and said, "There are two pieces of paper in this envelope. The address to the P.O. Box that your ID is registered to is on the top sheet of paper. On the bottom sheet is the address of the apartment that you will be staying at. Please arrive Wednesday night anytime after eight."

"I work Wednesday till nine," I told her. "I'll come by after that."

"Excellent. There's just one more thing we need to address. When you arrive at the apartment, make sure you have all of your Emory Walden means of identification with you. Your driver's license, your social security card, even your library card."

All that stuff was in my rucksack. Just about all my worldly possessions were in that rucksack. It wouldn't be too hard of a move out of Pat's and into the new place. Just one big bag of stuff.

"I'll have your license and your new keys ready for Wednesday night. All the loose ends tied up." Ella Alice smiled. But the smile was not for me. It was for the mirror.

"Our business here today is complete, and, if you don't mind, I've some things to take care of before Fletcher returns." She glanced at her watch. "I expect him within the hour."

So she walked me to the door, her heels clicking down the hallway before me, and I left the condo with the two envelopes tucked tightly under my arm, out past the costumed men and into the city.

* * * * *

Carolyn lay on her stomach in the green grass of spring,

her legs crossed in the air behind her, her chin propped on her wrist bent forward. I watched the skin on her back collect the sun as I finished eating and told her I'd better get on back to work.

"I can't believe it's your last day," she said.

"I know."

"Are we still going to hang out?" she asked.

"Of course," I laughed.

"I'm so excited for you."

"I'm so excited *about* you."

She smiled and giggled, telling me I was cute and ridiculous. Things had been going so well with her and in this way I hated to be leaving my job. I never thought I could do so well, not with a girl like her. We spent time together after work whenever we were on the same shift. We hid from Brock and waited for one another in the park like secret teenage crushes hiding from our parents. I'd ask her what she wanted to do and she'd shrug and in time we'd find our way here or there to window shop or gaze at the monuments, or just sit and let the night overtake us.

We were in that curious stage of excitement and potential where I think neither of us wanted to take the leap and ask for formal plans. So it was always after work that we hung out. But I never asked her to hang out if we weren't working that night. That way I hadn't felt too forward. And then, on this particular day, I asked her to meet me for lunch because it was my last day and we weren't both working the same shift.

"I'll call you."

"It's a beautiful day. I think I'll lie here a while before meeting my Mom tonight."

"Sounds good." I turned and begin walking away to hear her call, "Emory."

"Yes?"

She looked up at me over top her glasses and asked, "When?"

* * * * *

After work Wednesday night I ventured over to my new home. My very own place of residence. No roommates, no sleeping on the floor, no couches, no sleeping with hideous girls to stay out of the rain, no farm houses or train stations. There would be a bed all my own. There would be four walls and these four walls would be shared with no one. I would be alone. Free to be.

I stopped by Pat's apartment to get my rucksack. He was gone. I wasn't sure where to, but he'd been gone a lot more in those days. So I left him a note of thanks and took off. He had given me a key but I couldn't lock the door without it so I wasn't able to leave it behind for him. In the note I mentioned that I'd give it to him next I saw him and said we were still on for the Mezzanine that upcoming weekend.

The apartment could not have been situated more perfectly, I was thinking as I stepped up to the front door of a brick row house. The apartment, which I gathered was an old three-story townhouse converted into three or four individual apartments, was about midway between Dupont Circle and Adams Morgan on Florida Avenue NW. Its location was almost centered in my street art playground. The Dupont metro and the circle itself, where I slept that one night with Renton, was maybe a ten-minute walk from the front door of the apartment building. Adams Morgan, the wasteland of bars, clubs and late-night pizza shops, the very breeding grounds of the vitiated niche of my generation, was perhaps a six or seven-minute walk in the other direction.

Oddly, the apartment number was 1 despite being at the very top of the stairs. It was past a short, unmarked door that led to some sort of electrical closet or perhaps the roof. The apartment door was just above from there, plop, when I turned the corner in the narrow stairwell and headed about five more feet up to it.

I gave a knock, waited a minute and gave a bit more this

time. When the door opened, there stood Ella Alice, her green t-shirt snug around her breasts about eyelevel from where I stood on the second-to-top stair. From there, the t-shirt hung down just barely covering the top of her low-rise jeans which clung to the bone of hips and down her legs where they flared out just above the ankles where a pair of white sneakers were strapped to her feet.

"Welcome!"

I stepped up and into the apartment which was about the size of a college classroom or so and took up the entire top floor of the building. The room was all one with a sleeping area in one corner and, in the other, a little kitchen against a far wall that held a window the size of a cereal box above a white porcelain sink. Huddled in the kitchen was a stove with a range top, a ventilation fan overhead, and a small refrigerator that clicked on and off in a loud hum every ten minutes or so. In the other corner, the roof slanted down by a window with a metal cage outside of it, a fire escape. Just to the left of the window stood a small black desk with computer chair, which was about a body's length from the bed. The bed, which was also black, sat with its width sort of tucked under the slant. In the middle of the room, a few feet from the front door, was a round wooden table just big enough for two or three people to dine on. Two wooden chairs sat tucked underneath. Mounted on the wall between the bed and the kitchen was an empty Hungarian bookshelf. Across from it, resting against the near wall with no windows, sat a tan couch similar in shade to the wooden table which had to it a sort of orangish-green hue.

"The extra chair at the table is for when I am over," said Ella Alice. "To work, that is. I am much the artist in the kitchen I think you will find – if you haven't already. By the looks of you, you could stand to do some eating and should benefit from that."

She was saying a few other things, commenting on the furniture arrangement and the general set up of the place. But I wasn't listening. I was wondering how did they ever get furniture up into this place? No matter. The place was great. It was perfect. It was better than perfect. It was my first excursion in living alone. It was my first very own bed since graduating college.

I placed my rucksack down on the floor by the front door, leaning it against the wall with the couch up against it. "I have to run to the bathroom," I told Ella Alice, leaving her standing there in the common room.

The bathroom was to the right of the bed, a tiny room with a tiny sink, a toilet and a stand-up shower all crammed in almost on top of each other. The floor, what little there was, was tiled with white and black checkers one after the other.

I returned to the common room to find Ella Alice sitting on the couch, her legs crossed in blue jeans.

"Do you have your Emory Walden identification?"

I got my driver's license, social security card and my library card from my rucksack. "What do you need them for?"

"Collateral," she told me. "And safety, just in case something happened and you got picked up. Don't worry, we'll be holding onto them."

I grunted.

"Don't look so vexed. It's just for assurance. He's got all my stuff, too. We're in the same boat, hunny."

So I handed her the items. If this was the way it had to be, what good was my old identity anyways? What value did that person have? He was a criminal and an iconoclast. He had no money, no job, no line of credit.

"And your birth certificate?" she asked looking at the three cards in her lap.

"You'd have to go find my Mom and ask her for that one. She kept it. And I don't know where the crap she is, nor do I care."

Ella Alice nodded, seeming to understand. What about my passport, the one I used during my travels to Europe?

"I wish I knew," I shrugged. "I lost it. Unless it's in one

of my pants pockets in my rucksack. But I haven't seen it in a few weeks."

"Mind if I check your bag?" She rose to her feat.

"Go right ahead."

She scoured through the bag and found no trace of the passport.

"Satisfied?"

"I need to check and make sure it's not on your person."

I shrugged, telling her to go right ahead. So she frisked me the way I imagine a cop or a mobster would frisk someone. And still she found nothing. When she patted down my butt pockets with her paperweight hand I thought I could see the corners of a smile but I don't know. Perhaps it was just my loins yearning to reclaim fading memories of a woman's touch. Suddenly I remembered that alley night and Brock between her mouth's corners and the tickle inside me faded to acrimony.

"I told you, Ella, it's lost! That screws me more than anything 'cause now I've no way of getting out of this country if the air turns viral. You understand?"

To this she nodded. She put the three cards into her left pocket and pulled something out of her right one. Very businesslike she said, "Well here's your new license, Mr. Logan."

She handed me the card with the photo she took in Spivey's blue bathroom. It looked as real as could be, except the name wasn't mine and there was a P.O. Box address.

11

PAT YELLED SOMETHING I couldn't understand, his voice droned out under the bass thuds and all these people making a racket. What's that? He couldn't hear me. I leaned way over.

"Whattya drink?" he yelled in my ear.

"Whatever you're having," I shrugged.

He made his way to the bar, squeezing past, and sometimes pushing past, hoards of sweaty twenty-something salivating as they struggled for status – climbing over one another, stretching, reaching, oh so eager to get the bar tender's attention. To prove their worth. A few minutes later, he returned with two pint glasses of something or other that had a yellow and brown mix to it with a green lime and ice. We drank it down. And soon, Pat returned with another. We got that down, and soon yet another.

"Can I give you some money?" I yelled. But Pat shook his head, "I'm hooked up here."

I nodded and we sipped our drinks.

"Oh, here she is, our little hook up," he yelled pointing over my shoulder with the smile of the legitimated self. I turned under flashes and concussions of bass, doom doom ba doom doom ba-ba-bop doom. Some rapper was hollering about things I couldn't relate to.

A blonde approached us in a glittering top and a black

miniskirt that was so tiny it couldn't have been sewn of anymore fabric than a middle-school kid's cum rag.

"Hey babe," she kissed Pat, squeezing his upper arm.

"Heya, sexy. This is Emory."

She gave me the once over and the subsequent smile of approval common to girls that frequented these sorts of places.

"Hiya Emory. I'm so pumped you finally made it out."

I nodded, telling her it was nice to finally meet her.

I stood around trying to firm up my buzz while she and Pat tried to communicate by yelling in each other's ears. I knew I looked awkward and nervous like someone who didn't belong. Someone who somehow tricked his way past the bouncers. Someone who was now an embarrassing stain on the otherwise immaculately well-dressed and welcomed youth. The tawdry twenty-somethings. The aimless inert.

Everyone swayed with the music as I stood guarded, my eyes dashing about in the flicker. Sip. What a place. Sip. The place of young men and women with no other purpose in life than to crowd together like rodents to escape into alcohol and self-degradation. Sip. The males who slap their bodies against women, rubbing, thrusting, without discretion as to who's sweaty body capitulates. Sip. The females who slut themselves up in tiny little outfits carefully chosen to accentuate any feature they're confident of – tits, ass, stomach, legs. Anything that can be thrown at the throbbing male. Sip. The men and women come together here, drawn like lemmings. Sip. Crawling over top each other like rats in a cage. Sip. It is a dance of self-loathing, of depraved disregard for any semblance of self worth. Sip. Everyone slutting themselves out to the scene, to the overpriced drinks and cover, to being cool enough to hang out in the popular spots, to the in crowd, to the opposite sex. Sip. How do people start dancing in the first place - What do they say to each other? Sip. "Hey, I don't know you, clammy predator of the night. But, why don't you shove your private parts into mine like it's oh so casual. Like we're two people who've just met each other sharing a laugh. I'll just kind of bob and weave with you and throw my arm around your waste or shoulder and give you eyes. Here, let me rub my ass this way and that against you. Does that please you? Why don't you degrade me and use me as a sexual object? Why don't I disrespect myself by thrusting my body this way or that?" Sip. What self-respecting person would do such a thing? Sip. It is an enervated world. Sip. A world with no commitments, no loyalties. Sip. Not even to the impoverished self.

I felt the alcohol warming the back of my head and neck. Arms a bit looser. Legs not so stiff. Happily lost among the masses.

"Another one?"

I nodded.

Pat weaved between a few people and disappeared into the sea of bobbing bodies.

"So, Emory."

Lilleth and I were wedged between a cluster of sweat-dripped twentysomethings, bobbing up and down up and down to the beat. There were so many people all jammed together like one mass pulsating to a simple rhythm. Doom doom ba doom doom ba-ba-bop doom. It was so crowded we almost touched each other.

"So, Emory," she yelled this time.

"Yeah?" I yelled back.

"I know all about you." She had this drunken beam bent across her face.

I nodded. "Yeah?"

"I keep up with your writing – your blog," she yelld leaning her head next to my ear. "Also. My job. I hear some of the students talking about you in there. I'm down. People like me, we keep our ear to the street. We know what's good, what's hot. You know what I'm talking about?"

Perfume and perspiration rose past my face up towards the vents above. I nodded. Her mouth was resting right up by my ear so I wasn't sure if she noticed, but she kept right on either way. "I've been wanting to meet you for a while now. I've been kind of disappointed you haven't come around here. I told Pat that. You being who you are and all, I'd think you'd be in the crowd – the hot spots - a bit more."

"Not my thing," I yelled back.

"That's too bad. You're kind of a local celebrity. A cult hero."

"I didn't realize." I tried to give her an unaware, or even disinterested look but she couldn't see my face and all I could see was the skin poking out of her top with little dots of perspiration where her collarbone met her neck.

"You're off the menu."

"You wanted to meet me? Why didn't you just come over to Pat's?"

"This is where it's at, that's why. And Pitty-Pat's sort of – he can be sort of a stick in the mud sometimes. All that ganja keeps him strapped to the couch."

"It's just not my thing." I leaned away from her ear, trying to use facial expressions to get my point across to this intoxicated number in a cum-rag dress. But she just leaned back in.

"The suburbs are dead, Emory. There are a lot of girls who say your name in a certain way, a curious way. Say they want to meet you, girls that chit-chat with one-another about what they think you might be like, what you might look like." She gave my arm the same little squeeze she gave Pat's earlier. "I'm one of those girls, Emory."

I yanked back almost stumbling into the flesh cluster behind me. The film of sweat on her face glowed with triumph; triumph of the assertive, self-assured, twenty-first century fem. Her lips curled up slightly at the edges as she peered into me with cobalt eyes, little cobalt clefts between cakes of black eyeliner. The bass thudded in my skull. The warm tingling in the back where my head met my spine was spreading.

"Well, it's nice to finally meet you, Lilleth," I offered to this awkward moment. I tried to joke. "I hope I live up to the hype."

Up went the bottom of my glass and the rest of the alcohol concoction slid down to the cave of my belly. The alcohol swirled in the back of my head. She reached over with her hand, the hand that had clutched my upper arm a moment earlier and Pat's arm not so long before. Her hand slid between my legs and the palm of her hand cupped my life organ.

"Oh, I'm sure you will," she said leaning over, her lips practically touching my ear. With humid, lurking, intrusive breath, her hand massaged my genitals. "I'm gonna tell those girls you're hot as fuck. I'm gonna tell them you're big."

You rapacious little – !

"You and me should get together sometime, Emory Walden."

I grabbed her wrist, yanked it away. Her head reeled back and she gave me the face of an innocent, confused teenager who'd kissed a boy she mistook for her first love. Except this was no innocent girl. This was a rapacious Mezzanine groupie, a roach of the night, an officer of the flaccid youth. I had her wrist clutched in my hand and I could feel the blood, the intoxicated blood, pumping through her veins. I had the beast by the belly. I had -

"What're yall doin?"

Pat was standing to the side of us, clutching three drinks high up in a triangle before him. His eyes peered down at my hand wrapped around Lilleth's wrist. The alcohol sloshed in my skull, spreading to my appendages. The thudding bass. Lights dancing overhead and an entire room of bodies pulsating in sync. Say something. Say anything. No. Tell him the truth. Tell your only friend in this world God's evil truth.

"Pat. This –"

"Sweetie, Emory was just admiring the bracelet you bought me."

"Oh," Pat nodded. I let go her wrist which fell to the dangle of a silver bracelet. She leaned over and kissed Pat there on the lips. While doing this, her hand, charm dangling, reached up and extracted one of the drinks from his embrace. She pulled back and gave him a "thank you, sweetie" before wrapping her lips around the straw and pulling a sip. Then she shot a smile in his direction and then another, this time bigger, pull of the straw.

* * * * *

I sipped my fourth – fifth drink?

"Why don't you go slay some dragons?" Pat yelled, throwing me a wink. "Plenty of gazelles here tonight, my man." Holding their drinks high above the crowd, Pat and Lilleth trickled into the crowd to dance. And there I stood alone and lost.

* * * * *

I should leave, I thought. I should just take off and leave, push past all these people up the stairs and out the front door. I shouldn't bother to tell Pat and that licentious Lilleth I'm out of here. They wouldn't notice anyways.

Just then there was a tap on my shoulder. I moved slightly to get out of the way of some testosterone throbbing male trying to get by. That's what men do in places like this. They tap you on the shoulder and say, "yo, comin' through" or "look out behind ya" or some other pithy assertion framed to sound as masculine and confident as can be mustered when one must resort to something so feminine and vulnerable as words. And they tap you on the shoulder or, worse, put their hand on your shoulder. The latter is choreographed to imply they're exercising some superiority over you and have the authority to put their hand on *you* in order to manipulate *you*, the human object, who exists only as an obstacle in between them and their destination: most likely the bar, or the pisser. So, like I said, I moved slightly.

"Hey."

A female voice.

"Hey, Emory is that you?"

I turned to find before me the last thing I would've ever wanted to find in a place like this, but the one thing I wanted to see at such a time. Carolyn was standing next to another girl and the two were smiling with sweat beading off their cheeks and foreheads.

"Hey! I thought it was you!" She yelled, her smile growing. "This is my friend Adia. Adia, this is my Emory."

Her Emory! Oh, the long summers of my lost childhood! Sunburned shoulders, scabby knees, running and playing until I could take the heat no more and was forced inside by the sun to recuperate to mom's lemonade and the swivel fan.

I say "hello, it's nice to meet you" to Adia who stood about Carolyn's height but was droopy like a tired balloon. She was squeezed into a silver top with a low cut front where her fleshy chest crowded onto a shelve bra causing each fatty swell to lump practically over the silver fabric on out into public domain. Her matching miniskirt hung about eight inches or so above the knobs of her knees.

I turned to Carolyn who wore a t-shirt and designer jeans with calculated rips at the knees and around the thighs.

"What are you all doing here?" I asked.

"Just came with Adia to check out DJ Fosta Kidd. I never really come here often, but –"

"But it's basically the greatest club in the tit-sucking world!" proclaimed Adia, cutting Carolyn off – or maybe finishing the thought for her.

Adia threw her arm over Carolyn's shoulder and, gazing about, threw up her other arm and with her free pointer finger – as the rest were occupied by a half-empty mixed drink – she swept the room pointing out the evident glory of the dance room, the upstairs balcony and the bar. It was as though I should be looking on, following the tour of her finger. Instead, I looked past her, over her shoulder to where I saw Pat and Lilleth dancing. The two were dancing an arms length away, but each with another person. Lilleth had some fellow working and thrusting into her while Pat flailed around on some jiggling body with golden hair whipping about. Adia stumbled, slipped off of Carolyn and caught herself on me, her drink splashed all over my shirt before crashing to the floor.

She laughed, "Oh, hey there. Sorry about that."

I grabbed her by the shoulders, righting her.

"Whoops. There goes Mr. Drinky-Drink." She turned to Carolyn, "I'm gonna reload, hun. I'll be right – oh, hey, hey, there's Taylor. I'm gonna go say whatsup to Taylor." She laughed, "He'll buy me a drink" and began stumbling off with an eager smile and empty eyes. Then she added, "Maybe 3 or 4. I'll catch you birds later."

I watched her as she swayed and zig-zagged her way up to a tall guy and throw her arm over his shoulder. He turned to her, this serendipitous little fly in silver who, by no effort of his own, had just landed on his web.

"Well, I guess that's it for her," said Carolyn with a bit of a laugh and a shake of the head.

"Yeah, I bet."

"So, I'm glad to run into you here."

"Yeah, me too. I never thought – I mean, I thought you didn't like this place?"

"It's okay. I don't come here often, but once in a while it's nice to get out and have some fun, ya know? I mostly prefer the bars to the clubs. But the Mezz can be a good time if you come on the right night of the week."

"Oh, cool," I said. "Yeah, not really my kind of place."

"Then why come?"

I pointed over her shoulder to Pat and Lilleth. Pat stood with a drink in his hand and a lost look across his face while Lilleth continued to let the big man grind away on her.

"My good friend," I said pointing to Pat, "and his girlfriend." Carolyn followed my finger, then turned to me with a nod.

"I was actually just getting ready to leave."

*****

Outside, in front of the club the streetlights illuminated our inebriated state.

"So I guess we both got ditched, huh?" She said clasping her arm into mine.

"Typical."

We stumbled up the street a ways. "Your friend, Pat was it? He seemed nice."

"Yeah, he was pretty smooshed when I introduced you all."

Carolyn laughed. "Smooshed? I never heard that one before."

I laughed and she pulled tighter, gazing up at me with a haze in her eyes.

"I could tell," she said, still smiling. "He kept calling me Cara. Hi Cara. Emory's told me all about you, Cara. It was great to meet you, Cara."

I laughed.

Carolyn asked how Pat and I knew each other, her head on my shoulder now as we walked, and I told her we went to high school together. That we were just old friends. We engaged in small talk like this for a while and stopped to get some of that big-slice pizza to help sop up the poison in our bellies.

Any pizza craving drunkard in Adams Morgan who came to this particular stand could gaze up across the street and see a piece of street artwork plastered to the side of a brick building. It read "Happy Hour" and underneath was a stenciling of Dick Cheney with his infamous smirk sipping a Martini glass that read "BLOOD & OIL" across it. I'd painted it a while ago, the week the new administration had come in because I didn't want people to forget that slippery otter that had gotten us into this mess and I knew he would soon duck out of view, and out our of our minds. But truth be told, I'd completely forgotten I'd painted it.

As I ordered us each a slice Carolyn laughed. "That's pretty clever," she said, pointing out the artwork hovering above the street.

"What's that?" I collected the change from the cashier.

"That graffiti there. I see those a lot, more and more. They always strike me here or there when I'm going somewhere. Kind of gets me to stop a second and smile to myself. Like it's meant just for me." She laughed again, seeming to feel a bit foolish, and said, "I don't know. I like the wit, the social commentary of it all I guess. I mean, to do all that just to leave a message for people the artist doesn't even know. It just, it intrigues me."

"Yeah." I handed her slice to her as we walked out into 18th street where a crowd of drunks and pizza gobblers stumbled around, yelling and hailing cabs. "I see what you mean. I guess I never really paid attention before."

She grabbed a bite and stared at me while she chewed as if to say 'how could you not notice? They're everywhere.'

So I did my best: "But I mean, I'll definitely keep my eye out now that you mention it." And, then after a moment, I added "They're definitely interesting."

"Yeah, I just wonder if it's right, you know?" she asked, peering back toward the mural as we walked on. "I mean, whose gotta pay to repaint it? The Mom & Pop shop renting the building? The city?"

"The city belongs to all of us. It's our collective tapestry." I shrugged without looking back. "So if it speaks to you – then?"

She replied with her own shrug.

"I guess it's difficult to know these things," I shrugged again.

She smiled.

I leaned over, "Did I tell you how beautiful you are today?"

She shook her head.

"I didn't?" I exclaimed. I leaned further and planted a drunken kiss on her forehead.

After the pizza I needed to rinse and spit. I was embarrassed to do it in front of her. But what was the alternative? Excuse myself? Go around the corner? Oh, sorry

– had to disappear a moment. No reason.

When I finished: "I hope you don't mind. I know it's -"

"Why do you do that?"

"For my teeth. I know it's a turnoff. I'm sorry."

"You carry that around with you?"

I nodded.

"That's kinda silly."

"Beat's smoking."

We walked towards the park bench where we'd met for our first date some time ago. We sat for a bit, my arm around her shoulder and for a while I thought she was asleep.

I started to nod off myself when she piped right up: "I used to want to be like Adia," she confessed under the serum of alcohol. "I always wanted to be able to do what Adia does. To live carefree, to use womanness to my advantage. I know it sounds stupid as all hell, and immature and just, just – I just always wanted to bask in the attention of men instead of fearing that I'll be used up, used for my body and not desired for who I am. For me. I was like Adia for a while, years ago. I can't anymore. But, Adia. Adia does it so well. She doesn't care. She's taking advantage of them, not the other way around. Does that make sense? It makes sense to me."

She paused a moment. I opened my eyes to look at her and saw that her eyes were closed. Soon she began again. "I always wished I could be more like her in that regard. It's not you who's getting used. It's them. You're using them. You're winning the game, they're losing. You dictate. They think they're the ones in charge. But Adia, Adia is always the one who wins no matter what anyone thinks and she knows it. I mean, I'm confident in who I am. I get attention from boys. I get more attention than she does. But it's just. Well -"

"It's not you."

"No. No it's not. Not anymore at least."

"I'm glad it's not."

"Yeah?" Her eyes opened.

"Yeah, that business's no good. It's just no good. You've got to be who you are. And you're not Adia. What Adia does, whether she thinks she's winning or not – well – nobody's winning that game. It's a game where everyone is the loser. It doesn't get us, I mean our generation and all, it doesn't get us anywhere. You know?"

Carolyn gazed off down the sidewalk. "Have you ever contemplated a raindrop before?"

"I don't think so. Maybe," I told her, my body struggling to egest the murk looming in the back of my head.

"I think the raindrop is more important than the puddle," she said to the sidewalk. She reached into her pocket and garnished a translucent orange bottle. "My life is just beginning," she mumbled. "I read that somewhere." Carolyn unscrewed the cap top and poured a green mound of pills into her hand. She picked at them one by one and tossed them in either direction. They pinged off the concrete, bouncing this way or that until they fell to rest on the curb, on the street, in a patch of grass, or wound up floating in a puddle from the rain storm earlier that evening.

What are those?

"My little raindrops," she said, gazing over the gray landscape ornamented in green freckles.

"You don't need those?"

"I never needed them." She gave a sunken laugh. "I no longer want them."

She pushed herself up onto her feet and peered down at the little green raindrops. Towering over them, she said to me, "I don't want prescription raindrops in my life anymore. I want a new puddle to splash around in and I want that puddle to be made up of – of -"

Lifting myself to my feet, I asked why she was crying.

"I – I'mm get-tting rid offf all tho- thow-se r-r-raindrops t-too!" she cried, the words sputtering out in convulsion.

I wrapped my arm around her shoulder, pulled her head to my chest and tried to steady the body as it shook with little bursts of crying erupting against my chest.

"When I was a teen, my mom told me about the birds and the bees. This is what she said. She said, never give another the responsibility of caring for your heart. And I understand now what she meant, with my father and all," she paused a moment. "But carrying your own heart your whole life is such a heavy load. I want so bad to lose control. To be a passenger."

With women there is always more to comprehend than the words they choose to let seep through the dam. I wanted so bad to open her up. To be a part. To be a cure.

I leaned into her. "Baby, baby. I understand."

"Promise?" She glanced up at me.

"I'm not using you. I'm not, I'm not anything. I – I – I just. I really like you, Carolyn. I want us to be something that I've never had. I'm serious about us. You know that, right?"

She sniffled and nodded. "Yes, yes I know."

And I wondered if she did.

12

I GUESS I'D GOTTEN USED TO sleeping in my own bed in my own apartment. Sometimes I would lay awake at night and stare at the ceiling. Sometimes I would wake up in the morning alone with my four walls and expect someone to be in another room, a room that wasn't there, when I emerged for breakfast. At times, I found myself talking to the windows, the bookshelf, the humming refrigerator. I walked around the apartment naked just for something to do. I'd masturbated in every conceivable place: the couch, the shower, the bed, in the desk chair and even one time, about three in the morning, out on the fire escape.

Ella Alice was apt to come over unannounced from time to time and check in on me. She always wore street clothes when paying me a visit, her paperweight hand in tow. And, always, she cooked me something new with organic veggies and other foodstuffs that complied with that fad.

I'd have liked to tell her she was the best one armed cook I'd ever seen. But I didn't think it would go over too well. Still, I sat and watched her magic at work, and I was always amazed at how graceful and effortless her performance was. I couldn't cook that well with four arms, I wanted to tell her. I wondered how she got by with just the one and why it was that way.

She never brought me anything other than food, but

sometimes she hinted to me to check the P.O. Box which I had a terrible habit of neglecting for weeks at a time. Never having had an address for so long had left me without domestic habit.

Sometimes there were blank envelopes with my allowance in them. Other times there was a letter from Spivey, always written in Ella Alice's handwriting, commenting on my excellent 'pen' and 'stencil' with some recital of verbiage lauding radical social change. Sometimes the letters had updates about little achievements here or there on Fletcher's side of things, but mostly inconsequential gains written in the style of some corporate newsletter. Seldom, but sometimes, there were print outs of online zines and independent online news publications tucked in those tall clamp-close envelopes always with a sticky note in Ella Alices' handwriting. A lot of the articles made reference to me and the stuff I was writing. Some of the articles reported on the burgeoning population of disgruntled and increasingly active men and women, many of them young. There were new types of online movements using networking approaches that connected people together to get them to go out and do something like protest a common grievance. And sometimes there were URL links to these sites and groups. Spivey lauded these social media and it was written in one of his letters about how people were using these tools to self-organize in ways Spivey had never seen before. It made him very happy. It made me think of this guy I knew from before I went to Europe after I'd quit my job. I'd gotten involved in an activist group stateside called The Brigade and there was this guy Derek who was maybe in his thirties and wore hemp sandals and his hair down to his shoulders. He'd been at the Battle for Seattle in 1999 – drove clear across the country from Virginia because of a post he saw on a message board or something. He always preached to us about how the Internet would change everything. I wondered what became of Derek. What was he doing? I hadn't heard anything about him since I cut ties with The Brigade. As far as I knew, The

Brigade had disbanded or merged into another group or something. But Derek was probably still out there. He was probably working on our side doing a lot of the heavy lifting at the street level – pounding the pavement, waving the signs, shouting the slogans, and firing people up; the sort of stuff that I was now so distanced from.

With no employment responsibilities, I had a bounty of time to invest in writing and coming up with ideas for new street art. I had a few big schemes planned: One for a green highway sign over the beltway, another for a spot visible from the Metro stop on the Washington Mall.

I'm not sure how long it'd been since I had become Liam Logan in my private life and retained Emory Walden only as a pen name, a phantom radical icon for public consumption. Well, not *only* I suppose. There was Carolyn, Pat and Lilleth who knew my face as Emory's. Anyways, I guess it'd been about three months or more, and in that time period I'd recovered nicely from that short lull I was having in creativity.

Some reporter from the *Post* had strapped himself to my backpack and got by writing these shoddy pieces in the Arts section likening me to an aesthetic nuance like a decrepit bridge or a derelict metro stop that the city government should eviscerate. This reporter, a Mr. Trip Carpenito, was competent enough, at least, to see my street art as art, and as a statement of the world's status. He knew enough to know that there were street artists like me in cities across the world. In one article he referred me to as "Animus' wrath" stating:

> *Like a Phoenix, the socially--pointed graffiti art that riddled the district a year ago and was thought eradicated after the arrest of tagger Animus, the seventeen-year old graffiti artist and self-proclaimed Situationist, has risen anew with the emergence of a more prolific, and some say more daring artist. While his talents are certainly more honed, and his art more pervasive, police are not fully committed to stating whether they believe it is a matured Animus*

> *back to his old tricks, or if they have settled on the more likely theory that a new artist has picked up the torch for a fallen delinquent brother. It is hard to tell, say police officials, because this art is not 'tagged' with an artist's signature. Police Captain Kyle Yates has stated that the new art appears to be "of a different style and mind than the so-called Animus, however at this time we cannot rule out the possibility that Animus is responsible." Whether it is Animus or someone new, what is known is that the lull is over and graffiti art has reemerged with a vengeance to haunt the dreams of all city property owners.*

Spivey never left me any of this sort of thing in the P.O. Box, but I came to know of the articles when I met Pat and Lilleth one morning for coffee. Lilleth was gawking over them, and I was worrying someone would hear her.

I scolded her, saying "swallow it, Lilleth! Bother thinking once in a while, will ya?"

"Pitty-Pat and I are just proud of you, that's all."

I smiled.

"Is it all as bad as you make it seem?"

"We can't get through the morning without our coffee," I replied. "Doesn't that make us all sick?"

We sipped.

That night I sent Pat an email telling him to tell Lilleth she needed to keep a lid on that yapper of hers. So, I guess Pat gave her my email address because she wrote me an email apologizing, very sorry-sorry and that she didn't want me to get in any trouble and would be more tact about her knowledge of me.

Since then, I'd heard no mentions from Lilleth about my work, but I scoured the online collections at the library and read all six of the articles from Trip Carpenito.

Sometimes Lilleth would send me these brief, almost cryptic emails like old-time telegraphs that were strictly social in nature, the likes of which I labored to decipher. The easier of them went something like this:

Jammy jam 2night. A blast. Place called 'De Zire' URL? U can find. Address on site. Be there. – mmmeee

I never reciprocated, neither the email nor the invite. And still they came.

*****

One day I decided to metro down to the Mall, and hump over to the White House for a peacetest of the War on Terror. I was always in compulsion for rallies and protests. Any young person should be. In all truth, I missed them. I missed the days of The Brigade and being on the street taking direct action. I missed the rage you felt in your belly when a crowd of people seemed to scream in unison and your voice was magnified and you felt powerful. It made you feel like you were accomplishing something, to scream so loud, as though you could scream yourself to change. But of course, nothing had ever really come from any screaming I'd done. And although I knew I was doing much more with the writing and acting as the face of a movement to motivate others to scream and pound their fists, the action was far away and I never quite felt that same visceral satisfaction that I did before Europe.

But on this day I had an ulterior motive. I wanted to catch up with Renton. I'd seen him sparsely here or there around the city. I was tired of the confines inherent to a life with few friends. It was difficult and tiring navigating Pat and Lilleth all the time. Licentious Lilleth. That lush. That sneak. And Pat, poor Pat. Hapless, clueless Pat. Oh, and Ella Alice was no friend of mine. I enjoyed her company and all when she came over to cook, and certainly we were amicable. But I held her at a distance, as I knew I should. So Renton was what I went looking for.

I found Renton inches from the metal fence dividing the White House compound from the citizen. He held a candle before him, eyes closed, lips whispering to heaven above as if this were not a midday amassing of the discontents with their fiery passion, feet pounding and fists stirring, but a peaceful Christmas Eve vigil.

At the far edge of a long moment he opened his eyes, reached out his hand, and we shook.

"Hiii bromine. It's *really* good to see ya."

He rested his scarred hand on my shoulder, his arm snug round the back of my neck pulling me close to his side, and another long meditation ensued in which I joined. Thousands and thousands stood behind us raving, fuming rage, a pack of misled? misguided? – once complicit fools now with a vendetta, ready to erupt like chemicals haphazardly mixed. Elements on their own, they were freckles of potential energy easily made docile. By the chemist's hand of common grievances they bonded. The economy had tanked. They became kinetic. Everything they hadn't cared a damn about a few years ago now enraged them. The war cost too much damn money. Oil prices were too damn high. Our national security was at risk. America was losing its place as an economic power in the world.

They began to chant. It boiled off as if from the chemical reaction of all these people mixing and effervesced into the District sky. The chant grew behind us, repeating over and again. Each recitation built on the tempo and volume of the one preceding it. Fists shook, feet slammed against the pavement and grass. Placards littered with accusations and pictures of oil barrels and dollar signs waved high overhead. Like blood-stained walls, they were a sight that could not be ignored.

Renton said not a word save for his mumbled chants to heaven above. The resentment in the voices and movements of the people behind us was that of children whose parents thought their kids would simply shake off the burden of the terrible condition of the world being passed down to them. The children revolted, calling their parents out as miscreants, poor stewards of the children's future, mendacious once-demigods no longer to be trusted. All of this, it seemed, was to the parent's astonishment.

The aristocracy that had gotten us into this mess had fled

the castle when new administration took over in 2008. Those who left the White House and who had been around for Spivey's generation must have sniffed out the telltale signs. The old guard must have realized what perfect timing they had. It was someone else's problem now. And things wouldn't really change, anyhow.

*****

After the peacetest, I accompanied Renton to a homeless shelter run by a church nearby. I helped him while he volunteered handing out bowls of soup, mostly broth, on a warm spring day. When we were done, we each got a bowl and some bread and headed out back.

Renton slurped up mouthfuls while squatting atop a crate that I half thought would burst in two beneath him. With each slurp some broth trickled into his beard.

"I wonder who invented sweatpants and how they could be so awesome," he said.

"I'm not sure," I laughed.

We slurped a bit.

"How did it go?" I asked.

"*Really* good and kinda shirtarsky all at once." He told me as he slopped up some soup with a plastic spoon. "Us in the front – the thirty people or so – we do our vigil. And that's the biggest we've had so I feel like I'm makin' a difference. But the peacetest gets drowned out by them protesters that come 'round. Too much people yappin' and wavin' signs and makin' threats like that'll scare 'em. And so it gets weird. We're sayin' give us peace. Stop the killin'. But ya can't use anger, ya know?"

I didn't want to talk about that. I'd have been back there with the screamers and fist shakers if I could've. So I changed the subject, confessing, "I think I'm falling in love."

"Love is like mercury."

"I thought that was blood?"

"No, no. It's love. Love is like mercury. It rises in the

heat of passion and falls with the bitterness of time. Love, like all things, is part of this Earth cycle. It is meant to blossom and pass like seasons."

"I'll take the elder's word."

He laughed. "Oh, I'm not so much older than ya. Six or seven years, I'd guess."

I told him I was in my early twenties and he congratulated himself for his accuracy.

"I had true love once," he reminisced. "But not with a girl. With things – the true romance of our time. I had this affair with things. Stuff. And like all love, it blossomed and I was so blindly high. Then it crashed. It crashed with the dot-com crash round the turn of the millennium."

"What do you mean?"

"I'm runnin' from the IRS." He said, insouciantly. "I amassed debt, debt, and more debt. Credit card mostly, but car loans, mortgage, school loans. Ya name it."

"Gold collar – right?"

He nodded, tugging at a tuft of tangled wire on his beard, "That's what those people who are outside of it call it."

I nodded back.

He continued, "And so, eventually it compounded and I paid and paid. But the money's always goin' to interest, never principal ya see.-I got new cards to pay off the old ones on down the well until my accounts dried up. Had my back against the wall. A car, all the toys in the world – nice TVs, spiffy computers, stereos, clothes, bar bills. Everythin'. I had it. But back against the wall. Spent money like life depended on it. Just keepin' up. Ya know? Just keepin' up. And when it all – when it all became too much I was sued. And I realized that I couldn't do it anymore. I could file for bankruptcy. I got in my car this one day, it was a Thursday in June, I remember and I had all the intention in the world to go begin the process. But when I got to the end of my street I found myself headin' to my mothers. And I went there and had lunch. Leftover meatloaf. I loved her meatloaf, bromine, I tell ya. Then I said goodbye and that I was real sorry about what'd happened to me. And when I got back in that car I drove, drove, drove till the gas ran out and I left the car there on the side of the road. Middle of nowhere. No one has seen or heard from the person who got out of that car and walked away since."

"Jeez."

"Yup. Somebody, I'm sure, came to my door lookin' for me – the IRS, the credit card company, the banks, the Pigs maybe – and found I was gone. I jumped aboard a train like an ol' timer. I stowed away on a freight and found I liked it. Not so bad to be alive just to live, I found. Since, I've lived in just about every big city in the country. Just another vagrant, another vagabond. Lost in the hustle bustle. Maybe people assume I'm a meth addict, alcoholic, run away kid that's grown up. Maybe people think I used to be on those postcards they send ya in the mail: Someone ya see lyin' on a bench here, or diggin' through a dumpster there, and for a moment you're reminded that such peons exist in the world. Then a blink, out of ya sight, and forgotten. I carry no ID. Couldn't recognize me today with the guy who drove that car back then if ya had our pictures side-by-side. Was worried for a while it'd catch up to me. That about, oh, 7, 8 years ago now. That was way before the economy crashed for real - this last time, I mean. I guess I beat the latest rush to poverty," he chuckled. "Anyhow. Not so much as a worry about it has crossed my mind in 3 or 4 years, bromine."

We both chewed on that disclosure for a while as the humid air lingered with us in silence.

"I'm sorry" was all I could think to say.

Shaking his head, he said: "My point, bromine – if you love her, or him, or whoever, know what love is and understand it for what it is. Love it while it is love. Love that person. Let them know. Be love to them. Do ya *over*stand?"

"I think so."

"Make sure ya do," he slurped a spoonful, "Because if it passes without being reified between you, without either of ya calling it by the same name, then it will have been just a memory that ya mind masturbates to."

I laughed.

"I'm serious. I don't mean playin' with yaself in a literal sorta way. I mean ya conjure the memory up when ya lonely and fantasize about a reality that never was. And that'll be the only solace you got."

"Isn't that better than leaping head first into something that you know, as you said, is doomed to crest?"

He stood, patted a fist to his chest, let out a belch and said, "it's time to go."

"Well?" I asked, standing.

He tied me up in a man-hug, replying, "don't worry, bromine. You're *really* good. It'll be Swayze."

I laughed.

"I've got a massive deuce to drop," he shrugged, waddling off. "And ya got shitarsky ya gotta do too."

13

ON A TUESDAY IN LATE JULY Ella Alice cooked dinner as she had been doing at least once a week for many months. It was always something new, always something fresh: organic this, humanely raised that.

This night it was Thai tofu.

Lifestyle politics.

After dinner, and I had rinsed, we perched out on the fire escape, our legs dangling between the bars. I gazed down at an Asian man pacing back and forth dragging on cigarettes. He came out from across the alley every so often to have a smoke, grinded the cigarette on the concrete when he finished, and retreated down some steps and through a door. Above the door was a sign that read "Number One Bus Service." It was one of the dozens of little companies spread around the city that ran busses back and forth between DC and New York City. I'd seen him smoking all hours of the day and even weekends and I thought he was the owner. When the busses came in from up north, he'd send a couple of younger guys out there to unload the people. Then, he'd have them load more people on and send the bus on back.

"How's Spivey?" I asked, watching the man pace.
"Fletcher's pleased. Very pleased." She said. "We're raising consciousness."

"Yeah?"

"Yeah. This year's been great for him. It's been – you've been so good for him. His health. It's made it all worth it, he tells me, you know?"

"It's been great for me," I said glancing at her. "I just hope I can really be the change Spivey wants me to be. I mean, I'm just writing you know."

"You don't believe you're just a writer," she smiled. "You're a catalysis. Would you have given up everything like you did just to write? Just to type words and send them into space?"

"Well I get to do the street art too."

We laughed. The man descended the stairway and disappeared through the door.

"Try not to be so humble, hunny. It doesn't look good on you."

"What I mean is - Gramsci's writing didn't cause any great change. He was just a guy rotting in jail. Foucault imploded on his own beliefs and became a right-winger going around trying to morally justify attempts to infect others with HIV. You see it's -"

"Listen to you," she interjected. "Where's that beaming confident Emory?"

"He's with Liam."

"Not the writer. The writer's still Emory." She gave me a playful jab with her elbow. I leaned away and rubbed the spot on my arm where she'd hit me as if in great pain and again we laughed.

"Then again," I said, shifting towards her. "Marx's revolution didn't come as a product of his writing. It took others, people like Lenin, to enact the change. But he was the educator. So it depends on how you look at it. Without Marx there'd be no Lenin, right? Without me there's just a fledging old man regretting his life as he rots away, right? But now there's a possibility that one of these sparks will catch."

"Exactly," she said. "Do you feel the energy in the streets these days? That's because of you, Emory. You know the Situationalists are resurging – more popular than ever before.

There was even another communiqué by Animus' buddies, those kids - it drew a few hundred people and turned into a street party. And everyone was celebrating because those kids were promising more onslaught. That's because of you. And those college professors – the arm-chair revolutionaries that've been trying to one-up each other on how radical they are with their little theories that don't do bananas? They're getting active again, like back in Spivey's day. That's because of you. And the coffee shop uppidy's? Have you been in a coffee shop lately? Rather than reading fantasy books or trying to see who has the fluffiest scarf and all that watered-down pseudo-intellectual bullshit like they were doing when I was working at Spivey & Frettington– you know what they're doing? They're reading your blog, sitting around talking about your ideas and getting amped up, trying to attain critical consciousness. You know that protest that turned into a black bloc over on K Street and all those lobbyist's offices that got their windows knocked in? That's because of you. Look, change isn't something that might happen on down the line. It is happening right now. There is no other way about it!"

"Listen to *you*, Little Miss Radical. You're starting to sound like you're ready to grab a pitch fork! You must be reading those books?"

She smiled proud. "That and your blog."

We laughed.

"That's awesome."

"Thanks hun." She seemed to blush but I couldn't tell for sure in the fading light.

"Can I ask you a serious question?"

She nodded.

"You've really come to believe in this stuff?"

"Of course."

"Because I just wonder, you know? How does someone like you who comes from where you're from, who lives where you live, and the crowds I imagine you're in, and dresses like you and all of that – how does someone like you believe in what we're trying to do?"

"You know there are a few things they bother to teach us before we can get our business degrees," she quipped, her hands on her sides. "Look professional. Act professional. And believe in the work you do."

I laughed and she joined me and we laughed as the last of the day's light faded.

"You've got a curious smile."

I thanked her, wondering what that meant.

"Are you happy?"

"You know, I think I am. I think I am for the first time in a while. Is that strange?"

"No. why would be it?"

I shrugged that I didn't know.

"I'm happy for you. I'm happy for Fletcher."

"Thanks."

"It makes me happy, too. I guess it's just my way to care for people. For Spivey. And now, for you. It feels good to feel needed."

"I know what you mean."

"Where is it that you think I'm from?"

"I don't know. You look like a Congressman's daughter."

Again we laughed.

"I'm nobody's daughter. That's exactly why I came to this city."

"I understand."

"Now can I ask you a question?" she said.

"Sure."

"There's something I'm interested in."

"Ok."

"The graffiti."

"What about it?"

"I don't know. It's interesting."

"Do you want to see it? I mean, do you want to see one that I've done? Up close?"

She looked at me and smiled.

"How well can you climb?"

"There's a lot I can do," she said, sliding her paperweight hand behind her and out of view.

I looked at her and thought a minute. "Just walk down to K and 16th Street. There's a stencil on a gray building of a little boy saluting a bank. It's pretty obvious. You'll see it."

Ella Alice frowned.

"Better to be safe." I meant it in more ways than one.

"Well, at least tell me why you do it."

"I don't know. It started off as a teenage hobby, one of those anti-social things you do because you feel trapped by something you don't understand at sixteen."

"That's all?"

"Well, I guess in time, graffiti seemed like a direct way to get a message to the public. They say art starts revolutions." I gazed at her legs dangling below. "But I've lost the illusion that people can be deeply inspired by art, at least in a political sense. It's more vandalism than anything else."

"So why do it?"

"It feels good to be a shadow, I guess."

She looked at me a moment, then down to the pavement where the man had stood before, pacing, smoking his cigarette. "You're really talented," she said. "It's hard for me to admit that sort of thing."

I wondered, as we sat in silence in a night too dark for reading intentions, was that really her in the alley with Brock? It didn't make any sense.

* * * * *

Carolyn's fingers pressed my lips apart and I could feel them rubbing my teeth. "Do you want to kiss me?" she whispered.

I wanted to taste that I was falling in love, and not just feel it inside of me every time I saw her, or smell it every time I was close to her. We'd been drinking a little to celebrate the fact that her Mom was out on her first date since the divorce. I was happy for Carolyn and her Mom.

Her Mom seemed like a nice lady and in the picture I'd seen of her she had a smile like Carolyn's, but her hands had looked damp and arthritic.

Carolyn and I were lying on a hillside, the highway just below, and streams of light streaked by from fantastic machines. That, and the loud churning of engines one after the, other made for a time and place in which it seemed that Carolyn and I were the only two people in the landscape of a flowing sea of metal and plastic. It was as if this were all a show just for us, like our own personal Fourth of July light show or something equally brilliant and celebrated.

And here came Carolyn's finger. I pulled her wrist and her hand slid away from my face. And I could not taste her. I leaned in and pressed into her and I realized that I was not tasting her the way I thought I would. It had no taste. Rather, the sensation was simply one of being part of something. Something so much more than taste and smell and all of those things I'd been thriving on in all my lust for her. This sensation was like part of the great stream of lights and sound that seemed endless and eternal. She leaned back into me and her arms wrapped around my neck and pulled at me until I fell on top of her and everything was bright and crisp yet surreal and opaque all at once. My heart churned; a little engine. My hands rubbed her face and neck and I was a young boy again of sixteen getting curious on a bright night in the wet grass.

"Tell me this is real," she said. And I kissed her up and down. And it was more real than anything, except of course, the heartbreak that eventually constricts every man and woman who ever made love.

"Do you know what this feels like?" she asked. But I was kissing her neck and I was here in this moment and if she told me what it felt like then it was possible that this moment wouldn't last forever and that this feeling would be whisked away with the passing cars. I said nothing. And when I was inside her she moaned, "How do you do that? How do you do that, baby?" She kissed me wildly, and her hand, her hand was in mine.

*****

Happy I remained for the rest of the summer and on into the fall spending my days writing, my evenings with Carolyn, and many of the late nights on rooftops or climbing billboards. And each week came a check from Fletcher, praise, and visits from Ella Alice where I learned about all that we were accomplishing.

14

IN NOVEMBER THE TREES SHIVERED. They leaned naked in the wind as it howled through the corridor of buildings on my street and I clasped my hand against my jacket breast pocket; an envelope tucked inside. The envelope was not the normal kind I received in my box with Ella's handwriting on it. This one was white and it had been sent through the mail rather than dropped in my box by hand. There was no return address and my name and P.O. Box had been written in someone else's handwriting.

Finally, I got back to my building and up the steps to my apartment, then inside where I locked the door behind me. I peered around the room. The desk? I went over to it, looked around. No. This wouldn't do. The corner kitchen? Nothing good there either. The Hungarian bookshelf? I walked over to it. But where? I'd done little to fill its shelves. This wouldn't do. The couch? In the cushions? This would have to do for now. I unzipped the edge of one of two seat cushions and slipped the envelope inside. Then, I zipped it back up and got everything looking back to normal. Undisturbed.

I locked the apartment door behind me, and racing down the steps, I nearly tripped. I spilled back out into the wind. I scurried toward the nearest Metro station and hopped the metro and grabbed the rail and the shuttle raced beneath the city.

I emerged at Foggy Bottom and I guessed it was about a mile's walk so I lowered my chin and got to it, fighting the wind with every step. Finally, I ducked under the awning at 506301 and the doorman opened the door from inside and I was up the elevator and down the hall a ways to 4700.

I grabbed my breath and gave the door a few thuds. No answer. I waited. Then I gave it a few more. Still no answer. I thought on leaving for a moment. And before I'd made up my mind, I reached out for the handle and gave it a turn. I applied some weight and the door swayed wide on its hinges.

The empty entry invited me in to that smell of plastic and vinegar from before. In the living room, a couch sat alone. In the dining room, the Formica table stood idly while the photos hung there doing little to liven the space. The desk, lamp, and chair in the office looked lonely despite the company they kept with shelves of books towering over them. Each book stood erect and singular.

I wandered past the bathroom where Ella Alice took the photo for my Liam Logan ID. I wandered toward the kitchen and a part of the condo I'd never been in before. And when I reached the kitchen, I found myself standing in the company of appliances.

I walked over to the refrigerator and had a look inside. I suppose it was out of homage to a former way of life that I grabbed an apple. Perhaps it was the comfort I found in slipping into old habits that I put a second apple into my pocket.

I had a seat on a stool and began to eat and it was then that I notice a balcony overlooking the kitchen. Down a short hallway around a corner, I found a spiral stairway. At the top of it was a door. I went through the door and I was on the balcony looking over the kitchen. In the corner, I saw a set of doors. I could see the glow of electric light sliding out from underneath the left one.

I pocketed the apple I was eating, walked over and opened the door. Lying in a bed was Fletcher Spivey, his back to me.

"Oh I suppose it's time for my meds again." he muttered. Then with a cough, "isn't it?"

"Mr. Spivey, it's me. It's Emory."

"Emory!" he called. "Come around this way, my good boy."

"So fine it is to see you," he said upon seeing me round the bed. Then, with a sigh, "But for you to see me like this."

He was the gaunt remains of greater days. His eyes appeared grey and seemed to wander through and past me, settling on something only he could see. A hand reached out from under the covers and I took it. The skin of his hand sagged in my palm. The bones felt as if they would crumble in my hand with just a squeeze. And yet he smiled. "So you got my envelope?"

"I went by the P.O. Box this morning."

"Good," he smiled. "Glad my pen remains steady enough for the mail man to read it."

"I don't understand."

"Understand that it is the first – not the last," he nodded.

"Why?"

"Because I'm dying, Emory."

"Isn't there anything?" I asked. "I mean, Georgetown – that's a good medical facility, right? Can't they do anything?"

"It's hereditary," he replied. "And so the question is, can we not overcome what we are born with?"

"I really don't know." I took a seat at the foot of the bed, feeling the urge to rinse clean the taste of apple from my mouth.

"I am afraid there is little to do at this point," he frowned. "My doctor and friend at the hospital over there," he glanced toward the window, "lives with the notion there's a favorable chance he could save me with the auspices of some aggressive treatments. Yet, you see that such a feat involves a dual organ transplant. And, quite ironically really," he chuckled but it sounded hollow, "this is one of those rare times that both the wealthy and the wanting do truly live with equality. And there is not one thing money can do to propel me forward on the waiting list for those organs."

I frowned. "But –"

He cut me off. "And to have lived this long already! Oh! As you can imagine, such a fate places me quite low in the queue. You see the best for the most is the ethic. And given that I'm this old, what value is an old man who'd deny a younger person an opportunity at life? The medical field reminds us that it is always better to sacrifice the old so the young may live. We judge nothing of the conditions of either of the lives. What do they live for? What are their aspirations? What do they contribute to society? It is simply a matter of mathematics. And this I must learn to understand in spite of my own yearn to live."

He coughed and firmed his grip on my hand. His eyes glared into mine. "What if this other individual wastes their life away in front of the tube? Worse yet, what if they are a bad person? What if they are beholden to the ravages of addiction? What if they beat their spouse? Their children? What if they steal, cheat, or exploit others? What if they ruin the lives of thousands or millions by running a company into the ground, or a country? How can civilization – in this day and age - rely simply on a system of measure as our ethical guide in a situation like this? Young is and will always be better than old. But what if the old would have been far better for the world than the young will ever become?"

I sat a while in thought, the weightlessness of his hand in mine. "I guess I never would've thought about it that way."

"Well you can afford the luxury."

I felt a sense of shame on my cheeks but I didn't know why and so, confused, I tried to console, telling him I saw his point. "I bet your family would happily -"

"What family?" he grumbled.

"No one?"

"A pancreas can come only from a deceased donor."

"I didn't know."

"No family," he muttered. "No one to wait for to die."

He let go of my hand, and after a long minute in which he seemed again to be looking into something that I could not see there before his eyes, he said, "Ostensibly. Ostensibly it's no dilemma. The doctor asserts that aggressive treatments today mute the necessity for a relative donor, that compatibility issues and such complications can be largely overcome, although he would not die finding out, mind you. Special immune drugs, immuno-something, and something else about plasma, I can't recall. A bucket of damned doctor speak! But I shall admit, in some way it gives me hope, Emory. It's quite simple enough for me to understand that I can afford the best doctors, that I can afford to pay for such treatments when others can't. It is a notion worth clinging to."

"There's no doubt in my mind," I said, still wanting to please, confused, ashamed, uncertain, unable to stop myself at these words. Trying to fill the air, I said: "I don't know the first thing about medicine. But the doctor's right. The things they can do today. There's no doubt in my mind. It's just – amazing stuff - there's just no doubt-" And I stopped myself there. I breathed, eyed his hand, and thought about picking it up and trying to weigh it in mine.

"What a matter to shoulder you with," he sighed. And he was silent a while, gazing back toward the window. "But I'm glad you came. Though I should say I knew you would." He smiled. "That's why I gave Ms. Alice the day off."

"But when I came in, you called to her, didn't you?"

"Oh, just operant conditioning getting the better of me, I suppose." He pointed to pill bottles on the bed stand. "I'm taking those blasted little devils myself."

"Wait. She doesn't know?" I really did need to rinse soon.

"This move is between you and I, old boy."

"Well won't she know? I mean, she's your personal assistant? Isn't she-?"

"She has her jobs. I have mine. And you have yours."

"Well what am I supposed to do with it?"

"Simple," he said. "Carry the torch when my light has faded for the momentum musn't die with the exhaustion of a finite flame."

I nodded.

"If only I could prolong my time and put off this ravenous fate. If just to see around the corner. If just to be here to realize what is next. It is the tragedy of life, quite so it is, that we are kept from seeing through to their maturity the seeds we plant. I had done so little," he said. "Until I found you."

15

I TOOK CAROLYN TO THE NATIONAL ZOO and we trounced around in the cold. Afterwards, over hot cocoa she told me that her mom would like to meet me and she was inviting me over for Thanksgiving dinner the next weekend. Her mom's boyfriend would be there. His name was Ted. It was my first invitation to a holiday dinner since my high school girlfriend - my first love and the girl I lost my best friend over - broke up with me some time when we were in college. And so, on the following Sunday, I arrived dressed real sharp in a new jacket I bought, brown slacks, and a tie.

At the dinner table we sat for grace. I glanced around as Carolyn, Ted and her mother bowed their heads. Amen. Then her mother's gentle but damp hands filled our plates and I spent much of dinner telling her mother a made up story about what I do for a living. I hated to lie to her. But how could I be honest - what with the warm biscuits in my stomach and the way her mother leaned and nodded, "interesting. It just sounds so interesting"?

I brought a pecan pie and vanilla ice cream that I picked up at the grocer and after dinner we ate dessert while watching the game in the living room. Ted seemed nice. He was a football fanatic who got heated at a bad call, coaching decision, or boneheaded play. But he was otherwise laconic and he and Carolyn seemed to get on well.

After, Carolyn suggested her and I get out of the apartment and give the "young love birds" some time to enjoy themselves. At this we all shared a laugh and it was like a magazine.

Outside I rinsed and spat on the curb.

"I bet you couldn't wait to –"

"Oh I was dying."

Carolyn giggled. Carolyn kissed. "Oh!"

We meandered the holiday streets with no real place to go as windows gazed out upon vacant walkways.

"You look sharp in your tie. You didn't have to dress up like that, you know?"

"I wanted to," I said. "I can't remember the last time I wore a tie."

"I'm so happy you got to meet my Mom. You don't know how much that means to me."

"It was really a pleasure. I hope they liked the pie."

"Of course they did," she smiled.

"It's cute how much you and your Mom look alike and how similar some of your mannerisms are."

"What do you mean?"

"You both sort of eat with these little bites and cut everything up way beyond necessary."
"Are you making fun of us?"

"No, not at all. I'm serious."

"Why are you laughing?" she pouted.

"I'm not. I'm laughing because I'm happy. It just felt warm to see you all in there together. A family. To feel like – I don't know – like a part of it."

Carolyn smiled at this realization. "Yeah I guess it is. They seem happy together, don't they?"

I put my arm around her shoulder and pulled her tight. "I think they love each other."

She stopped and looked up at me. "I never thought I could be this happy."

Me neither, I thought.

"She really seems to like you."

"Oh yeah?"

"Yeah! She just seemed so interested in hearing about your job and everything. I'd told her how you were working at the restaurant when we met and that you were researching for a book you wanted to write and how that editor position came along and you just had to jump at it."

I released from the embrace.

"What's a matter? Aren't you loving me tonight?"

I laughed. "You're too cute." And then, "of course I am, silly. I love you with all my big heart."

She put her hand on my chest and whispered, "there it is." She pressed her cheek against her hand upon my chest a minute, then pulling back, she said: "I love to feel you right there. I've been missing you. I've been missing – and – just - well it's hard with you not around much lately."

"I've been busy with my work."

"I know," she sighed. "But I need you sometimes. I need you around. This summer we were inseparable. And now we're together maybe once a week. Are you sure nothing's wrong? Are you sure you're still loving me?"

"You know how passionate I am about us."

"You're sure your passion is not all sunk into your work?"

But the truth is that we do what we do despite the desperation with which we love. It is as though we don't know how to stop being the people we are. And even when we should have the foresight to see the direction we are going, we fail to truly have any vision. Our best effort is not enough. Our best effort is usually a fumble of words. The action never follows.

"Carolyn, listen to me." I grabbed her tight. "I love you like the mad man loves the night. Do you understand?" Staring into her eyes, I confessed: "You deserve better than I've been the last two months. I promise to you that I'll cut back on my work and devote the time to this relationship that is on par with the strength of my feelings."

"You better," she pouted. "Because I'm really good, you

know."

I wanted so badly for her to see that I knew and I folded her up in my arms and squeezed.

"It's cold," she said. "Just don't forget to love me."

16

"YOU DIDN'T HAVE TO DO THAT."

He danced around. Seething. Fists pulsating by his hips. Jagged violence in his eyes.

The spit fired from his tongue as the words repeated.

"You didn't have to do that."

"Calm down," I told him. "Calm it down."

"Don't you fuckin' tell me what to do. You think you're hard. You think you're – you're. Man, fuck you. Fuckin telling me what to do."

"What are you talking about? Telling you what?"

"Kinda audacity you got to come round here after what you been doin?"

"Hey man, I just stopped in to say what's up. Hadn't seen you in a while. I'm sorry. I've been real busy. I can see it's a bad time."

"Nah man," he said continuing to dance around like a boxer. "Let's hash this shit out. I'm glad you stopped by. I been lookin' for your skinny ass."

"Why don't you tell me what's going on?"

"I thought we were boys, man. I respected you. I looked up to you. And this is what you do? You take advantage of me? I let you sleep on my fucking couch man, for how long? And you go behind my back like this. Man, you knew I love Lilleth. You knew it and you did this to me."

"Woah, Pat. Stop it. Stop it. What the fuck are you talking about? Did what?"

"She left me."

"Oh damn. I'm sorry," I consoled, wondering what that had to do with me.

"She left me because of you."

Me? "I didn't say nothing to her. I haven't even talked to her in like months. What'd she tell you?"

"Yeah, she told me everything. Said she'd been sending you emails inviting you out and shit."

"Woah man, I never responded."

"So it's true?"

Scratching the back of my neck, I offered: "I mean, yeah she sent me emails. And, yeah she invited me to chill and shit. Like go to happy hour or clubs. But I never went anywhere. I never met up with her anywhere. I never even responded, man. I swear to you."

With this he charged me, fist swinging, tearing through the air. I leaped over the couch barely escaping his lunge. My shin slammed the coffee table. I rolled over it and onto the floor.

Fuck!

I leapt up ready to defend myself. But he didn't charge. He just stood there guarding the door.

Hopping on one leg, holding my shin, I screamed. "Chill the fuck out! Listen to me."

"You got nowhere to go, Emory. Stop trying to hide. Stop trying to delay. Let's do this."

"Listen to me. Listen to me. Pat, I never did anything."

"That so? What about that night at the Mezzanine? Huh? Tell me, Emory, why were you holding Lilleth's arm when I came back with drinks?"

"Come on man."

"Tell me!" He screamed. He grabbed at something on the table by the door and flung it at me. I ducked. A batch of envelopes hit the TV screen and dropped to the floor.

"Alright. Alright. Listen, you want to hear? You want me

to tell you? I'll tell you. I'll tell you but you're not gonna like the truth. But it's the truth. So fuck you, here it is." I struggled to stand tall on two feet, my shin throbbing. Putting weight on my ankle shot pain up my calf.

"Basically," I cringed. "What happened was she told me she was curious about me and I guess that she was into me and all that. And she was like trying to flirt with me and all. And I tried to show her, with my body language and the way I was acting and all, that I wasn't interested and that it wasn't cool. And then, I dunno, all of the sudden she just grabbed me. Like, right there in the club. She just grabbed my crotch and said something like about hooking up or bragging to her friends we were gonna hook up or something. I-I-I I don't remember exactly. But that's basically what happened."

The room sat swallowed in a silence that stretched out over a succession of hollow breaths.

Calmly, "I saw her do it," he admitted. His eyes turned to the floor. "I saw her hand when I was coming back with the drinks."

"So then you know. It wasn't me. It was all her. Like I said. I didn't do anything. Nothing. I admit that that happened. But I didn't do anything. In fact, I was gonna tell you right then and there. I was gonna tell you what happened," I pleaded.

"Why didn't you?"

"I don't know man. I don't know. You seemed so happy. You know? You seemed so happy to have her and so proud. It happened suddenly and I was. I was confused. And I wanted to tell you. But I just didn't know what to say. You know?"

"You made me look like a fool. You've been making me look like a fool all this time."

"You gotta believe me though. I didn't do anything. I didn't encourage her in any way. I never sent her any signals or gave any wrong impressions. I never egged her on. I swear to God. I played everything straight. I tried to honor you. I - I thought if I ignored it. Ignored her it'd go away.

But I never reciprocated in any way. In any way at all. You gotta believe me. I didn't do anything."

"You didn't have to!" he screamed. "You didn't have to!" And as he started to say it a third time his body fell limp and he melted to the floor. He propped himself up against the wall next to the door and buried his head in his knees, arms wrapped around them. "You didn't have to do anything. All you had to do was be you. Be this writer, this guy with these ideas and words and thoughts and actions. The guy who is where things are happening." He hocked back snot, "I hate you. I fuckin' hate you. She'll never love me so long as there are people - Get out of my apartment. Get your self-righteous ass the fuck out of my apartment. I don't ever want to see your face again. I don't ever wanna hear the name Emory Walden again."

"Pat, Man –"

But Pat cut me off, "I should've seen this coming. You don't change. You did me like you did James, you did me like you did James. You thief. I always stood by you, believed your side of things. But I see how you really are now. You can't just be happy. You've got to have everyone fawning over you and how damn great and smart you are. You've got to have everything be the way you want it." He hocked back more snot. "Well I deserve to be happy. I deserve -" His voice trailed off.

"Man, we're deeper than this. Can't we just forget Lilleth and –"

"Did you not hear me?" he screamed. "I said leeeeaavvee!"

I limped past the balled up mass of man convulsing in sobs on the floor and hobbled out of the apartment, closing the door behind me. I could barely keep my feet.

* * * * *

Ms. Alice had me picked up in a taxi to be taken to a doctor's office. She had to help me down the stairs from my apartment. In the back seat she got on her smart phone and made a call, dialing the numbers as she cradled the phone in her paperweight hand.

The whole thing was arranged. She hung up. We rode in silence the rest of the way as the afternoon light faded and the last streaks of melon were muted.

There was no receptionist to check us in, no nurse to take my height and weight. By the time we arrived, everyone had been sent home. The physician, Dr. Bend, a stubby man with hunched shoulders and the face of a banker, had me hop on the table and answer a few questions.

"So you're Fletcher's kid?"

"Yeah."

"Age?"

"I'm in my twenties."

Looking at me, then at Ella, he muttered "Ok then." And with a huff that seemed to weigh his belly down further to the floor, he jotted something on a clipboard.

"Height and weight?"

"Um, about 5'10". Maybe 140. I don't know."

He eyed me up as if judging for himself, then scribbled again.

"You exercise? Eat healthy?"

"Yeah, I guess."

"Allergies?

"Don't think I got any allergies – not sure."

"Medications?"

"Meds? No. I mean, I used to."

"When was that?"

"Couple years ago, I guess."

"Drugs? Alcohol?"

"Maybe a few years ago."

"Surgeries?"

"Not that I remember. I broke my arm when I was 11. But you mean, like -"

"How about hereditary stuff – any known diseases in the family?"

"Not that I know of."

Frowning, the stubs of his fingers tapping the clipboard, he asked: "You know anything about your medical condition? Blood type? Anything?"

"Yeah. It's 'O'."

He nodded, marking the clipboard. "The things we remember," he muttered, and I could sense the annoyance in his posture as he sagged toward the floor.

"When's the last time you've seen a doctor?"

"Few years ago. Maybe 4, 5."

He frowned, looking at Ella. I looked at her too, I guess expecting her to assuage his disappointment, but all she did was shrug. Then he looked at the clipboard when he said, "Let's do a blood test. Check out your functions. Run the whole thing. You're looking a little gaunt, a little thin. Not a big deal. But I can't not be a doctor. It's my nature, you understand?"

Soon, the needle went in. The blood went out. I felt it escape and I looked back to watch it move across the room in a vile with Dr. Bend. He stood it on a counter by a sink, the needle still in my arm. Then a new vile. Another draw. I looked away, then back to see the second vile placed beside the first. And then, one more vile and the needle came out.

"Thirsty?" I asked.

He chuckled with a creased forehead and placed the third by the other two, each vile cap its own color. "Running the whole thing," he affirmed.

I was told to lay back and I was spread over the table while he took a few x-rays. He gave the diagnosis with alacrity. "Just a small fracture."

I was less than upbeat. But the doc laughed. The way he saw it, we came rushing over here like it was some kind of exigency. I'd be limping out of here with a boot on my leg and crutches.

"Listen kid, have a little perspective," he said, neck billowing, "It could be worse. You could be stuck late at work doing favors for old friends when you should be at your 7-year-old kid's birthday party. You understand? Watching him open presents and enjoying a slice of ice cream cake."

Ms. Alice jotted down the doctor's directions on what I needed to do to nurse my leg.

Keep it propped.

Ice on and off the first two days.

Some Advil.

She gave the doc a check and the two of us were on our way.

PART THREE

ENTROPY

17

THAT'S THE LAST THING I remember with clarity. That I know really happened. It's spotty after that. But I am certain of some things. Certain of things that didn't happen. I know I wrote a hundred letters to Carolyn I never sent in the weeks spent boxed up in that apartment after breaking my ankle. I know I missed Christmas with Carolyn, her mom and Ted. I know I didn't see or speak with Pat after that. I know I didn't tell the police my real name or say anything about my blog and who I really am. I know I didn't say anything about Fletcher Spivey, or Ella Alice, or the whole revolt. I swear.

See, I remember things. I just need a little help filling in the gaps. Somewhere, somehow, we were infiltrated. Can't you sense it? I've just got to figure out how so I can warn Fletcher. I've just got to figure out who? Who wants me dead? I'm in this hospital bed for a reason, aren't I?

* * * * *

I think it was about 5 weeks into the healing process when I just couldn't wait any longer. I just couldn't stand to be pent up in that apartment typing away on the blog and emailing with supporters. I suppose I was impatient.

I came down in the alley and it had to have been after 1

in the morning. And as I came out of the alley into the street there was a guy who walked up to me and then another guy approached from the other side. And they were cops, they told me. I was busted.

I had on my backpack with my spray cans, and my stencils, and my clothes were splashed with paint. I'd got this one stencil of a B52 bomber in a peace sign and I think I'd written that famous maxim, you know, from Orwell's 1984. And I'd just tagged it up on a billboard by the Du Pont metro station. They'd gotten a call. Someone had seen me up there tagging the thing, I guess. So somehow they caught up with me. And this was it. So they took me in.

I remember the one cop was gloating. I mean, real in your face. He kept telling me how long they'd been wanting to nail me and how certain they were they'd eventually do it. And the other was telling me oh what a big fine I was going to have to pay and time I was going to probably spend in prison. Who knows if it was true or if they were just blowing wind. Either way, they'd finally put a name and a face on a faceless menace defacing the good city. I was through.

The first cop then started telling me how this was going to deflate the movement on the streets and how it was a moral victory for the city. I've always hated the way cops laugh.

So I played it cool as I sat there in the interrogation room. But underneath I felt asthmatic. The room smothered me. The cops were fucking with me. They knew everything, everything I'd tagged. Then they kept asking me if I knew Walden and where to find Walden. And I told them I didn't know who or what they were talking about. But they persisted. They looked real relaxed – real patient. And here I was in a room with walls collapsing around me. I insisted. So they both left. Then they came back a few minutes later with a laptop and sat it down in front of me. Guess what? They pulled up my very own blog in front of me and asked me if I didn't recognize any of the writing. If I hadn't heard anyone talking about it. And I said I wished I could help, but I was just a Situationist and my loyalties were to Animus, artistically, and Guy Debord, philosophically.

After a while they seemed satisfied. So some time in the pitch of the night, after admitting to tagging every building on the 16th block of K-street, the Happy Hour on 18th street, and this and that and the other, they dragged me down to a cell for the night. I was offered one phone call somewhere in all that. I thought long and hard about calling Carolyn. But what to say? Say I'm sorry? What good would that do?

The next day I woke up to find my bail had been paid. And as I walked out of the police station, who did I see?

I saw that bowl-headed swine in an officer's uniform heading in my direction. Brock. Mr. Mosquito. 90s Boy. Whatever you like. That pathetic piglet sucking at the teat of power had managed to suckle his way onto the force. I scurried down the steps, trying to keep my head down. But as we passed he recognized me and I heard him call, "Heya Emory." – smiling under that brimmed cap with the gold star medallion – "Heya Emory" – glossy shoes glimmering in the morning sun – "Heya Emory" – the eyes of the law staring into me. I hobbled by trying to ignore.

As I passed he reached out, stopping me.

"Heya Emory. Hey, stain. I'm talking to you," he clamored.

I looked up into his eyes. "What? Oh, hey. Oh, hey Brock. Is that you?" I played.

"You didn't recognize me?"

"Oh no. I didn't realize – you're a pig now?"

"It's been a while," he smiled, poking his chest out for the world to see his copper nameplate, Officer Brock Grismore. "What are you doing down here?"

"Overdue parking tickets," is all I could muster.

A laugh gurgled up, an undercurrent of mockery in his throat. "Jeez Emory. Really? You've got to be a bit more responsible."

I nodded. "Well, I better get on along, then."

It was far too early in a day to be faced down by inimical forces when the shards of morning frost still menaced the grass stretching between the sidewalk and the street. But as if sensing something, he raised an open hand before me as a crossing guard would. "Woah, woah," he stammered. "Not just yet. I want to ask you something."

"Yeah? What is it, Brock?"

"How's it going?" His eyes tightened their handle on me from there under the brow of his cap. "You botch that yet?"

I shrunk before his aplomb, yanking my eyes away, down to the ground.

Our two pairs of feet aimed at one another.

"She'd have been better off with me." He tilted my head up with his fingers. "Look at me." He ordered. "You were a novelty, Emory. You were a whim. I could see that. Anyone could see that. It's too bad she couldn't. It's too bad she couldn't or she'd have avoided getting hurt by you – which I'm sure you did. I'm sure you hurt her. Where is she now? Emory, where is she now? Huh?"

I brushed past him, scurrying off as best as my leg could hobble and he turned after me and I heard him call, "What good is a novelty when she's all alone in bed crying?"

I remember after that I stumbled down the escalator into the metro station unable to breath. I remember having scurried as fast as I could away from the police station, into the crowds and down into the city's belly. I remember that no matter how hard I sucked at the frigid air it wouldn't quench my lungs. The memories of nights with Carolyn flickered past in the lights that streamed by through the window of the metro car as it raced and rattled in the hollow.

This train was racing towards nothing but destinations carved out decades ago. There was no way Carolyn would have been happy with Brock. This I knew for she said it in no uncertain terms. But perhaps Brock was right. Just as certain as Carolyn would have never been happy with Brock, maybe it too was certain that my ability to warm Carolyn's heart was inherently finite. What were his words? I was bound to "botch" it up. It had been a prophesy seen by all but her and I. A prophesy in which we both naively partook in a tango doomed to expire just as certain as the music was written with a final verse to which the band is bound to oblige.

Had I known the song was on its last verse, I would have held her a little closer through the beginning stanzas. I would have listened to the chorus of the song a little more intently. Because when I saw her next she said something like, "I don't understand it" or, "I can't understand it." She was holding the Metro section of the *Post* her mother had shown her that morning at the breakfast table. There on it the headline, austere blocks:

A CITY UNDER SIEGE NO MORE: ELUSIVE GRAFFITI ARTIST FINALLY TAGGED BY DC POLICE.

Under that was my mug shot. Bony cheeks. Scruff on the chin. Vapid eyes like empty calendars. All spelled out in black and white. And the worst of it? Below the neck, printed in italics "Liam Logan." The byline: Trip Carpenito.

I begged for her to calm down and listen as she scurried from the foyer to her bedroom. I went after her to catch a door before it could be thrown shut. Through coaxing and crying we arrived at the floor in her bedroom. I tried to reach out to touch her but she recoiled – crawled back on her palms and heels, settling only when she ran up against the radiator. We held our positions, clinging to the comfort of little else but the certainty of the floor beneath us. Afraid then, we were, for some time to remit the territory claimed when we crashed to the floor. I was otherwise an intruder in her room, but on this plot of carpet I staked my claim. There I was safe. If I could hold this ground – maybe there was room to move forward in time. Yet every time I went to speak she asked me "who are you?" Over and again she shoved it at me and every time I fumbled it.

By way of time I found the means to calm her and move down the path toward disclosure. She said not one word. It was only her eyes that urged me on in my confession. I suppose they needed to know what it was before them, the boy she laughed her evenings away with that summer past, or the stranger in the newspaper photograph who had crawled with her under the sheets. She feared she had loved them both.

I'm comforted knowing I can't remember what all was said, and what she said to me. We live selective lives and construct our own realities. It is how we survive the perniciousness of our time.

These things I know. In that tornado of tears and hands tremoring, I remember coming clean; telling her about the blog I started while in Europe and how big it'd gotten and my work as a graffiti artist.

I remember having to go sometime before her mom was due home from a night spent at Ted's and before I left her room I grabbed the desk lamp and lit up my entire face for her to see.

We stood in the hallway to her Mom's apartment and had our last conversation.

That morning, for fear of the white walls and the naked bookshelves of my apartment, I went to Dupont Circle and looked for Renton. I waited an hour. Maybe two. After giving up, I meandered to a coffee shop. I sat to listen. And it was as Ella Alice had said. Without introducing myself, I borrowed a pen and a tear of notebook paper from a couple of GW students talking about the inspiration they were finding in the student uprising in France during the late 1960s. I wrote Carolyn a letter. This time I was going to send it.

Carolyn. You are the kid in me. I need you in my life the way a raindrop needs a puddle. I will seek you out no matter how far or near. I will not stop until I pour into you. No matter what happens ever, no matter if we ever become the things we want to become, or live the life we wanted to live. No matter if you move on, having met someone much gentler and loving. Please just know, that you have made me happier than I have ever been in the life I've lived here on this spiraling ball. My love for you is stronger at this moment than it could ever again hope to emulate. Please. No matter what ever happens, or how mad I may have made you, feel in your heart the enormity of the love I hold for you and find it in your heart to find your way back to me.

With adoration, amazement and amore,
Your Emory

As I got up to leave, I eyed a copy of the Metro section with Carpenito's article left on a coffee table. At the post office I bought a stamp and mailed the letter. After, I checked my post office box – a half-dozen white envelopes with Fletcher Spivey's handwriting.

I was due in court soon. I knew I might be going to jail.

18

I REMEMBER SITTING AT THE TABLE and watching Ella put together a bagged lunch, her one-armed magic at work. We'd decided to go out in public together – something previously thought to be a bad idea. But there were things to witness today. Things I wanted to show her.

I put my skully on low over my head, put up my sweatshirt hood, and popped on a pair of sunglasses.

"Is it that cold?"

"For May it is," I said. "You think this face scrap is helping with my cover?"

"Yes," she laughed. "The arrival of your beard – it's – well – an interesting development."

"You know it looks good," I joked.

"Yes, of course. Who wouldn't want to go to lunch with a guy who looks like the Unibomber?"

"If your yuppie friends could see you now."

Ella put on her coat, her sunglasses – which, if I remember, were big bug eyed and black – and handed me my bag and said, "shall we?"

We walked up my street, hopped the metro and rode into the caverns of the city. At the Smithsonian stop we exited the car and ascended the escalator to emerge onto the great lawn. She kept asking me where we were going and what we were doing but I didn't say. I just led her along, playing the quiet leader.

"You're a peculiar guy."

Her walk was brisk as usual. Very business-like.

"You were right," I said after a bit of walking.

"About?"

I told her to just wait, and directed us to a park bench where we sat and ate a while in silence.

"Well?" she had said, glancing at her watch.

I told her again to be patient and just as I finished I remember seeing it coming. Down a ways towards the Washington Monument was a parade of people marching in our direction and as they grew larger we began to hear them.

"Are you watching this?"

She just nodded, chewing.

"I did some research online and you were right," I pointed. "There's a bunch of articles about it all."

She chewed on, nodding, "You didn't believe me?"

The parade grew louder and nearer. At its front, in t-shirts that read "Fear the Art of Youth," a line of kids no older than college Freshman carried a banner spread across them that read: "Your Investments are Our Playground." Behind them, the party was led by a man with a mask-covered face, dreadlocks pouring out the top. He donned a purple vest and bright orange pants as he peddled a tri-bike with speakers propped across the rear axle. Party music blared as he rode, swaying down the street.

Following in tune to the beat were the hundreds who grew into thousands. Chanting. Marching. Their signs waving high, thrusting, jabbing at the skies of democracy. Feet pounding the grass and dirt. There were some dressed goofy in costumes like monkeys, giant teddy bears, fast food chain mascots with their heads shaved and blood dripping from both ears, fat cats with pocket watches, a three-person horse costume pulling a casket with the word "democracy" spray painted in black.

Some waved signs. "Fukt the Grammer Poleece." "Profit War." "Debt is Sexy." Ben Franklin in a warm up suit and a gold necklace around his neck shook a sign that read "Freedom to Buy Sweat Shops Shoes." Some danced in wedding dresses, zoot suits, pink pajamas. Some held giant puppets of Uncle Sam with money signs for eyeballs or Lady Liberty holding up a designer handbag. The puppets danced on long sticks. They taunted, twisted and swayed.

They were screaming. They were yelling. Their signs pounded the sky.

She called through the cacophony something to the effect of, "You know you can trust me."

Another band of the masked kids in "Fear the Art of Youth" shirts held signs, "I am Animus." A bit later I saw one that said, "Think For You: We Are All Liam Logan." But what had me really smiling were the signs and t-shirts that read "Emory Walden Reads To Me."

"I love this city," I called as the protesters marched by. Their yelling. Their jovial chants. Their fists punching the sky. Their dancing. "I love feeling like I'm in the pulse of it."

"You are the pulse of it," she replied.

We watched a while and I remember feeling whole. I remember telling myself, this is what it must feel like to have a superstar athlete for a son, or a piano prodigy. To watch yourself grow beyond your body. This is what it must feel like to be Bill Gates or Warren Buffet, Michael Jordan or David Beckham. To be an empire in name.

At the back of the protest were masked kids with backpacks laying cinder blocks in the street to sabotage the caravan of police cruisers and SUVs, their lights flashing. One kid with a megaphone called to them, laughing something like: "Go home pigs. You're not invited to the party."

They stopped in front of the Capitol a while where the party continued and the signs jabbed at the sky. Ella Alice and I watched in silence for maybe half an hour before the protest re-organized and turned left up Pennsylvania Avenue. When the last of it had trailed away, and the music had faded, I turned to her and said, "I wish Spivey could see it."

She told me don't worry. She took some photos. I guess I hadn't noticed.

"The protests don't really come through Georgetown," she said. "But every now and again when we know there's going to be one Fletcher rents a hotel and we watch from the window."

"There must've been 30 or 40 thousand people."

"It's the biggest I've seen," she nodded and pulled a pad of some sort from her purse and jotted some notes. I'd forgotten my sandwich. She had too. So we picked up and continued eating. There were things I wanted to talk about. I was in need of a friend. I had no one. But I didn't know what to say or how to say it. I was afraid of prison. And I wanted someone to know it. To at least share the knowledge of my fear. Mostly, I missed Carolyn. I wanted someone to know that too.

We spoke at the same time "I –" "So"

"What?"

"Oh nothing," I said. "You go ahead."

She asked me if I was sure and I nodded that I was just making small talk.

"I was making small talk too," she laughed. "So anyways, did you grow up here?"

"Sorta. I'm from Nova," I said.

"Oh, a Nova kid."

I nodded. "What about you? You're not a Congressman's daughter, right? So are you from here?"

"Oh, no." She wiped the corners of her mouth which she always did when she fished eating. "I came here on scholarship. Went to GW and haven't left since."

Yeah?

"Yeah. Actually, I grew up in Troutville where nothing happens and everyone's daddy's a farmer or an alcoholic. This city opened my eyes to a world of consequence. This is where the decisions are made. I wanted to be a part of that. I told myself this was it. Make it in D.C. If all these other people can, why can't you? You don't need to come from some rich family. You just need ambition. Will. Know what I mean, hun?"

Completely.

"You're going to laugh at this."

I promised not to.

"Before Spivey took me in and changed my whole view, I had this ten year plan. I was going to own my own marketing firm – the most prominent, most influential firm doing business for all the big swingers. I was going to be in charge – not just playing support." She kicked at the ground. "Sounds kind of corny, doesn't it?"

"Not really," I told her. In some strange way I felt maybe I could relate. The glow I felt from the protest must be something like how Ella must have wanted to feel. So I told her I thought that maybe in some way her and I were similar. But perhaps I was just lonely.

"Thanks," and then, after a pause in which she scanned her paperweight arm dangling there beside her, "It's like, 20 years ago the attitude was 'make it in New York City and you can make it anywhere.' Today – this is where it is. All the money and power has gravitated here."

"You must be hella smart. GW?"

She smiled at this, proud with that fake humility at the edges where the lips curl.

"You know my college psych professor said motivation is highly correlated with intelligence," I retorted. "Most of the time motivation is wasted on the wrong things."

"The best of us have dreams," she fired back.

I laughed for myself and she gazed off toward the crowd as it marched away, as if looking through it and towards a younger self glancing about the great future she has built gleaming florescent across a silver building. I interrupted her moment with, "It's a bunch of Congressmen's kids there."

"I know." Breaking her trance, she turned to me and said, "Jealous much?" She gave me a poke in the stomach. I smiled, pretended to laugh and thought a bit about the prospect before I gargled and spit into the grass beside me.

"You know that is a total turn off, don't you?"

I didn't care.

"Hey I really appreciate this," I said. "But I'd better get along now. This whole revolt business is a lot of work."

She agreed, thanking me for the chat. "I'm sorry if I offended you with the jealous thing, hun" she said.

"It's nothing," I said. "Thanks for coming along."

We sat a moment because I was unsure how to tie up the conversation and leave and so after some dawdling I asked, "What are you going to do tonight?"

She laughed. "I dunno. I'll probably hang out with my Clarendon friends. You know, the ones who don't think past 5pm or care who I really am."

I told her to have fun and at this we parted ways. And so, on this moonless night when the air tasted like the sap of leafless trees, I climbed the hilltop above the highway where Carolyn and I fell in love. It is strange how when you become infatuated with someone you feel as though they can see everything you do. As if you are showing off for them. I had felt in some blind way that everything I was doing – that if Carolyn could see – she would approve, smile, think I so smart, different, passionate and intriguing. I had felt that she laid in bed smiling, hugging her pillow and feeling close to me as though she were watching me in a movie, her hero out there risking his own hide for a great ideal she naturally sympathized with. Some common passion. If only she knew, I had thought. If only I could break my promise to Spivey. It was all in all some delusion – although not common between her and I.

It seemed romantic. Yet, being alone in a room. Not talking to the one you love on the line. Wondering if they'll call. Wondering if they're thinking about you. These are not the things of romance.

I am a loyal person. Even when failed or I fail myself. I do not believe in second guessing. I am not buying a boat or a lawnmower for my 3-quarters acre. I never broke my promise to Spivey so that Carolyn could truly know me. And I will not. I love Carolyn but I wonder if she would've loved me had she known me. In five years, I don't want to be just another person living a suburban lie. But I miss her.

"I need you around," she had said. Simple task. Show up.

I felt her fingers press my lips apart. I wanted to kiss her.

I need you around.

And I wondered how the sky would look in a world where I could have held her in honest arms.

I laid in the grass as the cars whizzed by below. I stared up at that sky and planned its alignment. This is not second guessing, I remember telling myself. This is moving forward. Formulating a plan.

I could see Carolyn sitting there with her mother, two beautiful women sharing supper. Their smiles, so similar in the warm halogen glow, wanted for nothing.

But I wasn't there.

Instead, out here where I was in an empty park above the city, I listened to the cars scream along the highway that cut through the natural world. One hundred years ago this park would've been a farm, or a forest. And I bet I could have laid there and been okay with myself.

But, not now. It was hard to be by myself. And I did not want to go home.

In the city, I looked for her everywhere. I knew that if I saw just a glimpse of the back of her neck exposed, I would recognize her.

19

"YOU NIGHT OWL!"

"Oh, look at you with your name calling." She shook her head. She was dressed like one of those toothpick-thin 'multicultural' women, women with complexion far too light for their heritage and who just happens to have Anglo features, right off the store window poster. I remember the irony of those ads.

That's America, right? Homogenization nation: You can be different, so long as you're not.

"Why not try and relax and get over it? What's done is done." She presented the chair before her with an open hand, "Have a seat."

"He was my friend going way back to high school," I spat. "We practically grew up together."

"Something wrong with your leg?"

"I'm fine," I snapped, pulling out a chair.

"I figured you'd be a teensy bit upset," she confessed. "But come on!"

"Of course I'm upset!" I protested. And then, "Why'd you email me?"

With a shrug, "cause I wanted to see you. It's the twenty-first century. Why else?"

"Sex & The City on re-run this week?"

She sipped her drink. "Why'd you come?"

I hesitated a bit. A waitress stopped by our table to see if I wanted something to drink and with my hat pulled low over my face I kept my eyes on the drink menu.

"Cause I thought I might get a glimpse into what the hell you were thinking," I said after the waiter moved on.

"I was thinking it was time to be honest with one-another."

"About what?"

She giggled, "Oh come on. I know you're into me. Listen, it's over between he and I- his eyes are off me. So why keep ducking?"

I said something like: "I don't know what planet you're living on Lilleth and what the view's like from there, but I'm in love with Carolyn. And she left me the other day. So I'm really not in the mood for your space ship fantasies."

She gave me a watery apology. A spoonful of sarcasm.

"Well don't you worry. I'm gonna get her back."

"I wonder what'd happen if I told Carolyn everything I told Pitty-Pat," she delivered the threat nonchalantly; as if it were just a thought passing by on a waitress's tray.

"You're not gonna do that. You're not gonna do that because if you do, not only will I never speak to you again, I will ruin you," I clutched the edges of the table between us ready to launch myself over the slab of wood and wrangle her by the flesh of her neck. "Your credit. Your reputation. Your bank account. Your job. Your condo. You know who I am. But do you know what I'm capable of? Do you? The connections I have? You think you're living in a fantasy world now? You're gonna be out there in the woods with Bambi and the fucking Lion King cause that's the only place you're gonna be welcome after I'm done."

"I liked your picture in the papers," she retorted.

"Eat one!"

"What do you care about this girl? What's she got so special?"

"We have no choice over who we fall in love with, Lilleth. So why bother asking? If I could sum it up, I would, but you wouldn't understand cause you don't know anything – you think love is a possession. It's not. It's an action."

"That's not true, that's not true at all! I loved Pitty-Pat. I did. But we grew apart. We're no longer those people each of us loved. You think I have no heart," she shook her head, fighting for dry eyes. "I still love him in a way, but I grew out of love with him as I grew into being my own woman. And there's a world out there he was holding me back from." She sniffled then said, "Pat lives in a cocoon."

Don't we all?

With that I felt the urge to leave. My drink had yet to arrive. No bother. I told Lilleth I needed to be going and as I began to stand she said something that really resonates with me now. She leaned in close and with a sharp whisper:

"Listen up sweety, you think you're the only one who can lean here? You forget, I know who you are. I know who you really are. And once the police know who you really are, and they've got your picture on file, and your prints, and whatever other shit they collected when you were arrested, they're not gonna have much trouble tracking you down. You won't be hiding in plain sight anymore. So I'm not so sure it's me who should be worried and I'm not so sure it's you who should be making threats. Don't you get it?"

"If you're gonna do justice, do justice to Pat," I retorted.

"Don't take your anger out on me, sweetheart. You're the screw up," she yelled as I walked away. As I headed for the door, I saw the waitress approaching the table with a stout and she gave me a confused look as I brushed past her.

20

COURT DATE. Fuck the justice system and fuck the cops and lawyers who pimp for it, I thought. Fuck Brock. That stain. That little teat-sucking piglet. Fuck Lilleth. Her unrealities. Her threats. And fuck Pat too. The world was a giant public bathroom.

On my way to the courthouse, head ducked down, I slipped a marker from my pocket and etched onto a newspaper dispenser "Think For You."

Some reporter tried to stop me for a comment but I just coughed in his face and shoved past him, limping up the courthouse steps.

Inside, I was shoved before some judge who was ordained by the Power's law in his costume robe, his eyebrows like Justice Scalia's, a gobbler for a neck, and Nancy Reagan's mousy little smile. He had that "I'm better than you" aura of the upper crust. The place smelled like musty hallways and stained oak.

He gave me this spiel, this petulance, this real run about "property" and "symbolism" and the "pestilence" he saw standing in paint-spattered street clothes before him. I can't remember all what he said but I remember it sounded rehearsed. He waved the marker removed from my pocket by the security officer upon my entrance as if he'd known I'd bring it and rehearsed that, too.

"Liam Logan. You represent a pimple on the face of this beautiful city. What you've done is meaningless. What you stand for has been defeated. Do you have anything to say for yourself, other than to pour excuses upon my court?"

"Yeah," I spat back. "Do you dine at the Ritchfield Steakhouse?"

I had planned ahead of time to stare into his eyes when he delivered his ruling. I don't remember if I did.

Expelled from the city proper. Banned from the mere possession of any form of paint or, "markers such as this." Just like Animus. And, community service. 250 hours. A $10,000 fine. A parole officer for two years. His name, Fred. And a friendly reminder, "mind the court or your undercarriage belongs to the prison."

I was told to "consider myself fortunate." He'd have liked to throw me in prison; his smile gone when he said this. Why hadn't he, then? Fear of a backlash from the spray can crazies? Had they thought Liam Logan was just a byproduct of the muting of Animus? Who would seek to continue my legacy once I was excommunicated?

After meeting Fred and setting up our parole schedule, I was led out a back door by two guards. There, in a parking lot between buildings, stood a row of squad cars polished and glimmering in the late afternoon sun. The guards chatted, disinterested, as we strolled along. No hurry. At the last car they opened the back door, still sharing the same buffoon story and laughing as I was chucked in the back of the car, and the door was slammed closed. I watched over my shoulder as they meandered back toward the courthouse.

The car started up. I closed my eyes, rested my head against the window and wiggled a bit to ease the discomfort of sitting on my hands. "A bit overkill with the handcuffs, don't you think?" I called to the back of the driver's head. He didn't reply.

We drove along for some while. I pretended to sleep. Pretended I was so at ease with all of this, so unfazed that I'd the vanity to nap. I peaked one eye open when I felt us cross the Roosevelt Bridge.

The driver, he started humming. Started humming Stone Temple Pilot's "Plush". A few of the words were thrown in here and there: something about a missing body.

Some minutes later the car pulled off the highway and the driver got out and I just laid there on the glass pretending I was asleep.

My door opened and I practically fell out. I was pulled up, dragged to my feet. I faked a yawn as best I could. Opened my eyes. Before me trees swayed in the evening breeze leaning out over a ledge. Below, the brown water of the Potomac bent toward Georgetown. Across the river, a forest speckled with light.

It was a beautiful summer dusk; orange stirred in a blue horizon. The air lingered thick over me and I could hear the rush hour traffic humming behind us.

I was marched from behind to the edge of the parking lot of the overlook, made to step up and over a stone wall by way of a baton jabbing my right kidney, then down a path to a switchback at the cliff's ledge where stepping spilled dirt over to join the flowing brown below.

The path doubled back toward the stone wall embankment which propped up the overlook above. We stopped at the path's end where a clearing no bigger than a bathroom stall rested hidden below a canopy of green.

Next thing I knew, I was whacked on the back of my leg. I stumbled forward toward the cliff before dropping to my knees to stop myself.

I righted myself, stood, turned around.

Standing there. Crisp. Smiling. Brimmed cap. That medallion. Black uniform.

"Surprised to see me, stain?"

His smile grew.

I was the Washington monument.

"How is she?"

I was the polio virus.

"Quit staring at your nose!" he commanded.

"Yeah, she's fine," I blurted.

"Oh?"

"Just saw her a little bit ago," I lied. "should I tell her you said hi?"

"Just shut up!" he fired. "Now you listen to me, Emory," his finger pointing me down. "We don't want you here. Understand? We don't want you around anymore kicking up shit. For a while, you were just a nuisance. And that was tolerable. But now. Now! Now, listen to me. Go give all this shit up! Walk away! Go get a job! Get occupied! Run away to Europe again! I don't care. Understand? Just get out of my way and stay the fuck out of my city! Cross that bridge to do anything but meet your parole officer and I will be forced to repeat the lesson I'm about to teach."

* * * * *

Have you ever been thrown into a wall?

Funny, it doesn't hurt as bad as having your nose pounded into your face like a nail under the hammering force of a baton crashing down on it. With the wall your body serves as a large surface across which the force is distributed. This lessens the detriment of the impact on any single area of your body. The same cannot be said about the baton.

Pain is relative.

Pain is better off distributed over a large area or over long periods of time.

The crack of the baton. A chirrup. Blood. Wheezing.

He laughed. "Holy shit did your nose explode!" He was giddy. Giggling. My nose gushing.

I could not see him standing there above me. A tower of spite, abhorrence wadded up in his hand. My eyes were open. Weren't they? I could not see his giggling. His gaping. His glee. But I could hear his smile. Hear the satisfaction in his belly as the laughs came up like little bursts, carpet bombing the air; detonations of contempt well-fed by this satiating display sprawled and bloodied before him.

He urinated on me.

He pulled it out. That same prick from the alley. I could not see. It splashed me. My clothes. My face. Warm.

I vomited.

He laughed harder.

"I'd shit on you, you pathetic piece of shit. I would. But I don't gotta shit just right now. Consider yourself fortunate. Piece of shit."

And I heard him walking away. I heard him get in the car. He drove off.

I cried.

I could not see. I was glad.

Yes. I remember that now.

* * * * *

"Heya Bromine!"

"Renton? Renton? Is that you? What are you doing here?"

"Looking after," he said.

He picked me up, tossed me over his shoulder and waddled off.

I cannot remember.

"Baby. Baby what'd they do to you?"

"Carolyn! Carolyn, is that you?"

I cannot remember.

* * * * *

"Emory?"

I emerged into time from that place between.

"Emory? Are you?"

Sensation returned. My fingers. Toes.

My face. Swelling.

Knots.

Pulsating pulp.

Piercing pressure. Like a wrench had been jammed up my nose, between my eyes, poking at my frontal lobe.

"Oh! Emory!"

"Baby" I muttered.

"Oh Emory, you're awake!"

Tried to open eyes. Jammed. Swollen. A sliver of light.

A puddle through which to see.

A beautiful figure. Outline. Smiling blur.

"Is this real?"

Laughter. "Of course it is." And then cries of "oh you're back!"

"Where – how did you?"

"Hunny, I came by your apartment. Like I always do to make dinner."

Blink.

Ella.

Crashing.

Sigh.

Oww!

"Try not to move" she said. "I found you. Oh it was a fright! I saw your legs poking over the edge of the couch as I walked in. I knew in my heart something was terribly wrong. And I called to you, and you said nothing. I came around the couch and, oh, it was the worst sight I'd ever seen. I nearly lost control. You were sprawled out, horribly messed up. Your face looked like it had been chewed up by a dog, or a dinosaur or something. There was blood. I screamed. I did. And I think that woke you. I called to you. 'what happened?' But you sort of gurgled - you were coughing blood when you tried to respond. So I told you to lie still. I'd call someone. You were in and out of consciousness after that."

Blink. The puddle in my eyes began to calm.

Unfamiliar ceiling.

"This isn't my room."

"You don't remember?"

Cough.

"You slept," she went on. "You slept and slept when we

brought you here. This was evening, oh, two nights ago."

"Brought me where?"

She pulled her good arm around me, her paperweight hand resting on my chest.

"I'm so happy. I swore that was the end. But the doctor says your fever has subsided, and I knew you'd come to soon. I've been sitting here all night. Reading." She paused, waving a book in front of me that appeared only as a red blur passing left to right and back.

"You need to rest," she said. "I'll return in the morning, hun."

* * * * *

The moon gazed out over the city. The city sprawled out below us, a haze of electric light, humming streets, mechanical humanity. Sprawled out forever over in every direction; the horizon glowing halogen.

"Oh, my moon!" She gasped. Her hips leaned against the rail. Her black dress cut above her knees where the muscles in her legs balanced her as she perched up on her toes. She swung forward and back under the twilight.

"Isn't it something – up here?" I whispered.

"Oh, it's celestial!"

The rooftop was adorned with an upside-down wooden crate which sat beside a blanket. On the crate: wine, two glasses and mason jars stuffed with flowers. Candlelight and music decorated the air.

"What's that over there?"

"That's Adams Morgan just over there," I pointed. "Meridian is between us, if you could see it. We walked by it once. Remember?"

She leaned into me. "Of course I do. And back that way?"

"Dupont. Beyond that, Georgetown, the Potomac River, then, Virginia of course." I spun us around, "And Ben's famous Chili Bowl is back that way. Oh, it's the best! And

Howard is over there. And the 9:30 Club is somewhere around there."

"Oh yeah, on V street!" she chimed in like a child calling the answer to a trivia game. "You know so much. You never stop impressing me." She adorned my cheek with soft lips.

We sat and drank wine. We gazed. We laughed. The moon watched from above, shifting its viewpoint as the night crested.

I poured the last glass.

"Come, come," I called. "I want to show you a secret something!"

"Oh, I love surprises!"

We leapt to our feet.

I led her around the rooftop, pretending there was something hidden under every unbuttoned brick or loose flap of tar, behind leaning boards, around the electric box, and just over there as we hopped needlessly over exhaust pipes.

I stopped us at a protrusion and lifted an exhaust flap.

"Watcha doing?"

"This is where my kitchen fan vents," I said sticking my hand in. "Romantic, huh?"

She laughed.

I pulled out an envelope.

She smiled.

Back at the blanket she read the contents by candlelight, the flicker, like wisps of gold breezes, brushed across her cheeks. She read the last words out loud, "With adoration, amazement and amore, Your Emory."

She rubbed the empty glass against her forehead, teasing me. Frogs went 'ribbit' 'ribbit' in the night yet there was nothing but concrete in every direction for a few hundred yards, save the rock creek winding to the Potomac. The song "The Long and Windy Road" by Ray Charles began to play.

"Will you dance with me?"

"You don't dance," she giggled.

"I love this song," I begged. "And I would love to

forever tie you to it."

We danced. We swayed. We floated on the rooftop among the clouds of the Mid Atlantic and I tasted the beads of sweat on her shoulder.

We kissed.

A thunderstorm flickered in the distance and we felt cool air brush over us and I rubbed the goosebumps up and down her arm. There is romance in vulnerability. There is tenderness in fear. "Let me in," she said, folding her arms up and pressing her chest to me. "Just let me in and I will love you forever." Trembling, dancing, barefoot hearts.

"Tell me about the moon," I whispered. "How is it now, again? A Waxy Gibbons?"

She laughed, "No, no. It's Waxing Gibbous." We laughed until our lips met.

On the blanket she called to me, "you are nourishing. You are nourishing."

I kissed her thighs to warm her and soothed her with my tongue. After, we laid awhile as the candlelight dampened. Soon the one remaining candle dispelled its last into a trail of smoke that winded upward and disappeared. I stared at her moon up in the sky, her head tucked between my arm and my side. Her body jolted a little, electric shots firing through her veins.

"Are you dreaming?" I whispered.

"Only children dream," she whispered back through a sleepy smile, "the rest of us reflect."

I fell asleep to her aura and awoke to the birds crying for daylight, their calls peeling away the darkness, and I opened the rooftop door and we descended the oblique stairway.

*****

The door opened. Peaking in was the doctor from when I broke my ankle. His shoulders sagged as he waddled in and he closed the door behind him.

"Good. You're awake," he said, eyeing me over. "How

do you feel, Emory?"

"It's a struggle."

He nodded as he scanned a clipboard.

"What day is it, Doctor?"

"Bend."

"Dr. Bend."

"It's Tuesday."

"How long have I? How long am I gonna be stuck here?"

"Well, that's - that's actually why I'm here,"

"Good," I said. "Cause I'd like to know. No one's telling me anything. Not Ella. Not Spivey."

"There is something you need to know."

"Let's get on with it," I begged. "I got a life to get back to."

"Emory," he frowned. I remember that frown.

"Look," I had cut in. "I know it's bad. But I'm getting better and I – I can see alright now. And it doesn't hurt so much to move. I mean, I can't stand lying in this bed much longer. I feel like I've been here for weeks. You know? You're the doctor. Give me some pills. I'll come back in a week. And -"

"Emory, Emory," he put his hand on my shoulder. "It's not the injuries you've sustained, Emory. It's something else."

"What do you -"

"Let me ask you this," he said, pulling over a chair and resting the dough of his belly beside me. "In the last six months or so, have you been experiencing any pressure in your head – any headaches?"

I couldn't remember. Why?

He leaned forward, his shoulders slouching. "Have you felt dizzy? Confused?"

"I said, I can't remember."

"There's no easy way to say this," he sighed. "You see, Emory, when we did a CAT scan of your head to assess the damage, we noticed something peculiar."

"Uh-huh."

"Upon further investigation, we stumbled across, well, see, it's really quite by chance that this was even caught. So, you can't really. Well, I guess in some ways it's quite fortunate. Depends how you want to. Well, anyway. You see, there's a tumor, Emory. In your brain. There's a growth. And well, I'm afraid. I'm afraid. Well it doesn't look good."

"How do you -"

"A malignant tumor. Very advanced stage. It's rare, I grant you. Very rare. Could be genetic. Could be environmental. There's no way to tell," he shrugged his shoulders and the dough of his belly raised and sank. "But I assure you it is real."

"What can you -"

"Fortunately there's an operation. But it's very risky. There's a – there's a lot of potential for things to go wrong when dealing with the brain. You understand."

"Uh-huh"

"I hate to say, but truth is there's a good chance you won't make it to the other end."

"Isn't there -"

"I'm afraid not," he said, stroking the strings of hair atop his head.

"And this operation – if I don't go through with it?"

"You'll be dead in three months, I assure you." He declared.

I swallowed this down, leaving it to anchor in my belly knowing I couldn't digest it. In times of crisis humans act irrationally and I guess I'm the type of human whose irrationality leads him to crack a joke.

"Looks like it couldn't be worse this time, eh, Doc?"

"I'm afraid you're right."

I laughed. All mad men do.

"Dr. Bend,"

"mmhmm?"

"Where am I?"

He looked confusedly at me, cleared his throat and sucked a wad of phlegm up into the chamber of his sinuses.

"What does it look like?"

I nodded.

"When you're in places like this, it's better to think about where you want to be."

I thought on this a bit. "I'm not sure where I want to be."

"Listen, I've got to get on home," he frowned. "I hate to be crass at a time like this, but it's late. And you've got a decision only you can make." He rubbed the top of my head, as if that could console me, and told me "take your time."

"I understand," I said. "You've got a wife. A family."

He sat a minute by me, conflicted by his need to leave and the knowledge that once he passes through that door he would leave behind a boy in an empty room digesting his own cessation.

As he finally stood to leave, he offered: "Listen kid, you want my advice? Do the operation. What you have – it isn't a pretty way to go, if you know what I mean. If the operation fails you can be comforted to know that at the very least you won't even know you were leaving."

"Thanks for the perspective," I said, watching him disappear through the door.

*****

I climbed on all fours up the stairs, elbowing my way up. One at a time. Opened the door. Crawled out.

I remember the mason jars with wilted, dead flowers.

I stumbled, colliding with myself until I arrived at the exhaust flap. I reached inside. Nothing. I reached further, further.

The moon looked down at me. I looked back. It looked at me as if watching TV; that slow motion fall of the silhouette to the flash of camera lenses. His face smacks the arena canvas. Those rides in the backseat of the car; those things that pass by the window when a boy is too short to peer out.

My first bloody nose.

Society. The violence. The cacophony.

Then suddenly, an empty sky. Desolate city. The space where sound once filled the air. Awkward lingering nothing.

I guess I was sleeping.

Sprawled, contorted, confused. Gurgling up from somewhere.

*****

Ella leaned in close, brushing her fingers through my hair. "I'm scared for you, hun. It's terrible. Everything's been going so well. And for this."

I closed my eyes to her calming fingers. At night she would come in and we talked a while. I liked my time with Ella. I could have fallen asleep to it. The rest of the time I thought of death. It was painted on the ceiling. It lingered in the dark corners on quiet nights as I lay alone in bed. It was the dryness on my tongue. It was with me in the layers below the bandages where I was rotting away.

"Have you made up your mind?"
"What choice do I have?"
"Yes, I suppose you're right," she said.

"How do I look?"
"Better when you smile."

I smiled for her and we chuckled. We sat awhile in that good moment. "Fletcher says he doesn't know if it can go on without you," she confided. And then a moment later, "Don't tell him I told you that."

"It's got to," I protested.

She leaned down, her pink lips hovering above me for a moment like glossy magazine prints as her breath kissed the mâché of bandage over my cheek. "You are so brave to be so committed," she whispered, tucking her head beside mine and wrapping her good arm around me. There we lay for some time. I knew the swollen pain would be there when she left. In time it sort of became comforting in its own way and

I think in the week or so since I met with the doctor I was beginning to accept the things that were now always there, lingering.

21

THE LAST GRAFFITI ART I did before the trial was not political. I painted flowers along the wall across the street from Carolyn's house where I knew she walked to work. I wrote her a message: "I never told you! My nickname for you was Unique Beauty. Please forgive me!" I couldn't sleep so I sat up all night in Dupont Circle only to fall asleep sometime after morning.

I awoke that evening and sat awhile on a park bench, watching the visitors march for the metro station to abandon the city they ruled and let the day be consumed by the night. Renton came waddling by when there was more dark than light and I called over to him.

"Heya Bro-mmminnne!" he called back. "How are ya?"

"Hanging in there," I said.

"It's *really* good to see ya," he replied, waddling toward me. Renton took a seat beside me and I welcomed his familiar scent of cabbage and grass stains. I asked him how he was doing and how his peacetests and peaceins were and apologized for not coming around to any lately. He said of my apology, "Stawwwp it!" and patted me on the shoulder and told me: "Pip, I been layin' low lately. The Pigs keep hagglin' my Minnesota mass-ass with their shitarsky. They don't get it. I keep tellin' 'em, hey, I'm not who you're after!"

"I'm sorry, man," I said. "You hungry?"

Renton told me he just ate some bread and pasta he found but could always eat so I told him to wait there and ran over to the convenient store where I got some jerky, candy, a bag of salsa chips and a can of iced tea. He smiled when I returned and laughed his har har har. "You're a good bromine, bromine. How's findin' things goin' for ya?"

"Things've been tough lately."

"How are ya? Tell ol' Renton bout it. I got time for ya."

I ate a while, then passed him the tea and said, "You were right about the mercury thing."

"Mmhmm," he nodded with a sip. Tea trickled into his beard.

"Except I don't know," I continued. "It seems like maybe it isn't that it's an inevitability that it has to rise and fall, but that the way we live today – maybe it's our own fault?"

He nodded at this, with his earnest look, his arm folded across the bench and his entire body turned toward me, "We all want a better world, bromine. If you can find peace maybe you can find peaceful love." He nodded at this, his beard waving up and down, and said, "Yeah, I think so. Maybe. I've found peace. But I never found no one to love me peacefully. But what does Renton know? I'm a fat smelly bottom feeder!" He laughed, shoved his hand into the bag and pulled out a wad of chips which he stuffed into his mouth. Pieces of chewed up chip fell out into his beard and onto his shirt as he spoke "I promise the world peace. I want to build it up. Maybe I'm not gettin' it done 'cause I got no one and never had no one lovin' me in my life."

"You're a good person. That makes me sad," I said. "You really never had anyone who loved you?"

He laughed. "I went to high school prom with a girl I loved. She turned out to be a lesbian and left me standin' there at the dance all by my fat self to go into the back of a limo with the field hockey captain." I laughed too at the thought and together we sat a while enjoying one another's company and ate and watched the people of the night retake the city.

"Just don't go livin' your life in a fake reality 'cause you've taken loss in life," he said. "There's meaning out there. There's a purpose for all of us who can survive ourselves. That I've learned. Ya just gotta go find it. Ain't nothin' what it seems when you're blinded by ya own self. But when ya smile at the end ya see so much clearer. Do ya overstand?"

I nodded and sat a while enjoying my friend.

22

IT WAS AFTER SOME TESTS, I THINK. He rolled in in a wheelchair pushed by Ella Alice as the straps of his brown robe dragged along the floor.

"Emory, Emory, my good boy."

He was faded, limp and hollow. He looked as if he'd been staring at a television for months without sleep, the now ever-present greyness in his eyes. But I acted like I didn't notice as I'm sure I was no sight myself.

"Mr. Spivey!"

"Yes, it's me, my good boy! I've returned as there is a transcendent matter over which we must converse." Ella wheeled him up to my bed, put a blanket on his lap, and asked him if he needed anything. He said he was fine. She leaned down in close and told me "you're looking better, hunny" with a smile.

Spivey agreed, adding "I struggle to think what we're up against."

Ella turned to leave behind two men seeping into the Earth. We sat awhile after she closed the door behind her until he said: "I know you like apples. I brought you this." He reached it toward me and asked, "can you eat it? It's from my fridge."

I took it. "I'm embarrassed," I said. "I – I didn't mean to steal from you."

"No, no. What's mine is yours, Emory." He nodded as if agreeing with what he just heard come out of his own mouth. "Diet is so important."

I nodded back, taking a bite.

"It is swell seeing you. But not like this, you know? Not like this."

"It's been hard to accept. But I'm getting there," I replied, unable to bring myself to look into his eyes. For in him I could see my expiring, wilting self, as though he had rolled in with death dragging behind him. "I feel like people are looking at a corpse," I said.

"Health," he nodded, breathing the words in. His trembling hand elevated from his lap to find its place on his chest. "Health was paramount to that which we have sought to accomplish. Yes, indeed. Should I be the first to admit I took for granted your health? How was one to know?" he asked himself. He gazed down at his hand a while before beginning to speak again, "And to think, we've accomplished so much. Quite so! We have. And then this. This perplexing turn of events which has been the impetus of many a night without sleep. Nights pondering how do we go on? How do we continue so that we may realize what we have risked and given so much of ourselves for? The movement is almost self-fueling now. We stand at the cusp. At the gate. To look at what we have engendered! The groundswell! Is it proper to reminisce of the days of our beginning?"

He nodded affirmation to himself and continued. "Our life trajectories took us in such different directions. And yet our lives have become so intertwined by common ideals. Yes, ideals; having arrived at them from opposite sides of the same reality. I remember the day you arrived at my condo. You were potential. Glowing. And I, a fading, disenchanted businessman. Both iconoclasts yearning to engender something." His voice trailed off as he said this last fragment until I almost could not hear him.

Then, without warning, he continued on loud as a horn: "I never doubted the feasibility of it. Indeed. Years defiling myself as a businessman afforded many lessons. Ah yes, my greatest achievement was to learn the art of discerning an investment. And in you I have made my best investment. Very much so. The catalyst which has helped me to achieve paramount things is what you are Emory."

I watched him sink back into his chair from the exhaustion of his emotion. He had refused to let his garrulousness wane with his health.

"It has been really something," I nodded, again gazing away. "I could never express to you how lucky I've been. I never could have known meeting you would change my life. I apologize that it is coming prematurely to an end. I am ashamed. I feel impotent to have let down the movement." I could feel the tears swelling but damned them up by biting my lip for sake of posture. "I have let you down after you have afforded me so much."

"No," he waved off my apology. "What could one do? What has been done through our collective wills has been monumental!" He rose, smiling, then sunk and said "Life abrades us. You mustn't be ashamed."

"It looks like our bodies have betrayed us both," I admitted.

"Yes, indeed. You had only your mind to lose when you came into my condo that day long ago now," he recalled. "And I suppose during our time you will lose that too." With a sigh which seemed to sink him further into the wheelchair, "I'm the one who should feel a sense of letting the other down."

Talking to Spivey like this was what I imagined it must be like to speak to someone close to you on their death bed with the irony being that you too are dying and so neither of you know who should say goodbye. So I just sat awhile without speaking and finished off the apple.

For some time Spivey seemed to understand and gave me my peace. His breath was labored, his hand had fallen to his lap. He closed his eyes and sat a while until I thought he had fallen asleep and I was prepared to try and rest myself until

Ella came to wheel his old carcass away. But just as I closed my eyes he began to speak. "Now that you may appreciate the perspective I've been forced to endure for some time – may I ask, what does a dying many want, Emory?"

Without opening my eyes I waited a moment. I knew the answer but I did not yet want to speak. I should have known better than to underestimate the probability that he would go on blabbering, I thought. Is this what he had come to talk about? So I laid there, and then I opened my eyes and gave him his pleasure. "To have a legacy."

"Exactly," he replied, excitedly. "And you have built your legacy. And you have helped me erect mine. Oh, plenty you have done in this world. Much more than most shall ever do. The lot of humankind are their own anchor. May you go into this operation knowing that! You have been true to yourself. True to that which you hold close to your heart, your fire, your ideals. Now that time has revealed that it is entirely finite you see that there is nothing else but that which we believe in. We dedicate ourselves, and when time goes on beyond our life, may it move steadily in the direction in which we have pointed it!"

He leaned in close, "Those envelopes I gave you, what use do I have for their contents? Nill! Likewise, they mean nothing now for you, don't they? Little matters. Just to see your feet at the start of the day. We want to look out to the horizon and know that after we are gone the horizon will stand where we stood because we stood there. Who cares of the other stuff? Wherever they be, let they be lost to the world."

I understood.

"We keep our promises to ourselves," he professed. "That's the variable that separates us. That enables us. If something is our life's work, we die doing it."

I agreed. "Although I want so bad to live," I told him.

"Of course you do. As do I. That is a different variable - the variable that ties us to the rest of humanity. I too want not only to know what is over the horizon – but to see it come to fruition. It is so close. It is so close that I must be confident at least one of us will last long enough to experience it."

"I never got to thank you for paying my bail or for the lawyers."

He waved off my apology. "I was overall pleased with the outcome we were able to get with the sentence. I wasn't too worried about that judge."

I suddenly remembered Frank. "I guess I won't be checking in with my parole officer. I guess I won't be doing any community service."

"Quote so. Quite so."

I laughed at the thought that to know you're dying is to truly be free.

"I know that laugh and now is not the time to give up," he said. "I've thought on it. And I must say that you were right - few things stand the test of time. But we must not let despair be one of them," he said. "Rather, we must participate. We must take action. Isn't it that whom we both are? Men of action."

"I've tried to be," I replied.

"Do you remember when you came by and found me in bed – the day you took the apples?"

Of course.

"Do you recall our conversation?"

"Yeah, that was right after the envelopes began showing up and I asked you why you were giving me them."

"Precisely."

"We were in different shoes then, huh?"

"I will not tolerate such pessimism from you," his voice peaked. "Listen to me Emory. I know we can only see things from our own perspectives. This is the shortcoming of man, that we live by the rules only we are the exception to. But we must see the opportunities we have left."

"Opportunities?" I laughed.

"Let me ask you to understand my perspective, knowing that you cannot see from its point of vantage. That is, let me be straightforward as I can only be. We must be prepared in the case that by some chance you do not make it to the other side." He lifted his hands off his lap, aiming a jagged pointer toward me. His silver ring dangled from the bone between his knuckle and finger joint. "There is a need to be prepared. This you must understand."

"Prepared for my funeral, yes." I laughed again. I'm not sure why. I felt anger, but to laugh at my own death? Was this really how I coped?

Ignoring my laugh he continued, "Do you recall the doctor I told you about? The one who believes there is an operation which could save me."

"Yeah, the two organs thing."

"Emory. I can only be candid. We can no longer afford the luxury to not consider radical action. Not in a political sense this time mind you, but as a matter of science. As a matter of health."

"I don't understand," I told him.

Fletcher leaned as far forward as he could without tumbling out the front of the wheelchair. "One of us must see this thing out. Don't you agree? If you do not make it to the other end I am asking you to make the greatest sacrifice, the greatest gift that any idealist could ever give. I am asking you to donate one of your good kidneys and your pancreas so that the doctor can transplant them to me. And thus, I may live and realize our collective dream. What greater demonstration of commitment to the cause than to literally dedicate a part of yourself, post mortem, as your legacy to ensure that it lives on. Yes! Just as I invested everything into you so that you may carry on the torch after I died." His hand grabbed the edge of the bed sheet as he locked his eyes on mine, "Would you do that Emory? Would you give those parts of yourself to the cause?"

I don't know exactly what I said to this. You can imagine. I remember I sat there awhile staring ahead at my own body spread out before me wrapped like a broken-down appliance under a white sheet. I remember thinking that I had not seen my toes in some time and I remember thinking that I would like to see them again but also that I'd give them to someone if I did not need them.

Was I an organ donor? I couldn't remember. Was that little heart printed on my license, my real license, the one with my real name on it? The one I got when I was 16? It was a checkbox on a government form. Had I checked it? Had I bothered to cogitate the decision? Check "yes"? Check "no"? Did it mean anything to me at the time? What about my Liam Logan ID? Was Liam Logan an organ donor? I didn't recall being asked by Ella Alice on that day over a year ago now when she snapped my picture in Spivey's bathroom.

My immediate reaction was to hop out of bed and run. I had nowhere to go. I wasn't even sure I could walk. I wanted to crawl under the bed and hide. If I was going to die I wanted to die the natural way – alone with the quiet moments that fall over us in a calm. I had imagined the calm felt something like the instant when we are fully submerged after jumping into water and we are overcome with tangible feelings of being refreshed and scared as the water engulfs us.

With nowhere to go my body lay there before me. Still alive. Still of some use. And I could live on and maybe that would be okay. It was much to consider, to look at the self not as a whole but as a million pieces that could be diced up and put to work, which felt to me – in some way – no different than living. The parts of ourselves that we dice up and leave here and there? We hope they will have some use, some impact. Our words. Our deeds. The things we build. The things we destroy. We leave dust of dead skin behind on all of them. Perhaps that is why we are always afraid and always feel alone, because we are constantly losing a part of ourselves. I'm not sure if these thoughts make sense. But you can imagine. It is hard to tell another person that everything is okay when he asks you if he can have a part of your body once it is no longer of use to you so that he may live.

But that's what I did. That's what I decided was right. I had thought Spivey was my benefactor, thinking myself some kind of twenty-first century Pip. And in a way I was, for I was a stupid, naïve boy clinging to his flashlight under his sheets looking for a reason. It was clear to me in that moment that it was a different sort of partnership with Spivey. There was nothing greater I could do than to pass along a part of myself to try and ensure my beliefs were realized.

And if I believed he would live to see through all I had worked toward or if I doubted it would ever come to fruition perhaps did not matter. If I were a businessman, it would have been an obligation for the reckoning for all he had done for me; a balancing of the ledger. But that was not it. It was for the ideal. It was to live with the understanding of potential. Of what could be. That there could be a better world. Why else should I have bothered to wage this battle had I expected it only to come in my time? Yes, it made sense in that moment that there is no selfish revolutionary who is a true revolutionary. A radical does things for the sake of others.

Yes I would do it. I was terribly afraid.

23

I AWOKE. THE CEILING WAS THERE. I had that dream again, I told myself. The room was empty; darkness tempered only by the light gliding into the room from under the door.

I had that dream again. Brock's standing there in uniform and I think Carolyn is there but it's a blurry dream of shifting depths and things fall in and out of focus in a tunnel upside down. They're both looking at me.

"Give up," he says. "Give it up to me."

Carolyn doesn't speak. She is floating over me and appears to be gazing down. Brock's hands are on his hips, his belt buckle shining in my eye.

His baton is dangling by his side. "Give it up." He reaches way back, steps forward, swings. But he misses. He laughs. And then he does it again, missing closer now. "Tell me I am right," he demands. I try to speak. I try to beg him to kill me. Nothing comes out. But I feel as though I somehow tell him without saying anything, as if he has put his baton against the side of my head and pushed it right out.

Just a dream.

I awoke.

My heart was racing. I pulled my hand from under the cover and placed it on my chest to find something laying there.

I grabbed at it and it crinkled in my hand. Paper.

I pulled it up before my face. "It's a newspaper," I whispered to myself.

I laid and waited until my eyes adjusted to the darkness. A front-page article in the the *Post*:

Protesters Attack Tourist: Police Chief Vows Crackdown
Staff Reporter

Not since the early 1970s has this city seen such political agitation. What has been an abnormally hot and humid summer has seen a seemingly endless parade of rallies and protests. Early demonstrations were largely peaceful and although characterized by vitriolic language and accusations against the government and corporate globalization, officials say up until July no arrests of protesters had been made.

The character of these protests appears to have changed. In the last month, DC police have made over 250 arrests.

"[The protests] started peaceful about 8 months ago. They were respectful, just marching and exercising their First Amendment rights," said Police Chief Roland Ozell. "But it's gotten ugly. Real ugly. Real suddenly."

Yesterday, a demonstration estimated at 100,000 strong near the Washington Monument turned violent when words were allegedly exchanged between demonstrators and a tour group from Arkansas. According to authorities, witnesses saw perhaps a dozen young men attack a tourist after a heated exchange. The attacked, Dennis Janson, admitted to calling the mob "un-American commie idiot [expletive]"and questioning whether they supported Bin Laden. However, Janson maintains he did not provoke them with threats of physical violence nor did he commence the fighting.

No suspects have been identified but authorities are hoping witness descriptions will lead them to the culprits.

The string of violent protests are being blamed on what is called The Fear the Art of Youth or FAY Movement, an emergent grassroots political movement. Police have vowed to crack down on the protests and Authorities contend the FAY Movement is not a serious threat to public safety and the security of the city. When prompted, Police Chief Ozell would not comment whether the city has made preparations to step up their forces with riot police.

"Let me say this. This city has a history of witnessing protest and we have learned and are better prepared to handle this sort of demonstration. They have a right [to protest], if done so peaceably, but I will make this promise to our city. We are prepared to confront these agitators and vow to protect the rights of our Government, our businesses, and our citizens. If any law is broken we will act swiftly to catch and punish violators. If demonstrations get out of hand, we will act swiftly and with appropriate force to quell them."

But others are singing a different song.

"We love our country and want to take it back. This was a sign of things to come. You've got some pissed off citizens here and I don't think a rebuke by some cop is going to stop that," said a young women who spoke on the condition of anonymity.

Asked if he believed the protest would continue despite the Police Chief's warning, an individual who also spoke on conditions of anonymity added, "Yes. All of us - we're not about to give up. We're sick of the sales pitches for The Capitalist War, man. We don't want a strip mall covering a desert on the other side of the world. Our country's been hijacked, man. All of us - we're sick. We're living in a Corporatocracy and we're not stopping 'till we change the system."

The young woman and man identified themselves as participant in many recent rallies and supporters of the FAY Movement. *(For more on the FAY Movement, see article "Political Party" on page B1).*

I turned to the second article, this one by Trip Carpenito which was a full spread in the Metro section of the *Post*:

Political Party or Political Agitators? Emergent FAY Movement has Murky Roots

Their breed of political activism involves protests, vandalism and political graffiti. Their leaders are enigmatic and diffuse. They call themselves the FAY Movement.

"They don't have so much leaders as they have idols – who they think are visionaries - graffiti artists, inscrutable political commentators," said D.C. Police Chief Roland Ozell at a press conference yesterday.

One name authorities connected with the protests is Liam Logan, a graffiti artist from suburban Washington who recently admitted responsibility for a string of graffiti vandalism that plagued the metro area.

Sasha Gupta of the Department of Public Works said Logan's work prompted numerous phone calls to the city's call center. "His works were everywhere," Gupta said.

Logan refused to comment before a private hearing last month in which he pleaded guilty to 1 felony charge for destruction of property. The plea agreement, which was struck by Logan's team of high-powered lawyers to prevent Logan from being legally associated with the FAY Movement, therefore absolves the graffiti artist from any blame for the FAY Movement's actions. It is a mystery how Logan, who is unemployed and appears to have few assets, was able to arrange for lawyers from the prominent Washington firm Thurston & Fabos to represent his case pro bono. When contacted for comment, Thurston & Fabos refused to field any questions regarding their arrangement with their client.

It is indeed the mystery surrounding Logan that has attracted so much public interest. In the right circles, his influence and connection is not clear but appears to go without words. In the weeks following the sentencing of Logan, the city has seen an evolution in the character of the FAY movements. Yet, by all accounts, Logan is nowhere to be found. Records show he did not show up to his first parole meeting and a warrant for his arrest is outstanding.

It is the evolution of the FAY Movement that appears to have city goers on tip-toes while most seem to know little about who the FAY are and what they want. According to its website, The FAY Movement, which calls itself a political party, is a rallying cry for citizens concerned about the "corporatization" of American democracy.

"I was ecstatic when Logan was arrested," said Archie Pannengrav, city resident and small business owner. "I was worried my building would be vandalized. Now I'm worried about rocks being thrown through my windows. I don't know who they are and I don't care but it needs to stop. It's maddening is what it is."

Was Logan a Red Herring?

But, as it turns out, Logan may not be the city's biggest concern. Police Captain Kyle Yates, who led the investigation into Liam Logan, says the city is better off for having caught him despite the uptick in violent protest.

"I don't think Logan is really all that important to the movement," said Yates. "We have reason to believe it's moved beyond him. He was a rallying cry, a reason for a demonstration, and now they've moved past him."

Yates believes Logan is not a priority and has asked Police Chief Ozell to shift focus towards apprehending a man named Emory Walden.

Emory Walden is an unknown blogger who is widely credited as the grandfather of the FAY movement. While Walden did not officially start the movement, and in fact his name is not listed as a member of the governing body of the FAY Movement on its website, his writings are widely discussed on the movement's website and are a topic of discussion in their message boards. A popular blogger for a number of years, Walden's blog took off as the political climate in the country and around the globe grew increasingly unsteady following the economic crash of 2007-2008.

Although a political fixture in the Internet age, it appears Walden is even more enigmatic than Logan. Numerous sources within the FAY Movement admit to having never seen Walden but state that some supporters are rumored to be in communication with Walden via email and Internet chat.

Police Chief Ozell refused to comment when asked if his department has any leads as to where Emory Walden might be.

"I will say that this is a man who is inciting violence and vandalism. He's indirect, but he's inciting violence [and] agitating the

peace. He's given the order to 'change the world,' which is to say he has directed others to carry out crimes. His words have influenced the actions of many and he's culpable under law [for his actions] and will be brought to justice."

So far, authorities have been unable to track the IP address, a unique computer identifier, of the computer or computers from where Walden is blogging. While authorities who have analyzed the blog writings believe Walden is an older male, perhaps in his forties, young adults make up the Movement's largest block. Psychologists who study young adults believe the Movement is particularly attractive to persons who feel a sense of loss of direction.

Youth in Society

"They seem to be struggling to cope with the demands of twenty-first century society," says Professor Jen Yoon of George Mason University. "No generation before has been held up to such stringent pressure to succeed. Many appear profoundly maladapted and envisage the world as a place without purpose. Some appear to have rejected our society in search of something they see as better. Modern society has witnessed this wholesale psychological exodus of a generation previously, such as the counterculture movement of the 1960s and the Lost Generation after World War I."

Whether these psychological evaluations are accurate or not, it appears there is something appealing about this movement for many Millennials. Yet, those critical of the efforts of the D.C. Police Department say that if Liam Logan can be soon forgotten, who is to say that Emory Walden is really a target worth pursuing? According to social movement theorist, Olivia Henderson, "Walden is simply a banner. He's not so much a person as a psychological sign of the times. If authorities want to find Walden, they need only look in the face of the kids in the streets."

Whatever the case, it appears the D.C. police have their hands full in a political game of cloak and dagger.

I let go of the paper, feeling it slip from between my fingers and slide off the edge of the bed to the floor. Dying is a bit simpler than other forms of loss, I said to myself. To lose Carolyn was to live without her. To go to prison was to live without freedom. At least dying was to be without alternative – no time for regret, no time to feel shame. No time to wonder what might have been or what will happen. This was the conversation I had with myself every night.

*****

If I remember right, about two weeks before the trial Ella came over to the apartment. She cooked dinner but, for the first time, it didn't taste all that good. She seemed preoccupied as I watched what was usually a master chef fumble around the kitchen, dropping a few things and cursing at the mixing bowl she couldn't keep still.

We ate burritos. I remember clearly. That was it. Burritos. She didn't even bother to tell me what was chic about it – was the beef grass fed? The onions, tomatoes organic? What about the refried beans? Is it possible to even get organic refried beans?

After dinner, Ella got down to business. She had come over to council me on the trial and was acting as a liaison between myself and some hot shot lawyers Spivey had gotten me hooked up with. The stipulation was that I didn't go to their office, they didn't come here and we didn't meet nor communicate directly. So Ella did her usual duties – the loyal assistant ensuring everything went to plan.

"It's critical you don't talk to anyone about the trial. No media. They're going to want to talk to you and they'll know their best chance will be before or after the trial, understand?"

Leaning back in my chair with my arms folded across my chest, I let her go on like this for some time. I had a knack for tuning out – an effective strategy honed in adolescence for coping with angry parents and authority figures. It wasn't that I didn't care about the trial. I cared deeply. My hide was on the line. What bothered me was how it was all being handled.

"Emory? Emory? Hey – are you listening to me?"

"Can I tell you about this friend I had? He was a good friend to me and now he hates me cause I'm a bad –"

"I need you to focus," she snapped.

"What about this other friend I had? A long time ago –"

"Emory. Focus!"

"What about –" I cut myself short. I suddenly didn't feel like telling her about Carolyn. She wouldn't care. She was all business. "Alright, what is it you want?"

"Well I'm trying to brief you on our strategy but you're just off jumping on rooftops or something."

"I can deal with the flippin' trial myself," I shot back. "I don't need some pricey district lawyers with their marble-sign clout looking out for me."

She slapped her paperweight hand upon the table blowing papers all about. "Oh? You're gonna deal with it yourself are you?"

"I-I-I just don't get it. Where's Spivey in all of this? Sitting back in the shadows like always? I never see him. I never even hear from him. Not a sorry about your luck or even an inquiry about what went down or how I feel about it. I'm just supposed to –"

"Oh! You think he doesn't care? Is that it?"

I shoveled back in my chair and shot to my feet. "Yeah. I gotta be honest. I wonder a little. He's not sticking his neck out . He's -"

"He paid good money for these lawyers," she yelled. "Where's your thanks? Where's your sense of appreciation? You seem to think Spivey's a bottomless well."

"Hey," I retaliated trying to match her volume, her intensity. "I don't ask the guy for nothing!"

"Oh, don't you?" She fired back.

"Yeah, that's right. I never asked the guy for one thing. He came and found me, remember? He's the one who made me quit my job and- and - you remember servicing any of those requests?"

"Don't give me that shit! It was like paradise for you. You were glowing like a fourteen year old with a swimsuit magazine in his hands."

"Hey, all I'm saying is I didn't ask the guy for any money or any stupid lawyer."

"You narrow-sighted, ungrateful, callow little shit! There's a lot he's sacrificed for you! You don't know what you're up against! You don't bother to consider what he's up against, what he's risked! His livelihood. His fortune. He could be imprisoned too and rot and die in a cold cell like a nobody! Or worse! These people aren't messing around! This is a serious game you're playing and you better figure that out quick! They'd love to get their hands on the two of you, trust me!"

"I need to trust the forces behind me," I retorted, glaring.

"Do you think he'd just throw everything he has at you for nothing? You think Spivey's a fool? You think he'd just throw away his safety, his comfort, his money?"

"What I-"

Before I could say anything she went on a tear. "This apartment," she grabbed her plate and threw it toward the sink as if to call attention to the physical presence of the space we were in. The plate crashed but did not break. It was one of those plastic plates but the effect was still dramatic. "All your graffiti stuff and your computer stuff," she grabbed a pen and threw that toward a stencil I was working on on the common-room floor. Less effect that time. "And your allowance! How much is he giving to you, Emory? How much?"

"You're the one stuffing the envelopes so you tell me because honestly, I don't really pay attention." I stormed around the table and got myself right up in her face going for the intimidation factor.

She launched to her feet, kicking the chair behind her, matching my affront with her own red fierce countenance. "He pours everything into you!"

"Well he ain't buying my love, hunny" – I emphasized the hunny, mocking her foothills twang. "You afraid Dad loves me more than you, is that it?"

"Go fuck yourself," she retaliated. "You don't know nothing about me and what I've been through, so spare me the psychoanalysis." With this she whacked me with her paperweight hand, a thudding rubber wrapped around a solid core that had a dense umph to it. I acted unfazed though my arm felt heavy and numb, saying "I just might not show up to the stupid trial." I gave it to her with a sort of shrug, a kind of nonchalant 'whatever' attitude, but deep down it was an idle threat.

She gasped "You have to!" She began herding her papers into her bag. I seized back the role of the aggressor, stepping forward, bumping up against her which forced her to stumble backward.

"I don't have to do a damn thing!"

She glared at me awhile aghast at what she had heard.

"Do what you will!" she spat, scurrying around me, grabbing her bag with her good arm and storming for the door. "Just show up!" The door slammed behind her.

* * * * *

"Is there anything you want to tell me about before all of this?"

"Can I tell you about Carolyn?" I asked.

She nodded.

"I was in love with a girl named Carolyn," I said.

"What was she like?"

I thought a moment, leaned my head up, "You know how here in the summer the air is thick and it sort of lays on you and you feel like you're being touched by something all the time? And if you walk outside on a summer night you feel like that thick air has this amazing quality that connects you with everything, the dew on the lawn, the damp on the leaves, the croaking frogs and the fire flies?"

"Yes."

"She was like that," I said, sagging back into the bed.

Ella pulled her head back off my chest and gazed at me a

while. "I understand," she said, erecting herself on her chair.

"I'd just like to make it right, you know, before I go through with all this? I wish I could talk to her again. Apologies seem important."

"They do?"

"They're something I never cared for. But there's a lot of people I need to apologize to."

"You want to apologize to me for anything?"

I laughed.

"You're a sweet kid, Emory," she smiled. "That's a real sweet thing you said about Carolyn. I imagine she'd like to know that."

I nodded. "Thanks."

"Maybe you should write her a letter and I could have it sent to her or something?"

"I don't know where she is," I sighed, knowing I could not bring myself to write Carolyn another letter. What could I say? I'd sound desperate – she'd be upset – but not because she lost me – because life is sad. And what good is it to bring her sadness if she will not be sad for reasons that cause change? Yes. It'd just be exploiting sadness.

"Oh," she nodded. She stood up, as if preparing to leave. Her paperweight hand fell to her side. Her good hand tucked a tangle of hair behind her ear. She sat back down.

"Do you have anyone you want me to give your belongings to if this thing –I mean, is there anything of particular importance that you want to make sure doesn't go forgotten - well, you know, just in case?"

I shook my head. "I haven't seen my parents in – they have no idea I'm here. No idea what's happening to me." The thought was like something had been blown from my grasp in a windstorm. I wondered if and how my parents would find out. I imagined my Mom reading at night, bobbing in her rocking chair in the shadows formed on the wall by the lampshade, bighting her lip as she rocked herself. I thought of my father listening to Charlie Parker and thinking it sounded flat.

They'd see each other briefly at my funeral. I suppose they'd say hello, make small talk. And before turning away, maybe they'd apologize for things they're not sure of. A neighbor would bring dinner to my father. Another would invite my mother to a function, probably something the neighbor ordinarily wouldn't invite her to. In time, people would stop coming. And they'd stop talking about me. And my mom would rock in her chair and my dad would sit by the silent stereo. Each alone.

"There's no one else?" she sighed.
"I have a friend named Renton. But he's homeless."

"Homeless?"

"You're right. I could bequest him the apartment!"

"Jesus Emory."

"Ok, bad idea. I doubt Fletcher would like that." I wondered - what did it matter? Couldn't Fletcher pull some kind of deal with one of his business friends and give it to Renton? What use was it to him? Material things have no value to people living in a finite world.

"It's not that."

"What is it? What's the matter?"

"Nothing, nothing," she stood again. "I just wish I could help you."

"I thought the apartment was a good idea. And my friend – I really want to help him. He could really use to get back on his feet. If you want to help me you could -."

"Forget the apartment!" She interjected, a sharp tone from between pink lipstick. "We can't just hand over the apartment to your homeless friend." She grabbed a breath of air and pressed her hands down her thighs, matting her dress. Calmly, "Is there anything inside the apartment I can give someone? That sort of thing?"

"Not that I can think of." I shook my head in frustration. "Just throw away all my shit. All my old shit. It's worthless anyway. Who would want it? A rucksack. Some clothes. Maybe donate it. Throw away my paint and my stencils. You can keep the laptop and stuff if you like, of course. Maybe clear the data and recycle it with one of those programs -"

"Well aren't you just worthless!" she bellowed, stomping her heal.

"I am dying you know!" She turned away. Dying is an angry affair. "Ella, what is it?"

"It's nothing. It's just. It's frustrating is all - not being able to help. You know?" She pressed down her dress and smoothed herself before turning back. She smiled. But in her altered tone I heard a cleft and I wondered what was wedged between it.

24

THE WORLD SPUN, contorted, confounded by the light like the Earth overexposed to a million stars of distant galaxies. The bleach-like sand that grinds away the enamel in our mouths while we sleep coursed through my veins. I slept with myself in my own arms the way the haze at sunset holds the light when the sky in pink-purple screams across the angelic awning like stretched moments that bring awe to the few who bother to look up anymore.

I teetered at the edge where sound shakes through to the marrow; where the atomic and galactic are seamless and the bright is dark and it matters neither because it seems to all make sense to the mind that isn't there. In the faraway – somewhere on the other side – was the hallway where the path led down to a dream room.

I grasped at the edge of something passing by, not with hands but through the forces of balance, fighting for a hold I couldn't keep. I felt myself drift down the hallway and into dream room. It was too bright to see. But I could hear a commotion. The four walls of the dream room echoed words in dampened reverberations, as though I was submerged in a pot of water. I pressed my ear against a wall, straining to hear. A man and woman were arguing.

"How the crap did that get there?"

"I don't know – you tell me. I thought you took care of

it."

"Well look at it. I did."

"This is what I found when I got here. Okay? What do you want me to do?"

"I thought no one knew about this place."

"That was the agreement."

"I mean – in that condition – someone must have helped."

"What are you trying to say?"

"I mean, look!"

I can't bear to. Okay? I feel sick. Let's just – come on – please – let's just stay focused, find it, and get the heck outta here. Who knows – you're probably right - maybe someone's on their way here right now."

"Is it okay?"

"Yeah – I don't think. I mean. I tried when I got here and, and, and no response. Nothing. Do you think?"

"Ok then - just shut up and look."

The enclosure was alive with commotion as my surroundings were disinterred. I took strokes against the force pulling me away, fighting to cling to some measure of balance. Fast and slow up and down – like a drunk clinging to a wall hoping for sleep. Yet different – for I fought to stay here in this world.

"Nowhere! I can't find it anywhere!"

"Me neither."

"Well what the crap?"

"Well it's got to be here!"

"How could you botch this up?"

"Me? Look at you! Look what you did. We didn't agree to that! This is way too far."

"This was your idea."

"This wasn't. This wasn't."

"You're right – your idea was that the place'd be empty."

"I'm scared – Goddamnt! What if?"

"Chill out! Okay? Who the hell cares. We'd all be better off anyways. You can't back out now, so just keep looking."

"I want to get out of here damnit!"

"Listen, listen. You've got to calm down." There was panicked breathing, panting and coughing and then the clammy whooping sound of flesh meeting flesh. "Listen to me! We've got to work together." The whole space fell quiet. Then a deep breath. Then quiet again. Whose breath was it?

"There's only one other place left to look," said the man.

"You really think?"

"We've got to check."

I felt my balance upset by shifting forces.

"Careful."

Something elevated then crashed beside me.

"Check under there."

"I did! There's nothing under there."

"What about the zipper there? Check in there."

I heard a ruffling but I had lost my balance and the sound and the space seemed to be drifting away. I felt suddenly not as a buoyant mass but as one sinking away from the lucid dream room. I clawed, scraping at the matter in which I sank. One last. All my effort. I reached, stretched, clapping my hand open and shut feeling only the rheum.

"We can't just leave like this!" cried the woman.

See, I remember things. I just needed a little help filling in the gaps. And the way I remember, I feel – I know that something is not right. I just don't quite know what.

PART FOUR

ANOMIE

Sometime in 2010

25

SO WE'RE ALL CAUGHT UP. That's everything I remember; everything that happened so far as I know.

And tomorrow they come. They come and put me to sleep. There will be a tube placed in the vein in my wrist, I am told, and I will drift off to sleep in no time. I don't even have to leave my bed. They can just put me under right here in my room and wheel me over to the operating chamber. I don't even have to see the room where they'll cut me open in my brain or something and stand over me in masks speaking hospital jargon. I don't have to see the room that I might die in.

Dr. Bend told me again this morning that if I don't make it, I won't even know the difference. They'll send me off somewhere to knife me open and remove a spongy gland. Then they'll flip me over and get the rest of their bounty. And if I do make it?

Who knows how long I've been laying here, staring at the ceiling, going back through everything, the light from outside leaning in from under the door. Me in here. In darkness. In thought.

Who knows? But the door just opened. His two feet roll in, followed by that brown robe with the strap dangling along the floor. Ella Alice pushes him up to my bed. "We've come to say good luck," she says.

"May we be alone?" Spivey motions over his shoulder. She nods, turns toward me, but I look away, faking that my attention is on Spivey. "I'll come back later," she calls to me, exiting the room.

"So this is it?" I say.

"Emory, my good boy!" But his cheer is insincere, just an attempt to blow good spirit into the room. We sit in silence, neither with anything to say. I gaze at perhaps the only future I have left. Little parts of me – the only parts that still have value – filtering away the problems of a gaunt old man's body.

"How do we feel?" he asks.

"I feel very good. I feel like I'm getting better."

My condition has clearly improved, he affirms. Dr. Bend even says so.

"I feel like I could walk. And I -"

"Yes. Indeed – I imagine you do," he interjects. "This is how we feel when we want to escape our problems. That we could just get up and walk away from them. Is it not?"

He pauses, breathes for a while. "Dr. Bend took the bandages off and I should say you look quite good. Yes, it is swell to see my dear Emory's face again. But we must remember that the problem does not lie here," he lifts his hand, the ring dangling, and points to my face, "but here." He shifts his aim toward the side of my head. "Dr. Bend says, indeed, you have improved a great deal. He reported to me on the matter - that you are healthy enough for the surgery."

I nod as that too was what I had been told this morning.

"Mr. Spivey." I know this is my chance to confront him about my suspicion that we have been infiltrated. It is now or never. I have no evidence. I don't quite know who it is or how. No suspect. No one to point him to. Just this feeling inside me that something isn't right. Maybe you can't see it. But it is a feeling of certainty and at least I could warn him. I've thought it all through and figured out nothing. I can't help him. All I can do is warn him. He'll have to figure it out without me if I don't survive the surgery.

But for some reason I don't say anything about infiltrators or how I've been up thinking about it nonstop for who knows how long trying to piece it all together. Instead I just ask, "- What's the purpose of it all?"

"Oh rest assured my good boy," he says, placing his hand atop my leg covered under the sheet. "It is not the end. Ms. Alice will take up the blog if things turn for the worse. I've spoken to her on this matter and we agreed she is ready. It is for the best that the movement believes – that is – continues to find inspiration in Emory Walden. Do you not agree?"

He looks at me – as if trying to gauge my reaction. "But such are merely precautionary measures," he continues. "Although difficult for us to toil over, they are necessary. Insurance policies, really. We know in earnest that all shall go splendid and we shall pick right back up in no time. Quite so! A mere bump in the road."

I forget completely about my suspicion that we have been infiltrated, and the thought of saving the movement suddenly seems very far from my mind.

"How long have you been searching for a pancreas/kidney pair?"

"Since I found out I was dying." He furrows his brow. "Years, I suppose."

I sit with that disclosure awhile, mulling it over in my head. I think of when I first met him in the Ritchfield Steakhouse and how he looked much thicker, much healthier. The only thing that has not changed about him is the few strands of white hair dragged across the roof of his head. Even his beard, which now clings to concave cheeks, is patchy and wilting.

"You know what I never figured out," I say. "How did you know who I was?"

"Oh, Emory, what does it matter? You must understand. People such as myself, we come to know things through a web of byzantine paths. If my memory will permit me – I sent someone who worked for me out looking for you in

Dublin. As luck should have it, it turns out you were here," he laughs. "So I tracked you down here. It was quite serendipitous, really."

"Interesting," I say. "I guess I wondered – you know – in the back of my head."

"Does that satiate you? I don't see why it matters," he shrugs. "Are we not best suited to spend what could be our last evening together speaking on things of substance?"

"Whatever makes you happy," I say. I guess it doesn't matter so much how he found me but why. I spent the morning thinking about it and could not make up my mind what I believed.

He leans in. At this closeness I can see that his body has an unsteady quality to it that he appears unable to control. "Can I confide in you," he asks.

"Sure," I reply, hoping he will disencumber the suspicion beginning to grow inside me.

"You know what I ask myself often?" He waits for a response but I do not give him one and so after a while he continues, "I ask myself – what would my father think of me now? That old bastard -"

I close my eyes. I do not care about his father nor do I care how he would react so I let him rant on for a while paying no attention. I spend that time thinking, trying to take it apart and put it back together, knowing something is not right, tossing it around in my head. If only I could remember just a bit more clearly to see what it is I am missing. Then, in pain of frustration I impulsively blurt out: "I'm not going to live you selfish man!"

"Now stop that!" he scolds, taken aback. "I earnestly believe you will survive the surgery and you must believe it too. This other ordeal is a rotten insurance policy on our investment."

I close my eyes again. This time I want him to leave. I want to be alone. I cannot believe that I will survive the surgery no matter how hard I have tried to convince myself through the dark hours spent alone after Ella has left for the night. To hear him say it is to be told winter is not coming by a branch of maroon and orange leaves. To hear him say it is to truly accept it. I will not survive the surgery.

"Ok, I will believe," I lie.

"Emory," he says and I can feel it is beginning to be that time. "I know not what to say. I feel that I have said it all and yet I feel I have said nothing. I promise you, without equivocation, it shall go on despite what happens in that operating room tomorrow. Categorically. It shall. It must! It is imperative! You know this. You do know that I know you do know? I know Emory Walden is an ardent believer. I have never met a man so committed, so loyal. Ideals unparalleled! I should reiterate – for it bears repeating - what I told you a week ago. May you go into this operation knowing that you have been true to yourself and to the verity of your ideals. You are indeed the catalyst to which I say thank you. You have afforded me the opportunity to strive to change the world. To realize my vision. To repent for the world I helped create. To realize the long lost dreams of my generation. I knew a catalyst of your caliber was out there – and I scoured and scoured. And it was all worth it. Quite so it was!"

His fist shakes in the air and it is as if he is trying to muster the energy to stand, yet nothing happens. He sits there reaching high, his fist in defiance of something outside, far away, going on without any knowledge of the two fathers of the movement who are all but expired rallying for their last bout of courage.

"It perplexes me to wonder where I'd be without you," he continues, settling back down into his chair. "Would I have found the will to live this long? We stand at the cusp, Emory, for we capitalized on the chaos of this decade! We stand at the cusp and we share the glory for we know what we have engendered. Yes, may you go into tomorrow knowing we have kept the promise. Your name will live on in perpetuity! They shall shout Emory Walden when the palisade comes tumbling down!" He pats my knee, a smile propping up his sagging cheeks.

I smile back for him as best I can. He has no more to say for the first time in all I have known him. With a struggle, with a great lurch powered by an aching grunt, he stands from his wheelchair. As he inches toward me, bracing himself with a hand on the side of the bed, I see the quivering unsteady of a determined man.

He leans down to hug me, saying "May I say thank you just one more time?" We embrace– his paper body against mine – and I grab hold of him and hold for a long minute the body in which I will take on a new form of life.

His breath, a wheeze next to my ear, incites in my head a swelling indignant tumor pulsing at the feeling of my own youthful body failing to outlast this frail tattered and fading page in time pressed against me.

"Who's in charge?" I beg, clutching his robe.

He pulls back, "What?"

"I said, who-is-in-charge" He pleads that he doesn't understand and I let him go with a flick of the wrist and he stumbles a bit, catching himself on the edge of the bed.

"I want to see the pictures," I clamor.

"The what's?" He gives himself a push backward and tilts himself toward the chair and when he is sure his aim is true he lets go, falling backwards into the vinyl seat with a thud.

"The pictures," I repeat. "The pictures of my brain. I want to see them."

"Very well then," he stammers. "If that's what you want. I'm sure we can arrange for the scans to be brought in. In the morning, shall I ask Dr. Bend to-"

"Yes," I insist. "Yes. Tell Dr. Bend I demand to see the scans of my brain the moment he gets in."

"Well, surely. I under-"

Just then Ella Alice pops into the room. "It's time to get you to your bath," she announces scurrying up to his wheelchair, grabbing it, swinging it around and heading for the door. "Sorry Emory," she calls over her shoulder, wheeling him off. "The nurses hate if he's late. I'll come by and see you later, Okay?"

* * * * *

I think. I think I remember now what transpired between Carolyn and I that night she confronted me with the *Post* article and I sat on the floor of her room for hours trying to explain the pernicious things I'd done. That tornado unwound something like this:

"Don't you remember the graffiti art that one night we were in Adams Morgan and you said you liked the graffiti and you thought it was playful?"

She nodded.

"That was me! That's all. You see. That was me. I did that. I did all of that. Shouldn't you be happy to learn that?"

"Why do it?"

"I want to be change. I want to do something important. I want to make the world better. You understand? It's just the way I am. It's inside me. And what's more is, I got this – well I write this sort of blog. Maybe you've heard of it. I'm not sure. But it's a real big deal in an out there sort of way."

"I know about the blog, Emory."

The ceiling looked as it did when I was a boy, so out of reach.

"You know? How come you never?"

"How come you never said anything about it to me?" she fired, cocking her head. "Why didn't you tell me about it? Or this, this new thing with the graffiti? Why have you drawn this schism between us and that life you lead on the side?"

"I didn't know what to say. I didn't know. You make it sound like I've been cheating on you or something."

"You may as well. I can't trust you," she snapped, heels now dug into the rug – legs coiled up; thighs and calves loaded like springs. "Plain and simple. You think I'll wait around for you. You think I'll always be there. You lose sight of us. And you keep secrets."

"I guess I'm kind of surprised you're upset about this."

"Really? To have my mom find your mug shot on the morning paper?"

I apologized – embarrassed – ashamed, remembering her mother smiling as I told her all about my made up job and my made up life.

"I didn't care about the political," Carolyn went on, conceding nothing of the momentum she'd built. "I honestly didn't. In fact, it was kind of sexy for a while, kind of intriguing. You're a really interesting guy. I mean, you're all kinds of smart and I can't take that away from you, Emory. And I love you. But it got old, can't you see? You're getting older. How long are you going to live like this 19 year old idealist kid who thinks he can change the world? These high school and college kids rebelling against authority – that's understandable. You're a grown man, Emory. Know what all other grown men know about the world."

"But that's just it," I said. "Don't you understand? You see what I want to tell you is after I got arrested I–"

"I understand, lucidly," she pushed on. "I understand that when you put yourself at risk, Emory, you put us at risk. When you risk your safety, when you go out and do crazy things, when you're off living some fringe zealot's fantasy, you're not thinking about me. Your fingers are in too many buckets of paint. You're not thinking about us. You're not honoring or valuing what we have. And that makes me wonder, why can't you just be happy to have me and to have a normal life and normal things and want to grow our lives together? Were we ever going to grow up and try and start a life and be happy – get it right like Ted and my Mom?"

"Yes, but – "

"I grew up - stopped chasing men and luring them to chase me. Why can't you stop your little game of tag?" she bellowed.

She dumped her face into her hands exasperated, rubbing the butt of her palms into her temples. Then, glancing up at me, nodding to herself, she declared "It's time for you to go."

Where was my strength? She sprang up. I rose too for fear of further angering her. We are crazy often to think a little good deed can overcome the height of our transgressions. This is a misunderstanding all humans have with the social world, that it wants to offer us forgiveness after it finds out who we truly are.

At the door I pleaded. "I understand. I understand, baby. I've sacrificed a lot for, for other goals and other people – for the cause of resistance - but -"

"Resistance?" She grabbed the newspaper and waved it at me as if swatting at a fly. "This isn't resistance. Resistance to you people is not a means to an end. It stands by itself. Resistance is just an end. It's not a tool for change."

She motioned me out to the hallway. "I can't do this anymore, Emory," she said. "Try not to look so surprised."

"But that's what I'm trying to tell you. Sitting in that jail cell I realized my entire life I've looked outward and upward for verification of my thoughts and feelings. I've looked in books, books, books, every type of book possible. I've read dozens of articles by scholars and so-called great minds, I've scoured quotes of erudite and leaders the same. I realize it now, I spent all that time reading every word not because I wanted knowledge, not because I wanted to be smart or get ahead, be a better person, bring myself up a rung on the ladder. None of those things. I learned all that nothing, that dribble, because I wanted affirmation of the viewpoint I already held; of who I already was inside. I never sought a bit of knowledge that disagreed with the person I already was and I haven't learned a thing I didn't already know. It is clear to me now that every vociferous reading was a desperate search for some string of words so arranged that they would prove the math and method in my stubborn, terrified mind. And sitting on that concrete slab I realized I'm not afraid – I'm not afraid of where the world is going, or whose doing this or that. And it's because the world with you is the world I want to spend my life exploring."

Carolyn gazed down at the skin wrapped over the rivets

of her knuckles, as if checking for something. Then, gazing up at me, she said, "That may be all well and true and good but I need more than to be the function of some guy's sudden self-awareness."

A knot of pale fingers grabbed the handle to the front door of her mother's apartment, twisted, and pulled it open. She stepped through, never looking back.

26

HOURS PASSED AS MY MIND STIRRED toward an unstable state as I thrashed my arms around in the aphotic cell that was to be my casket in a matter of hours. I felt the urge to scream, to burst into a tirade of primal bellows until my vocal cords scratched and bled, aching away the last sounds from my lungs. Yet I did not. For in the moments before I could, in my panicked, aimless thrashing, my hands dipped into something, somewhere in front of my face that sent settling over me a Buddhist-like clarity.

At this state of calmness, I fell back into my pillow, embracing a new warmth. I was engulfed by this clarity, which may have lasted only an instant, but which gave sight across time and states of consciousness; of all I had done and all I had been.

This was my celestial moment of rectitude. My ataraxy attack.

*****

I am sitting, waiting, knowing, accepting what is to come. For hours I stare into the blank space before me seeing it all. Childhood, youth, adolescence, the life-full sensations of scraped knees, first loves and first loves lost, not the pain, but the melody and elegance of our clashes with a force so enormous, so daunting that only a child understands its place against it. To age in this world is to reject what we know through the frivolity of stubbornly refusing to embrace our human imperfections - the one truth that paralyzes us all: the finality of life. We're all runaways, cowering, hiding in the corners, under desks, afraid not of the mirror – for we love ourselves – but of what lies spread out before us toward a horizon of musts, of righteous truths, of heart wrenching days where the world brings us to tears, exposing its true imbalance, its unapologetic harmony.

And so, in time it happens. The door yawns open just wide enough for a head of amber hair stretched and knotted tightly behind her to lean in. "Have you calmed yourself?"

"Yes, I'm sorry." I call back.

"You could've given that man a heart attack!"

"Yes," I call again, "I'm just so afraid and I lashed out. You understand. Please – accept my apology."

She edges into the room, "Are you sure?"

"Yes," I repeat myself. "I am terrified and I let it get the best of me."

"Ok. Good. I'm glad. Listen, I'm leaving now - going to head to bed. It's past three and the surgery is first thing in the morning. I just wanted to check if you were alright."

"No, no. Come here," I beg. "I want to tell you – I've had a remarkable experience. Like a vision or something. I really don't want to be alone right now. I need someone to know about this."

She steps in, easing the door closed behind her. "Ok," she says, flicking the light. "But just for a short while. I'm exhausted."

"Thank you," I say. "I really appreciate it. I can't stand to be alone here unable to sleep."

She eases closer until she reaches the spot where the visitor's chair sits. She clutches the chair back, using it as a barrier between her and myself.

"Ella, before I – before tomorrow, I want to ask you something," I say.

"Yes?"

"Ella. Are you attracted to me?"

"What?"

"I don't know – the way you've been acting lately. It's like there's something that's grown between us. Don't you think?"

"Is that what you wanted to tell me?" She asks, stepping around the chair.

I nod, "you're so beautiful. You know that?"

"Of course I'm attracted to you." She dangles her hand on the edge of the bed – picking awkwardly at the cotton fabric. I ask her if she is sure, and she repeats, "yes, yes, of course."

"Will you come here? Will you hold me? I don't want to be alone."

"Emory – it's late."

"Can I ask you a question?" I whisper, "Who's in charge?"

"What?" she asks, leaning forward.

"Who's in charge?"

"Dr. Bend will be taking care of you tomorrow."

"He's a brain surgeon?"

"Oh – hunny – I'm not a doctor. I don't know the first thing –"

"Good point," I reply. "Just want to make sure I'm in good hands is all."

"I understand." She sits at the edge of the bed, placing her hands below my neck, and peals back the sheet. "Don't you be afraid," she says as her hand begins to massage my chest.

"Kiss me," I beg. She leans forward, closing her eyes. "Kiss me or tell me the truth."

I grab the knot of hair behind her head and blunt her left cheek with my fist. I spin her around, throw my arm around her neck and squeeze her to me, bending her back as far as I can by thrusting my pelvis upward to abrogate any leverage she may have. She thrashes about, first with her arms and legs, then she starts whacking her head against my jaw. I lower my head, pressing my forehead against her ear and pull her body close to mine so that her neck is bent so far she has no room to cock it.

"Tell me the truth," I whisper. She tries to scream. I tighten my arm noosed around her neck depriving any oxygen to fuel her. "What's the game? You don't believe in what we're fighting for." I ease back my hand, and again she tries to holler. I bob left to right, left to right, gaining momentum, and then – peaking - tumble us over the edge of the bed to the floor.

On top of her, we wrestle and claw until I manage to firm a grip on her trachea with both hands. Squeezing the pathways closed, her face beginning to swell, I gnarr, "Why? Why? What is it? What is it? What are you trying to do to me?" I head butt her. I saw it in a movie once. I thought it would hurt me but it doesn't. I can feel nothing but than to be alive. And so I do it over and again. Five or six times. Blood begins to leak above her eyebrow and then it starts gushing, squirting out to her side. Her corneas swell, veins bulge along her forehead and below her eye sockets.

"I know you're doing this, I know you're doing this," I bark, overcome with life. Easing my grip, seeing that the world is darkening for her, I feel now my body trembling. Gasps erupt from her pink lips, grasping desperately for the air in front of her.

She coughs, choking it out, "I hope," choke, choke, "you die in that surgery!"

I sneer, "I know you do! That's the plan isn't it?" I cock back and let go on her, fist pummeling flesh. I have never punched anyone before this night.

I stand up, looming over her and glance down and that once immaculate, beautiful face of hers glares up at me an unmasked wad of blue-black rubble. "You'll never accomplish whatever you're after," I pant. "I can die – that's okay. But you'll have to live knowing that." I turn, heading for the door, expecting hospital security to come rushing down the hall. It is all over. It is wholly incomplete. I can embrace that, I think, as I open the door and step out.

27

I'M FINDING MYSELF not in a corridor of white but standing in the dim light of a balcony. No one rushes toward me. What am I doing here? I stand a moment in utter disbelief. Could I really be? All this time?

I am alone, gazing out over the granite countertops and stainless steel appliances of a kitchen. I see windows the size of doors leaning overhead and through them I can see for the first time in who knows how long the sky and the moon. To my left, a door. To my right, a door. Behind one are answers. Behind the other is freedom.

This is no hospital. I'm standing in Fletcher Spivey's Georgetown condo.

I turn left and start to run. I open the door and stumble down a spiral of stairs, through the kitchen, towards the hallway. I'm running. I pass the bathroom where I became Liam Logan and head to the end of the hall where I stop to find my way. To my left, the study where I gave up my own history. In front of me, the living room with photos of men and women whose message had been lost long before I went searching for myself. And to my right, the empty hallway entrance towards the door. I take off in a full gallop toward the door unable to halt myself before crashing into it. I lunge for the handle. Turn. Pull.

Stuck. Not a budge. I grapple with the handle again.

Nothing but a door clasped shut. The lock! I grab for the latch on the lock only to find a keyhole where a latch should be.

Shit! My mind races. How high up are we? The 4th floor, wasn't it? I race toward the study and I've not gone three steps before she comes barreling around the corner, a butcher knife glistening in the light that falls into the hallway from the lanterns outside the windows behind her.

"Give me the key!" I yell.

"Are we making deals?" She says calmly.

"Yeah, sure. What do you want? Just give the fucking key and I won't kill you."

She laughs. "How about you tell me where the envelopes are and I toss you the key."

"The what?"

"Don't be coy. The envelopes with the freaking money. The three million dollars that's missing from Spivey's account." She pants, "I know he gave it to you. I found one of his little white envelopes before he could mail it to your box."

My arms drop to my side. Before me, her torn clothes dangling from her, her face marred and bloodied, this fragile mind is tattered by money?

"That's what this is about! That's such bullshit. I can't believe this." I shake my head, knowing this is an attempt to stymie deeper truths. "Tell me, who are you working for? What faction, what episteme? This is some kind of government shit that has infiltrated everything – isn't it?"

She laughs and laughs, nearly keeling over, the knife waving recklessly about. "You ignoramus! Yes, yes you're right," she snickers. "In all your wisdom you forgot the one ideal that trumps the rest!" she screams. "Greed! The unyielding human philosophy. Call it a political philosophy, call it an economic philosophy, call it a fucking episteme, you loser. Call it by any name you wish. We're all tethered by it. The churning in us all, no matter how we try and hide it. That little voice in the back of the collective consciousness that says 'more for me.'"

"You've got to be kidding," I clamor, patting my stinging cheeks where her nails had sliced me.

"No," her head thrashes about. "No, I'm certainly not."

"What about Spivey? I mean -"

"The rich do as they please," she snarls. "If they want to lay a railroad across the nation, they will. If they want to build skyscrapers, they will. If they want to start a revolution, they will. They've been doing that for all of history. And they do with us what they will. To me, to work for their stupid company, or their revolution, it's all the same. And the same goes with you, Emory. We are puppets. Just like the rest of society. So who cares what happens to Fletcher Spivey? Who is he to you? Just a greedy old man who wanted to live and needed you to do it."

"Quit bullshitting me! Tell me. Is it the CIA? FBI? NSA? Who? Who wants me dead?"

"No one," she laughs. "Except Fletcher Spivey cause he needs your pancreas and your kidney. Life will always trump some bullshit idea some idiot wrote down in a book."

"He wouldn't turn on me like that!"

She wipes at her face with the back of her hand, hocking in a bubble of snotty blood. "You idiot, I convinced Spivey to get the dual transplant to save his life. If I saved his life, and you were out of the picture, I'm right back in. I was helping him keep everything afloat. I deserved that fucking money!"

What? I cannot believe or trust anything she says.

"Let me spell it out for you," she says. "Fletcher Spivey was going to – to use your fancy word - bequest his money to me until you came along and –do you like this one? - bereft it from me."

"This is ridiculous! You had a good job. You make good money."

"Get it through your head," she clamors. "I didn't stick around D.C. after college to be another yuppie going to bars in Clarendon, driving an Infiniti and living across the river looking over to the bay of power."

"So you're really serious?" I ask. "This is it. You're just going to come clean to me like that. I don't believe it. This is some kind of bullshit James Bond – here I am the evil villain coming clean nonsense. It's ridiculous. Tell me the truth!"

"Hey, you asked," she retorts. "And, hunny, I'm not no evil villain. You have your little dream. Your stupid juvenile revolution. Well you know what? I have my dream too. And I'm not gonna let you ruin it. I worked my ass off my whole life for an opportunity and here you come steal it out from under me. I refuse to let that happen. You fight for what you believe in. You think you're the only one? You think you're the only one whose passions and ideals matter? Who cares if it is greed, if it is to want to be where I belong? It is to want for something passionately. You of all people should be able to understand that."

"This is all over money?" I say. "Then you can have it. 'Cause I don't believe it. I call your bluff. What the hell does money matter to me anyway? Just about as much as it mattered to that dying man Spivey when he gave it to me."

The moment we come to terms with the fact that we cannot have something, we conspire to destroy it.

I rush forward, aiming at her bad side and she lunges, jabbing at me. The steel strikes my arm and slides in but it does not stop my momentum. I crash into her, tackling her to the floor and in the commotion her paperweight arm dislodges, becoming entangled below us.

"Give it to me, give it to me," I gnarl, slamming the roof of my head against her nose over and over. "Give it to me, give it to me, give it to me!" Blood explodes like fireworks over her face, splattering into her hair. She cries, shrieking horrid, macabre wails, like this rabbit I once saw whose baby was being eaten by a magpie. The knife protruding from my arm, nothing left to lose, an utter and desperate madness overcomes me. I grab at the knife and yank. A pain unlike anything I can describe; the nerve-searing screech of an evacuating sliver of metal, the gash and crushed bone. I thrust the knife high into the air over her head. "Where's the goddamn key? I got nothing to live for you bitch! I'll shove this fucking thing right through your eye!"

At this she capitulates, beginning to sob and moan. "It's on the hook in the kitchen."

I leap up for the kitchen. It is then that I notice him there leaning against the wall, watching; the ghost of a man barely able to prop up the robe draped over him. I shove past him, grab the key from the hook, then shove past him again.

"Emory!" he calls.

I step over Ella's contorted body – her gnarled fake limb bent beneath her. She begins to speak.

"What is it?" I say, dangling the knife above her. She lifts her head, looks at me as best she can through the red in her eyes, and mutters under a nasally gurgle of blood, "You're just an over-privileged kid who couldn't adapt to the fact that your life was good."

"You make me want to jump," I reply.

"You're no different," she manages through the swollen knot that is her face. "We're all licking the dick of power."

"You're right," I say, glancing over at the shadow of a man clinging to the wall. "What you said about the rich is true," I allow, turning back down toward her. "You used to read a lot, right?"

She nods. "I'm smarter," she groans.

"What about Fitzgerald. Did you read him?"

She murmurs something that sounds like, "Yes."

"Had you understood him you would have seen a privileged class where there are no entrances. Just gates." I turn toward the door, expecting nothing this time.

28

I WOKE UP IN THE INTERSTICE between two dumpsters behind a gas station near 2nd Street NE, my arms wrapped around my rucksack. I'd tied it to my waist. After leaving Spivey's, I headed straight to the apartment, climbed through the short door near the top of the stairs and onto the roof. I spared no time. Dangling down in the exhaust flap that led to my kitchen fan vent was a string. At the end of that string, a key.

Under the wooden crate sat a safe which I had drilled to the roof then stripped the screws so they couldn't be unwound. I picked up the crate, set it aside, and opened the safe. There were 25 white envelopes, each with my P.O. Box address written in Fletcher Spivey's shaky pen. $120,000 in bills was stuffed into each. Next to the envelopes, a small black case. I emptied the safe, shoved it all into my backpack, shoved my backpack into my rucksack, closed the safe, recovered it with the crate, and got the hell out of there.

I knew they – whoever they were – would be looking for me so I slept between these dumpsters and sat there all day until darkness returned to the city. At night, I ate two hotdogs and a soda from a food truck and went looking for Renton. I resolved to give him most of the money and the majority of the rest I would give to Carolyn, saving enough for myself to get out of town, head west, and live as long as I could before the tumor overtook me. I didn't know exactly where I'd go but I had heard there was quiet, desolate, gorgeous terrain in northern Idaho.

Yet, I could not find my friend. I searched the city every night, hoping he'd turn up sleeping under a bench in Dupont or behind a church somewhere. But every night I scoured the city to find he was nowhere.

I began asking street people. No one told me anything. They acted like they'd never seen him - never seen a giant homeless Santa Claus waddling down the street, eating from garbage bins, filling cups at soup kitchens. After two days looking for Renton I had thought it smart to find somewhere safer to stay so I hoisted myself up on a low overhang, then up onto a rooftop where I camped out during the day and hid my rucksack.

*****

After an unsuccessful week I've resolved to find Carolyn. I chose to look for her second because I was afraid to see her again. But I can't put it off any longer. Luck has kept me from being caught and I have no expectation that it will last. I need to leave the city soon.

I find her coming out of the alleyway behind the Richfield Steakhouse where we first met. So, from a distance, I follow her until I know she is alone and I run up to her and I call "hey" in a whisper.

She turns, "Jesus you nearly gave me a heart attack!" And then, upon recognizing me, "Oh my God, Emory! Where have you been?"

"Shh! I can't talk here. Meet me at the park overlooking the highway where we made love that time." And with that I take off.

An hour later she shows up at the park. "Oh my God Emory. What happened to your arm?" She says, pointing to the blood stain on my shirt.

"It's fine," I tell her. "Listen, I don't have long. I need to talk to you."

She stands beautiful before me, her radiant eyes gazing over an apparition from her past who smells of garbage and sweat, who hasn't showered in months, whose hands are caked black with dirt, whose face lays hidden under a tangled, soiled beard, "I never thought I'd see you again. I read in the paper there was a warrant on you."

"It's all gone. It's all wasted," I cry. "It's too much to explain, but I'm in danger and I'm leaving and I had to see you one last time."

"Are you okay?" She does me over again with her eyes, doubting what she can clearly see has become of me. I nod that I'm okay. "You were right," I say. "I threw away what we had, what we could have been because I just couldn't be happy with the world and accept it for the imperfect place that it is."

Carolyn looks up at me, forcing a smile with wetness in her eyes. "It's okay," she smiles.

"It's not," I reply. "You needed me and I wasn't there. I'm no better than anyone's parents."

She takes my hand, gives it a little squeeze and assures me that all is okay, that I'll find happiness. And she tells me that after her and I broke up she never thought she'd love anyone as much as me but that she's found someone. Someone named Garth. It empties the air from me to hear that. Garth. I try to smile but I can't. I just squeeze back and stand there before her concentrating on breathing until I've paced my heartbeat and feel I can talk again but all that comes out is, "I'm a failure. Everything I did. I thought it was change."

She takes up my other hand with hers and begins to speak, "I think you were a part of something. I just don't think you can see it from where you're looking. You've got to get out of it, ya know? Away from it. You've got to go where you can watch it with binoculars, or maybe even a telescope. You've got to have the context factored in, and stop looking through a microscope."

She smiles, "Yeah. You've done something, you've

accomplished a feat. It may not look the way you thought it would, it may not be understood the way you wanted it to. But you changed a lot of things. You changed me or maybe it's that you forced me to change who I was. I always wanted the attention, the notoriety, like I was some kind of beauty and that beauty would garner respect, admiration. Love. But I came to see that it's not where you are on the ladder, so long as you're holding on with the right person. I am happy with Garth. I am happy with who I am. And, honestly, without the things you taught me I don't think I could have ever found this, this place in life. I always felt that love was something I created with someone. But you taught me that it's not. You are the first person I ever truly loved. I had been loved before but I did not feel or share that love. I just knew it was there the way we can know it rained the night before when, in the morning, we wake up and before we've ever opened the windows and seen the damp street - well… anyways, I'm getting mushy or metaphorical. But, what I mean to say, Emory, is that you taught me how to love – how to love the rain, how to love knowing the rain is there when I awake in the morning. I am free now because of that. I am free from want. Free from wanting all those things I used to. I am free to be who I am and be happy with that. Do you see? You see, don't you, Emory?"

"Yeah," I nod, avoiding her eyes. "I see."

I take my hands back, turn and begin to walk away. There is nothing I can say or do. Behind me the beauty of the world, the only thing in it that I truly love, stands in the body of one woman who deserves nothing of who I am and what I have to offer.

Below the park, SUVs driven by average thoughts race over the Potomac, heading for sanctuary in the suburbs. The baby on board cries. The world is full of them. Dragging myself away, one step at a time, I hear her call, "Emory, I love you. You're a great person. Please take care of yourself."

I turn, rush back over to her and start rambling. "I know that it's over. I love you too much to try and change it. I love you too much to let you be with me again. But I want to give you something. And in that way, if it helps, it lets me love you from far away – through it."

I reach for my bag, open it, grab a wad of white envelopes and tell her, "Here, put these in your shoulder bag. Keep them secure. And don't open them till you get home."

"What is it? What are they?"

"I know you wanted to go back to school. You shouldn't be waiting tables, pinching pennies, never saving enough. You're way too smart for that. You have such a future ahead of you! Let me help you live your dream."

I kiss her. I do not care that she probably does not want to kiss me. I do it anyway. I lean in and give her all I have. "I will always love you too," I cry. And I turn and run. It is the only way I can leave.

I shiver on the rooftop by the gas station on 2nd St. It's a chilly night in early Fall and I cannot find sleep. During my travels to Europe I often slept alone in places like this. Sometimes they were worse. But I never felt the emptiness of a city. I never felt the cold against my back as I lay alone. I had wandered but never felt lost. I had never felt the nothingness of my possessions. And yet I have never held so much of value between my arms as I do on this night on this rooftop.

I stare with vacuous eyes out across the street where the light cast shadows on nothing but trash bins and a few trees and see that I have been running from something. And I see two things so opposite in myself. My feet had been running from something and my mind had been searching for proof of who I was all at the same time as if fighting myself. My arm throbs where Ella stabbed me. My head hangs heavy, stuffy from crying, from the rot and filth that is of me.

29

IN THE MORNING I WANDER along to the motion of the street, the place where others rule the day. The lawyer. The corporate grinder. The government official. Have they, too, ever questioned the logic of the buildings and streets before them, lined with cars and steel-framed madhouses? Yes, this is one of those days where the protests will come storming around the corner any minute.

I walk and wonder. When your ideas are everywhere, where are you? Where is that connection – have you lost it? I'm heading for the bus station near my old apartment. There is a bus and I could hop it and get off at the stop in Baltimore. From there I could hop a railcar and stowaway and head west until I find myself to northern Idaho where I could hide in the hillsides of evergreen mountains. There I could die in peace, naturally, alone, under a tree-top lined sky as the tumor swallows me.

I buy my ticket in the basement storefront from the smoking man and stand in a corner across the way from the fire escape, hidden in the throng of waiting, chattering passengers. Noon approaches. Two men begin calling, pointing, speaking in a language I do not know as they scurry toward me. Pointing. I turn to run. If only I had time.

I come to in the back of his police cruiser, he sitting in the passenger seat turned toward me with his arm resting across the bench-back.

"Heya, stain," he calls. "Looks like I caught up to you." He speaks in a quiet, sedated tone as if speaking to a sick child. He brings his arm to his lap where he seems to be rubbing something. I sit up, glance forward and see the gun in his lap. Underneath it, my backpack.

"You look great, stain," he laughs.

"Let's just get it over with," I mutter.

"That's what I was thinking," he smiles. "See I know who you really are, Emory Walden. And I'm the only one on the force who does. Everyone else thinks your some petty graffiti artist named Liam who skipped parole. So what does that make me?"

"A genius," I mock.

"No," he replies in his staid tone, "that makes me in charge."

I rub the back of my head, noticing he hasn't even bothered with the handcuffs and so I reach for a door handle.

"They're locked," he says, peering over the top of his police cruiser shades.

"So who are you working for then?"

He sort of hisses, "No one. This was my idea."

"Yeah?" I doubt that. "Then what's the score?"

"I'll tell you the score," he replies. "I want to know what's in the envelopes that Fletcher Spivey gave you?"

I gasp. Did he notice? How does he know who Fletcher Spivey is? I peer around, trying to think – trying to buy a moment.

"Well?"

I tell him I don't know what he's talking about. It is all I can think to say. Yet I know it is a pointless attempt at escape and he demands again that I tell him and this time I say, "I don't know, I never looked. I swear."

He hums a long "hmm," then scratches the underbelly of his chin a minute, "Were you loyal to Mr. Spivey?"

"I'm a loyal person."

"Was he loyal to you?"

"I don't know," I tell him. It's the truth.

"So he gave you envelopes. Did he give you orders? What to do with them?"

"No! He just sent them to me and told me to keep moving forward with everything when he died. That's all. There was no concrete plan or anything. Not like something specifically I was supposed to carry out or anything."

"So you had envelopes, you didn't know what was in them and you didn't know what you were supposed to do with their contents? You know, I'm a cop, Emory. I don't eat donuts but you're feeding me a big hole here. Do you catch my drift?"

"I'm telling you the truth. I don't know what they were for and he never told me what specifically to do with them."

"So where are they?"

"I don't know."

He holds the backpack up, shaking it, asking me what is inside.

"You're the one holding it," I reply, fearing what would come. He unzips it, turns it upside down and shakes. A wallet with my Liam Logan identification and a pink bus ticket fall out. That's all. He shakes some more, shoves his hand in and reaches around.

"So you were riding the bus with an empty backpack?" He picks up the ticket, crumbles it and shoves it through the one of the bar holes at me. Had he bothered to read the ticket he would see the boarding time read 8pm.

He asks me if I expect him to believe that I don't know where the envelopes are and I tell him I don't care. That it is what it is, whether he likes it or not. I've no intention of telling him what I did with them. There is little he can do to me that isn't already happening. "Listen, after you nearly beat me to death with your club there, I don't know what happened. I was in the hospital – or I thought I was – for I don't know how long. I got out just the other night and went back to my place and it was trashed. So I guess I got robbed and they were stolen. Okay?"

He appears to think on this a moment, scratching at his chin, "you were robbed?"

I nod.

"There's just one problem with your story, Emory."

"Yeah, what's that?"

He removes his sunglasses, looks at me through the bars and says "I'm the one who broke into your place and trashed it and I didn't find no envelopes."

I gaze back at him, confused. What?

"Me and Paige Lee, you're little friend. We came by your place after I gave you your lesson and turned your place upside down looking for them and they weren't there."

"Who?"

"Spivey's assistant," he says, raising his brow. "You know," making finger quotes, "Ella Alice."

It dons on me as I sit caged in the back seat of a cop car that I have never thought about it. I realize I should've known. Hadn't she spelled it out to me early on? Ella Alice. What a made up name. Like Liam Logan. I fall full on into an eddy of confusion. Wait, wait, what? So we were infiltrated, weren't we?

"Infiltrated?" he grins. That's right. The two of them. In the alley. They'd been following me, hadn't they? He got to her before I was ever even on board! Doomed from the start! They had their tentacles into it. But who? NSA? CIA? FBI? He was an agent. I knew it! They'd had their eyes on Spivey for who knows how long. Or maybe - maybe it was me they'd been watching. But Ella Alice, or Paige whateverhernamewas, was lying about the money thing, and Spivey, and Dr. Bend. That's what counted. That's what mattered. I'd been right.

"I'm gonna let you make a choice," he says. "See I know what was in the envelopes. Paige and I've been working to seize what ended up in those envelopes well before you came on the scene," he chuckles, frustrated, then snaps, "Of course we couldn't have predicted that Spivey would just start dumping his estate on you!"

He removes his cap with medallion, brushes his hand through that thick bowl of hair, and trying to remain calm, he places his sunglasses back on and asserts, "So tell me where's the money or I'm gonna drive you down to the station and turn you over to the dogs!"

"Alright, take me in," I retort, because that's exactly what I want him to do. I am right. Ella Alice had been protecting them, whoever they were. And, now, Brock is too. Of course the NSA or FBI or whomever knew about the money if they knew about everything else, having been watching the whole time. She and Brock talked and this was the piss-thin story they'd come up with. Or maybe it is the cover the People Upstairs told them to use if ever they got caught. I didn't buy it from her and I'm not about to buy it from him. I've been right all this time. We've been infiltrated from somewhere high up.

"You're serious?" he asks, poking his tongue into his cheek, struggling to remain poised. I can see that behind those shades are two throbbing eyes, below that pressed blue uniform are wound up muscles ready to crash through the bars and eviscerate me. He tries to laugh that frustrated dry 'ha', saying "Is that what you want? They're gonna rip you apart."

"I'll take my chances," I say, betting he isn't one to back down on his threat. He has already beaten me down with violence and is not likely to waste his time repeating it when he can hurt me through other means.

He starts the car and like that we are off through the streets of D.C. towards the precinct. The leaves are just beginning to show yellow and it is a fine day to go for a ride. In front of the precinct where he parks so he can publically march me in, a hero. I say through the bars "you have a small prick."

He cuts the engine, turns back over his shoulder, "What did you say to me?"

I tell him that he heard me. "When I saw you and Paige

or whoever in the alley that time, I saw your prick. It's small."

"You saw us?"

"By that club the Mezzanine."

"How did you?" He turns away, telling me to shut up.

"Did you ever beat her up?" I persist.

"You don't speak to an officer that way," he barks.

"The girl I knew as Ella - did you beat her up? You're a violent guy. Did you beat her? Tell me, did you beat her?" I press and press. "So why Carolyn then? If you had Ella, why Carolyn? Were you gonna beat her too? She'd be better off with you then, right? Maybe get her arm chopped off."

"That had nothing to do with me," he yells, bringing the cruiser to a silence. I'm not sure whether to believe him or not. The eddy spins on. He hops out of the cruiser, slams the door and opens mine and I try to rush him but before my body can lunge he blunts me in the gut with his club. I fall out of the cruiser smacking the pavement where I keel over and, with a knee into my back, he handcuffs me.

*****

Heads turn as Officer Brock Grismore marches a filth-covered, twenty-some-odd boy into the station door, his clothes ripped and blood-stained, his face obscured behind a wiry knot of beard.

Teetering on the edge of her chair in what must be a special-order junior-sized police officer's uniform, slurping her super cup, is a woman with black bangs and a nameplate that reads Yvette Cortez. She turns away from the depths of the Internet into which she has browsed, and says to Brock, "Whatcha got?"

"I'd like to take him straight to the Captain," he replies.

"Friend, I got a migraine so big it could wear a muumuu," she mutters, unimpressed. "Ya know the procedure. Don't waste my day 'less you gonna come on a lil' trip 'round the desk here, have a seat and type all these people we got waitin' here in, and type this Jerry in yaself."

She glances over at a throng of cuffed criminals in chairs with officers looming over them, checking their watches, then back at Brock. She smacks her lips and plops her jaw down on her fist which she has propped up on the desk.

"But I've got to see the Captain. I don't have time for -"

She eyes the two of us, unmoved and asks in a bored tone, "Do I *need* to get up?"

Brock grits his teeth. "Yvette, can't we do this later? It's important."

She picks up her soda, slurps a gulp, "have a seat."

After about an hour we get to the front of the line, with Yvette frowning as we approach. "Ok, then," she mutters and motions behind us with a nod to a room of empty seats, "looks like we took care'a that line" Glancing up at Brock, she asks: "So what this one in on?"

A crackle comes through the speaker propped on Brock's shoulder, a high-pitched voice, "Calling all officers. Calling all officers. Urgent. We have an 11-99. Requesting support from all available officers. Report of an officer down on K street NW and Connecticut Avenue - 10-108. Repeat. 10-108. Calling all available officers."

Cortez glares at Brock, his hand clutching my arm. "Well?"

"But I've got to –"

"I do this all day," she says, tiredly.

"This man is wanted! He needs to be placed into a cell until I return!"

"Friend, I'll take care'a it," she says, raising her eyebrows. Brock glares at me, then at Cortez, then back at me. He tosses my backpack on the counter, turns and races out the door.

"Ok friend, let's get started. What's ya name?"

I point to the backpack. "My IDs in there."

30

I KNEW THIS WAS ALL COMING. I made up my mind while shivering there on that rooftop last night. This tumor will have me dead in three-month's time. I simply have to know. I cannot let Ella Alice protect the infiltrators with her piss-thin story about the money. I cannot just run away. And so I went to the bus stop right by my old apartment where I knew they'd be patrolling and set myself as the bait. Once I throw myself at them they won't be able to ignore me. And I'll finally know who infiltrated us.

In the holding cell I think about what to ask Captain Kyle Yates. There are so many questions. I imagine he'll turn me over to the FBI or NSA in the morning where I'll figure it all out.

But it doesn't happen that way. Instead, after only sitting in the cell maybe an hour I'm dragged from my cell, thrown in the back of a windowless van and some cop drives me around D.C. When we park I'm escorted out of the back of the van inside a parking garage where I'm handed over to another man, this one an arm-shredded, buzz-cut military type in a black uniform with a gun strapped to his thigh. Without ever looking at me or saying a thing, he marches me through a parking garage, up an elevator, and down a corridor of doors where one is opened and I'm thrown inside.

The cell exists of four blank walls of unpainted concrete in a windowless room with a bare concrete floor with a drain in the corner. Far above, the four corners of the wall bend toward each other in a half circle where a single exposed light bulb is screwed in. I sit down against a wall, my cuffed hands behind me and wait patiently, feeling happy in a way to finally get my chance to hear they whys and the hows.

Some time later the guard returns and brings me through a maze of hallways to another room. The room's walls are blue and it too is windowless. A man can stand in one corner of the room and in one leap be at the next corner. Inside stands a wood table with steel legs and underneath are steel chairs, all of which are bolted to the floor. He marches me over to the chair, pushes down on my shoulders, forcing me to sit.

Later, two men, their shirts tucked in, one in suspenders, the other in a tie, come in through a steal door with no handle on the inside and sit across from me. It seems that to exit a card needs to be slid into sliver in the wall.

So this is it. The People Upstairs. I'll finally be told the score. I'll get my peace of mind, no longer having to wonder.

"Let's talk," says the one, "I'm Bud Marr, you can call me Bud. And this is –"

"Agent Cheggins," says the other.

Marr is stout and when he came in the room he had moved like a street sweeper. Cheggins is marker-thin with not much for a nose and wide, flat lips that express a perpetual state of 'hmm.'

"We know a lot," starts Cheggins. "We know what he's been doing. We've had our eye on him a few years now. We know what his plans are and the moves he's been making. We got servers-worth of files. So let's get down to it." His lips move little when he talks, the words seem to seep through the sliver of his mouth.

I nod.

"We know you were with him," says Marr, pulling a cigarette from its sleeve. "We know you were close with him." He lights his jack, dragging on it.

"Alright Liam Logan," interjects Cheggins, "Give him up to us and you'll be treated well. Come clean. Where is he?"

I'm both afraid and curious. I want to know who the People Upstairs are, how they'd infiltrated us, and what Brock Grismore and Ella Alive have to do with it all. Yet I cannot not, for the life of me, allow myself to give up anything of myself. I no longer have anyone or anything to fight for but myself. I know no matter what I will rot away in a cell for what will be the short rest of my life. Sitting here, toiling over how I have been betrayed at all other levels only hardens my resolve. I will not betray myself. I may not die free but I can die alone protecting who I really am from the wrath of whatever force I am up against. "Bud, Agent Cheggins, I don't know who you're talking about."

"Ok," says Cheggins, agitated. "Let's look at it from our perspective. We know all about your work. There's no getting around that. We know your association. There's no getting around that. Save yourself the pain, the time. All we're asking for you to do is tell us where he is. It's going to save me time, it's going to save Bud time, and it's going to save you time."

"It's in your best interest, kid," says Bud, calmly, dragging little pokes off his jack. "You cooperate with us – we look at that sort of thing very favorably."

"You shouldn't smoke, Bud" I say. I want so bad, in a completely irrational way, to change the subject. To just talk about something else and let's all forget this. "My best friend growing up, well, I bet him he couldn't quit smoking. So we shake on it. And he does it. He quits. You believe that?"

"Is that true?" he stares down the remaining white of his cigarette, half cursing the inevitability of its termination, half welcoming it.

I nod. "Saved his life."

"Yeah? That's great!"

"Sure is."

"He's doing great? He's healthy?"

"I don't know," I sigh. "I haven't seen him in many years."

"Thought he was your best friend?" Bud asks in a dejected sort of way.

"He was."

Bud frowns and I pull my arms close to my chest and look away, saying simply, "Life abrades us."

I say nothing of my role in all of it and nothing of the shame for what I did to my best friend. No, not Pat. Someone from years before. And I find myself thinking of the last time I saw him, his back to me as he walked out a restaurant door. But I was in love for the first time then. It didn't last. I think about my former best friend, and the girl we both loved, and I know it has nothing to do with this moment and where I am now. Yet it does in every way. Isn't life like that?

"It's a lose-a-little, lose-a-lot scenario," Cheggins chimes in. "You work with us, you lose a little. You don't, you lose a lot." We sit there for a while and it goes on like this. Finally, Cheggins grumbles, "Get this kid out of here. Let him wallow in it. He'll understand what's best for him."

"I don't know who you're after. Honestly."

The guard, that life-sized commando action figure from before, is called in to drag me back down to my cell. I'm thrown in, the lights thrown off. I try my best to sleep. The lights never come back on. No one comes by to check in on me. No food. No water.

31

TWO OR THREE DAYS HAVE GONE BY. My stomach is aching in ways I'm struggling to understand. I cannot think clearly enough to sift through my thoughts more than one at a time without growing confused.

I think it's the third day. Perhaps the morning. The guard comes in, drags me to my feet, stands me, prepares me to leave the cell then turns and shoves me to the floor. He walks out, closing the door.

Some hours later he returns, picks me up, preps me to go and then brandishes a roll of bread which he shoves into my mouth. He turns, leaves, closes the door and comes back with a paper cup of water which he slides through to me through a latch in the door.

This process repeats every day. There is never enough water to wash the bread down and yet I am too hungry not to eat it. So I sit hungry, eat bread, drink water, and sit both hungry and dry-mouthed, cradling my stomach in my arms, groaning, until he comes back the next day to start it over again.

No one is telling me anything. Why am I here? What's the score? Why did Ella turn on me? And what was Brock's role in all of it? Was he really a special agent, like Marr and Cheggins?

On the fourth or fifth day I can feel myself decaying. I

run my fingers over my body in the dark, feeling where the bones jut out. By this time I give up wondering about Ella and Brock and Spivey and the whole revolution. Instead, I try to pass the time thinking about my life and wondering what other decisions I should have made with it. I wonder if someone else were me what they would have done. But mostly I think about food and I think about water.

On what I guess is now the second week, I'm deprived of my clothes. A vent far, far overhead, much too far out of reach, begins blowing cold air and I cower in the corner in the dark cold and shiver, my undercarriage on the icy concrete. The guard comes in for his usual feeding ritual and all is the same except this time the bread he shoves in my mouth is rock-hard frozen and the water comes to me as ice cubes.

I eat, my jaw aching from biting the frozen roll. I crack the ice in my mouth and swallow. I shiver. I begin to hope for the end, for the tumor to swallow my mind and in the darkness I wonder if it is starting to happen. Perhaps this shapeless darkness exists more in my mind than around me. Perhaps the aching in my stomach is really in my skull. I pray and pray that it's true while time labors on. Day in. Day out. After many days of these frozen rolls jammed in my mouth I can poke my fingers between and practically feel underneath my ribs.

The guard comes in. I let him drag me to my feet where I can barely stand on wobbly legs and this time he throws me over his shoulder and carries me from the cell.

In the interrogation room sits Marr and Cheggins, each dressed about the same as when I last saw them. On the table stands a stack of files, a recorder, a pen and pad and Bud's cigarette pack. The guard props my naked body in my chair, my cuffed hands falling through the hole in the chair back, and I sag forward for I haven't the strength to hold myself up. He grabs me, props me back up, and stands behind me clutching my shoulders.

"We've invested a lot of our time and dollars into you,"

says Marr, fiddling with the pack of cigarettes now in his hand. "We bother to do this because our order depends on it. The threat he poses - you can understand." He puts down the pack, folding his arms, "I'll be honest, Liam. I don't like to see you suffer like this. I'm a compassionate person. I've got a wife. My daughter's six. I got a dog, Odom. I don't have the heart to go home and look at my family knowing there's someone like you being treated how you are. But I do it. I do it because I love to go home to my wife, my kid, my dog. Do you understand?"

I nod, "Yes."

I am trying to picture this fat man eating popcorn and watching sitcoms on his couch in a safe suburb somewhere. I am trying to imagine what his street looks like, who his neighbors are. Maybe he lives on my old street. Maybe I was his neighbor and I didn't ever know he got up before the sun and faithfully doled into the city, never complaining, never letting on to the other commuters on his block where he was going, what he was doing.

"I don't know where he is," I mutter.

"Well," says, Cheggins scribbling something down on a pad before him. "Do you know the definition of this word?" He slides the paper across the table to me, block letters that spell "T-O-R-T-U-R-E."

I tear my eyes away from the paper. "No, no!"

"In its origin, it meant the process of extracting truth," says Cheggins through his starchy lips.

"Are you going to beat me?" I ask, wholly afraid. "Please don't! Please don't beat me!" I cry.

"We do not beat," says Cheggins. "We understand that the body is stronger than the mind. Only a primitive nation beats its prisoners nowadays." He raises his hands over his head, stretching, then tucks them behind his ears.

"I'm hungry," I yell. The aching in my belly commands me to. "I'm thirsty. I'm so thirsty! You can't keep treating me like this!"

"We're no longer in charge," says Cheggins, "you're the

one in control."

"Is the third week hot? Is the third week hot?" I beg.

Marr is motioning for the guard to leave and when the guard lets go I sag forward like Spivey used to in his wheelchair. I wonder what became of him. Did they have Spivey too? Is he in a nearby cell? Can he survive without his medications? Surely he can't. Are they going to bring in Ella Alice, or Paige whateverhernamewas, to identify me and put it all to bed? Is that the score? Are they stringing me along letting me think they don't know who I am, waiting for my confession – to accept my responsibility? Yes. That's what they are doing. It's about getting me to tell them what they know. It's about betraying myself.

Cheggins places his finger upon the sound recorder on the desk but he does not press it, "there is no third week," he says. "The extraction doesn't take us that long."

Marr places his hands on his temples and rubs. He chews on his nails, picks the pack of cigarettes up, peers inside and places the pack back on the table. Cheggins continues, "You'll tell us today. Or you'll tell us tomorrow. After tomorrow, well-" he says. "There are really only two ways about this."

"Jesus, Joe," cries Marr. "The kids gonna talk, stop threatening him. You can see he's been through enough." Marr puts his hand on his chest and pants a bit. He's in terrible shape. He must weigh nearly 300 pounds.

"Hey, woah," says Cheggins, pulling his finger from above the record button. His lips are open wide enough to nearly see his tongue among the black void of his mouth, "We're not in control. You've read the Extraction Manual. Let's let Mr. Liam Logan decide."

Cheggins stands, motioning for Marr. "We'll let you think. We'll come back soon."

Marr stands. "Do you need anything?" he asks me.

"Water," I beg.

"Sure," he smiles. "I'll be right back."

I sit, waiting. 5 minutes. 10 minutes. Longer.

Water. The thought of it spilling down my throat is churning in my head. The pain in my stomach sits with me, thinking too. Together we wait. Stomach and I. Where's the water? Why hasn't Bud returned with the water? He should waddle in here any moment, a tall glass of water in his hand. Lukewarm. Ice cold. I don't care. Where is he? Where's the water? Time rolls along with my stomach and my mind, rolling over, over, over itself. And there is no water. My tongue joins in, rolling along. Dry, chappy – my lips smacking. Panting like a dog. I need some water says my stomach, says my mouth, says my mind.

The hours pass.

I'm trying to forget it, trying to think about something else. Carolyn. What had she thought when she opened those envelopes? But I can't keep concentrating, not even on Carolyn. My eyes remain fixed on the door. Where is he? Where is Bud? Why hasn't he come waddling in with that water? A glass? Or a whole pitcher of water?

Time keeps right along. No water. No Bud Marr. Maybe he forgot. Maybe he went to get the water and got called away on some urgent matter. Or, or perhaps he went home! Perhaps he's at home sitting his fat ass on his couch, watching reality TV and laughing with his fat little daughter and his fat ass wife, all drinking butter-flavored milk shakes and weighing down the Earth.

He isn't thinking about me, rotting here. Needing water. He's stuffing his face, satiated and satisfied with the world he's protecting. His little secret agent life. I bet he feels so special. Oh, a real tough job. Lots of sacrifices. Come in and talk to people when the work is already done for you, when you've drained the life from them. When you've drained- I fall forward in the chair, my face smearing across the tabletop. After a moment I begin to notice my face sticking to the wood, sweat on my forehead.

I leap up, screaming toward the handle-less door, "Where's the goddamn water? Give me the goddamn water!" I throw myself into it and the sweat trickles down my forehead into my eyes.

Unable to wipe my eyes and unable to see I lean my face against the door and rub my cheek against it, trying to clear my eyes, trying to abate the sting. I am rubbing the skin right off my cheeks and everything burns and everything aches.

I bellow, begging the tumor, "Let me die already, let me die, let me die!"

Nothing happens. No one is coming for me. I just keep right on living.

I awake when the door opens and shovels me aside. In steps the guard followed by Marr and Cheggins, lugging their equipment. The guard props me up on my chair then turns to leave. In a lot of ways, it is just like how it was when Ella Alice pushed Spivey in.

"Today's the day," says Cheggins uneventfully, setting up his recorder.

Chewing on gum, Marr leans forward, his elbows on the table, a bottle of water between them, "Tell us. Where is he?"

My mouth feels so dry I can barely speak what I want to say and I glide my tongue across my teeth a few times but feel nothing against my tongue.

"Give him the water," says Cheggins, halfheartedly.

The water pours down my throat. I chug it down, gulp, gulp, gulp, until I nearly pass out for lack of breathing. You'd imagine it's the best water I've ever drank. It isn't.

"Food," I beg.

Cheggins waves me to be quiet. "We're here, Liam," he says, resting his hands, "because The Agency protects the brand of power that funds The Agency. Now, the type of government he's advocating has no need for an agency such as ours. And that's why people like Bud and I work so hard. We don't want to go away. We're good at what we do. We find it rewarding. So now it's time for you to help us do our job."

He waves an ad flyer of a pizza in front of me. "Let's hear it. Where is he?"

"I admit it," I'm crying, "I'm him. I'm Emory Walden."

32

MARR AND CHEGGINS look at each other for a long while, and then back at me.

"It's the truth. I'm the guy who wrote the blog. I'm responsible for all of it. The stuff I said about the system, how I encouraged all those people to rebel and protest. I planted the seed for all of it. The FAY Movement. Everything. Okay? All that destruction. It's on my shoulders. I did it. I don't know why I did. I guess I couldn't just be happy with how I thought my life was going to go. I should've- oh – I don't know. What does it matter? Point is, it's me. I'm Emory Walden. I've got to take responsibility for that."

The two men stare at me, Marr chewing his gum loudly and Cheggins' thin lips not flat, but austere, crooked. Finally Cheggins says, "What?"

"How else do you want it?" I plead. "I'm Emory Walden."

I have betrayed myself. Why aren't they pleased? Shouldn't they smile? Maybe shake each other's hand on a job well done? This defeated emaciated body before them has been turned on by its own mind.

"Yes. We heard you," says Marr, chomping away. "What about him?"

"What do you want to know? Spivey? The envelopes? Is

it the envelopes? Is that what you want?"

Cheggins pulls a manual from his folder and flips through it, scratching his bald head. Marr leans toward Cheggins, glancing too at the sheets flipping by. The two whisper a moment and then Marr looks at me and says, "You have a strong will. You refuse to betray your friend – your compatriot. We can respect that. But you understand, the manual says that in the rare case the extraction is ineffective - "

"What do you mean? What do you mean?" I interject, desperately. "I've told you! I've told you! What do you want to know? I'll tell you what I did with the envelopes! I can get you Fletcher Spivey. Honestly, I can!"

"The manual says," Marr continues, "we offer you one last chance and if you do not comply your case becomes a failure. It says simply here," he takes the book from Cheggins and reads, following his fingers along, "Reiterate to the subject that he or she does not want their case to be a failure."

"So we'll ask you again," chimes in Cheggins. "Where is Tait Klaus, aka, Renton?"

I'm sitting up at this, looking over the two men, feeling afflicted. Both are glaring at me. Cheggins leans forward and presses the record button. Marr scratches his ear and folds his arms. Tait Klaus?

"What do you mean? Renton? You mean Renton the homeless guy?"

They nod in unison. "Yes." Says Cheggins.

"You got it," says Marr.

"You want Renton?"

Complete and utter bafflement overcomes me. They're serious, their eyes wide.

"I – I – I don't – I don't understand."

"So you admit you know him," says Marr. "Now, what we're asking is for you to tell us where he is."

"But why? Why do you care about him?"

I climb out of my chair, my naked body exposed before

the two sitting men. They watch me get up. Cheggins leans forward as if alert but Marr stretches an arm across Cheggins' body keeping him in his seat.

"Mr. Logan is in charge now," he reminds Cheggins. "Let's let him talk."

"I don't understand. Who the hell cares about Renton? I'm Emory Walden. I'm me. I admitted it. Isn't that what you're after? Isn't that what all this is about? To get Walden and Spivey and stop the whole uprising, the whole movement? Why else –"

I drop to my knees, the bone thudding against the concrete floor, "What stage of torture is this? What kind of psychological knob-turning are you are doing? You're joking right? This is a trick. What do you want me to tell you? I'll tell it all! I'll tell it all damnit! What is it?"

"So you're really Walden then?" Says Marr.

"Yes, yes!" I holler back. "Yes!"

"Interesting," says Cheggins. "We had no idea Klaus's associations crossed those kinds of boundaries."

"Very strange," says Marr.

"I don't see it," says Cheggins. "Why would Tait Klaus care about the FAY Movement?"

"It seems like he's using a diversion," replies Marr.

Cheggins thinks on this a moment, jotting some stuff down, and says, "Very sophisticated."

"He's aligning himself with –" Marr begins.

"For protection," interrupts Cheggins.

"What?" I ask, incredulously. "So then that's it? It's the FAY you're after?"

"Are you kidding," laughs Marr. "The FAY movement? They're great for business. They put bread on the table." He laughs further at what he's said, "I guess both figuratively and, in your case, literally."

"You're serious?"

The two men nod in unison.

"Ok," I nod back, my mind is in such an addled and exhausted condition, so jaded and demoralized that I haven't the cognitive luxury to truly comprehend what I am now being told. "You want Renton. I'll help you find Renton. Just please, can I have something to eat?" And at this I collapse.

33

I'VE COME TO IN A BED with an IV in my arm and a bag of clear liquid flowing into me. Not this again. But it's a hospital. A real hospital. Some kind of military place, with nurses bustling about attending to shaved-headed men in bandages, whose arms have been blown off or who look like ghost robots with masks on their faces and tubes coming out in every which way. Sitting next to me are Marr and Cheggins.

"Good," says Cheggins, "you're awake." I move a little and sense that my leg is cuffed to the bed.

"Food?"

"That's what the tube's for, hydration and sustenance straight to your system," says Marr, pointing. "Just take it easy. You'll be feeling alright soon and then we can talk."

The two men say they'll be back in an hour or so, then get up and leave. When they return they seem jovial and all in all glad to see me as if nothing from before in that place, wherever and whatever it was, had even happened. They ask me how I feel and I tell them Okay and then Marr asks me if I'm hungry. I tell him I don't know and they take a seat beside my bed. Marr's rump sags off a good six or seven inches on either side of the chair. I think he looks like a t-rex the way his stubby arms fall to his side.

"So listen," says Marr. "Now that we got that stuff

straightened out -" Marr pokes his head to one side as if motioning to something down the hall. "Let's see if we can't figure something out that's in both our interest. How's that sound?"

"Sure."

"We're ready to make you a deal. You lead us to Renton – to his successful capture – and we find a way to, shall we say, repay you for the discomfort you've encumbered."

"Yes, we always like to leave things on amicable terms with clients if and when at all possible" adds Cheggins. "It makes for good business practice."

Uh-huh.

"So, does that sound agreeable?" asks Marr, tapping his fingers on his thighs.

"Yeah, sure," I say in disbelief. I'm lost somewhere down the corridor of the ridiculous. Had these two men not just let me rot away in a cell to nearly die for some-odd two weeks?

"So you can bring us Renton?"

"I can help you find him – I know where he hangs out. He trusts me."

"Good, we'll bait him," Cheggins says to Marr. Marr agrees with a nod and Cheggins writes it down. The two men leave, telling me it's a matter of my recovery before we'll get underway, and they need to go home to their families for the night.

So I lay in bed alone, checked on now and again by a nurse who calls herself Francine and who would make for a sweet old grandmother. It is too surreal to step back and reflect upon. I have never been so confused in my life. The eddy no longer takes effect, nothing spirals, nor do I feel the warm clarity of the ataraxy attack from the night when I thought I had understood. My dendrites are fried. It's pure straight ahead, one breath at a time, trying to decide if this is a dream and if so whose. At every edge are tattered, misfit pieces. I need to understand.

I lay in bed all night thinking it over and over, tossing on the mattress, my leg chained, an incandescent corridor of obsession from which I cannot find respite. By morning it seems quite simple, quite silly. I've resolved there is but one way to get the answers I want. I need to ask. No one is going to just up and offer them to me as I had thought they would.

When they return after four or five days and sit down to see how I'm doing, I say, "It'd be helpful to me if I could understand some things."

"That sounds fair," says Marr. Cheggins agrees with a yes, his flat lips seeming to not move.

"I don't really get it – I thought you guys were after me, after Emory."

"But we're not," says Marr.

"But you're not," I repeat.

"Why isn't The Agency concerned about the FAY Movement? The cops seemed real worried. It was all over the papers. There was even a taskforce looking for me. I- I – I just don't understand."

Cheggins begins to speak. "What we do, Emory, is driven primarily by research. It's very scientific. Like the extraction manual. These are tried and true methods for maintaining balance. Does that make sense?"

I nod, uh-huh.

"The Agency is interested in dealing with the problems of society by assessing the variables that contributed to past outcomes, those that we favored and those that we did not. Say something happens, and an outcome occurs. We try to look at all the different factors that went into that outcome. We then take all those variables and look at many, many occurrences and find the patterns. From this we're able to use sophisticated algorithms to predict how society will behave when faced with certain circumstances. We're numbers people, not enforcers the way you think of the police or the military. We use social engineering."

"I'm not sure that really explains it."

"But you see it does. It's really about understanding what works and what doesn't in engineering the public mind. Take for example the Nixon administration in the late 1960s, early

1970s. You've got a public that's very angry about the Vietnam War. You just came out of a decade of civil unrest unlike any other. The Nixon administration was very afraid of the public unrest and that made sense at the time. The prevailing wisdom was that violence and mass discontent would undermine this great nation."

"Right," I say.

"Right," echoes Cheggins. "But then what happened?"

I shrug.

"Nixon got re-elected. Why? Not because McGovern was a bad candidate but because of the protesters. Because when you have a system such as ours, when people have nice things and can speak en masse through voting, the public will not stand by and permit their way of life to be taken from them. Sooner or later they will respond, either through their own will, but more likely through their approval of the actions of the State. Violence is always an acceptable response to violence, with few complaints from anyone because the violence perpetrated threatens the public's wellbeing. And our studies showed that this has always been the case in situations both big and small and this will always be the case."

Cheggins looks at me, and seeing that I do not understand, he turns to Marr. Marr seems to get Cheggin's body language and picks up explaining, "So what we do is, we sit back and let things play out a while. The public demands a response from the police, maybe even the National Guard. But in the end, order is restored and the violent ones are outcast by the majority. It is simply not possible to start a revolution with violence in what we call Media Societies. The majority will not accept it."

"What's best about violence," says Cheggins, chiming back in, "is that sometimes the public doesn't even need to command the power to squash the violent with violence. Sometimes the violence destroys itself."

"I think I get it."

"Good," they both reply.

"So the FAY Movement?"

"It'll flash. It'll flicker. It'll burn out. It's a matter of history. A matter of math and science."

"You don't care about Fletcher Spivey?"

Cheggins turns to Marr, "Spivey's, what, a few megabytes of data?"

"That sounds about right," replies Marr.

"Spivey doesn't get it," says Cheggins, turning back toward me.

Marr turns to me, "Do you get it? Do you understand why Renton is such a concern, then?"

I tell him I think so.

"It's interesting stuff, when you really think about it," says Cheggins. "What do Mr. Luther King, Ghandi, Nelson Mandella, and the Dalai Lama all have in common? Here's a hint – it's the same weapon used so successfully in the Velvet Revolution over the commies in Czechoslovakia."

"They used peace."

"Exactly," says Cheggins, "you see – nonviolence is the one true weapon that threatens power. Leaders can't go around yelling death when their enemy is a poem for peace. The public – sometimes within a nation and sometimes the global public of nations – just won't have it. Our studies show that's why the 60s failed. They grew impatient and took the easy road to violence."

"But Renton doesn't do anything," I plead. "He just feeds people who are down and out and helps people and lives off the waste of all of us."

"You can't quell peace. You can't integrate peace into a violent society. There's no money in peace. So you can't minimize it, marginalize it or co-opt it," says Cheggins.

"It's very dangerous," confirms Marr, shaking his head. "How do people like Renton start? They start by planting the disease of peace and in time it starts to affect others."

"We live in a delicate time," adds Cheggins. "That sort of thing could spread rapidly."

34

THE SEARCH FOR RENTON got underway about a week and a half later. It took a good bit of nursing and recovery before I'm back on my feet and there were legal things to go through. Yes, I had to sign legal forms stating that I was under contract with The Agency to perform certain duties by law and that if I fulfilled those obligations I would be subject to what was known as "favorability." I also had to sign that I would not discuss my relationship with The Agency or even acknowledge whether The Agency did or did not exist, taking the stance in such a case that the Agency were mentioned that I had no knowledge of such an entity. I was reminded that I did not want to break my agreement resulting in a failed legal agreement.

Along with that, I received a good deal of briefing from Marr and Cheggins about how exactly the bait would go down. Essentially it was quite simple, although they spoke of it as though it were rather complicated. What I would do is, go looking for Renton, find him, hang out with him, lure him somewhere out of public view and wham a team of G. I. Joe types would sweep in and take him away. Out of shame I asked to be taken away too in the whole sting because I didn't want Renton to know I had turned on him. Marr and Cheggins found that agreeable and so it was settled to cover up my betrayal of my friend.

In the time spent with Marr and Cheggins I learned a bit about both of them. Yes, Marr truly did have a wife and a daughter and his favorite show was the one where the celebrity-obsessed teenies would get on stage and sing or dance trying to win a million dollars and a record label. Not too surprising, really. It was watching the American Dream he had said with a smile.

Cheggins was divorced. He lived alone in a condo south and west of the city and he had a son who was a banker and maybe going into politics one day, Cheggins hoped. As people, they weren't so bad I guess.

They were both eager to talk to me, to tell me about their job. I suppose it was because they knew I legally couldn't say anything about anything we discussed and I guess they were lonely and had no one they could brag to about what they did. Not their families, their friends, not the person who cut their hair. I didn't mind. It filled the time.

What we did was, I'd sit around in their office like it was take your kid to work day until the evening. I did a lot of sleeping and I read the newspaper, skimming for articles about the FAY Movement. I'd search the obituaries just in case Fletcher Spivey was in there. I found articles about the FAY Movement, talking mostly about panics and threats and how Yates and Ozell and the rest of the D.C. police were trying to deal with them. But I never found anything about Spivey. Then, we'd drive around in a 4-door coup to one of the areas I knew Renton used to hang out and they'd drop me off. I'd spend the night looking around for him and, if I found him, I was supposed to be coy and send a special text message using a phone they'd given me.

In the morning, on his way to work, Marr would pick me up, bring me to the office, which was in a white building up on the hill by the Supreme Court, and Marr would go to work and I'd sleep on a couch in his office.

This went on for a week. Then two. Then a month. Then two months. I searched and searched, wandering Dupont at night, buying an iced tea or a plastic-wrapped sandwich at the drugstore for sick souls and high-school drop outs with holes in their stomachs. I went by the Church, checked out the shelter, checked the kitchen to see if he was back there helping out. I hung around on the Mall by the White House but all I saw were security officers with semi automatics trolling about and siren-topped cruisers parked at the ready.

The nights grew cold and I was issued a winter coat and gloves. Some nights it rained and I could do nothing but sit and listen to the rain and think of Carolyn and what she'd said about the rain while I listened to babies cry in nearby apartments. Sometimes I could hear their mothers cry along with them. Every day when I didn't find Renton and Marr picked me up I felt relieved. As we drove to his office he'd look at me and say, "no?" and I'd shake my head. Then he'd turn the radio up. He liked to listen to the morning shows and sometimes the Top 40 hits.

Today when he picked me up and after I shook my head no he asked, "You want to know something?" So I said sure.

As we drove east toward his office, the radio down, he said, "I haven't smoked in three months today."

Is that right?

He smiles. "Yep. Are you proud?"

"Of course I am," I tell him.

"It was because of you," he says. "Really. What you said to me got me thinking. So I asked Cheggins to bet me I couldn't quit. He and I are buds. I'd hate to have him get the better of me so it was a real motivation. Anyhow, I realized the other night that the last time I tried to quit I lasted exactly 10 weeks and two days. So I think this might be it," he says, smiling. He pats my knee with his t-rex hand on his t-rex arm.

"Well congratulations," I smile back. "I'm proud of you."

I realize I haven't rinsed with anticavity since my court date and we drive a while through D.C. It looks different from his car.

"Can I ask you a question?" I say.

Marr nods of course.

"What federal agency are you guys, NSA?"

"We don't work for a federal agency."

"You're corporate?"

Marr shakes his head no with a bit of a chuckle, "This might be hard to understand. But you see, there is no difference between the private and public sectors. They aren't really fighting each other. That's an either-or fallacy created to divide the public along political boundaries. The Government can look like it's regulating industry, which pleases some. The industry can appear autonomous from the government, which pleases the other half. But it's all the same. Does that make sense?"

I tell him it makes more sense than most things I've heard in some time.

"Internal analysis showed the public and private sectors would be more effective if they merged given that both are after the same thing: subjugation of the public. That's why there is simply The Agency."

"What about Brock?"

"Who?"

I don't bother to reply as we descend into the parking garage.

35

SOMEWHERE, ON ROOFTOP PENTHOUSES, in suburban living rooms, in college apartment parties and Main street bars, in clubs like the Mezzanine, in the dim light of the TV counting down to the lonely grandmothers and divorcees in the cave of their living room, in bedrooms where children stay up past their bedtime glaring out the window, the world looks wide-eyed and eager, rushing forward toward midnight. Ecstatic and hopeful, young and old celebrate the potential they project onto a specious ritual. That little lie we collectively make to ourselves: that turning the page on the calendar to a new number of year means something profound; that in some way tomorrow will be different.

It is inside us for a day or two, a week at best. We feel exonerated from the things we've done in the past as if born anew; a world of virgins waking up to pancakes and coffee. "Happy New Year," we smile, cleansed of our problems, our debts, our broken families and dreams, of all we are abashed. Yet soon our past and our problems seep back into view. And we are who we are. And we continue to be. And not much changes.

Some years we like our neighbors. Some years they get a new car. Some years we get a raise. Some years we lose our job. Some years a baby is born. Another, a relative dies. We fall in love. We fall out of love. We're young. We're old. We work. The world keeps falling apart. And every 12 months at a certain time of year we long, eagerly reaching for a change, and we find it again where it was a year ago - in a ritual that gives us nothing more than a brief escape. And we hope, desperately, that that little escape is enough to keep us holding on for one more year.

On this night as the fireworks lit the sky, as the young fools kissed, as the world cheered and hugged, and the lonely held themselves and smiled imagining someone was thinking of them, while many raised their glass, as children jotted down the first thing they said in the year 2011, laughing to one another, I wandered into an alleyway.

There had been two teenage boys, drunk and shoving one another in the snow. They were daring the other to step into the alleyway as I wandered past searching for my lost friend beneath the crystals of frozen water falling from the sky, the sky lit pale orange-white against the street light. Each stuck his chest out calling the other a 'poon' and betting the other didn't have the courage to go on and have a look.

I overheard the one with a puffy red coat and a red cap to match say he'd heard a rumor from his older cousin there was something no one wanted to see down there. I stopped, stood next to them and the three of us glared between the buildings where the far building cast a shadow across the void. We stood there a moment, the boys looking at me. "Check this dude," said the red coat passing a paper sack to the other.

"What's down there?" I asked.

"Dunno," said the other, a short boy with pin-thin eyebrows that angled down toward his nose as he took a gulp from the sack. "My boy's cuz says it'll give nightmares to anybody who go see it. Says he gots nightmares for two weeks."

I eyed over the two boys a moment, then into the void, and back at them. They were staring intently ahead, the snow beginning to collect on their shoulders.

As I stepped toward the void I heard the red coat behind me say, "check this dude." I felt something in the frigid emptiness before me that pulled me forward with this distant sensation as though I knew. I had a flashlight given to me by Cheggins a while back and I pulled the light from my coat pocket and flicked it on.

The alley was narrow, the crooked brick walls of the buildings seeming to lean inward. It was like any other alleyway. The one I used to climb to get on rooftops, the one I'd slept in between the dumpsters behind the gas station, the alley behind the Ritchfield Steakhouse, and dozens of others I'd used in a past life that seemed both faraway and always with me. These spaces were invariably much the same in any city in a comforting and welcoming way. But on this night, in this particular alley, as my flashlight lit up familiar spaces, damp walls and unwanted plastic and iron strewn about, I felt as though my feet and the body it carried forward were extrinsic to the path I stepped, as though watching myself in a dream.

As I got about halfway into the alley, I glanced over my shoulder to see in the distant light two silhouettes like statues in the snowfall watching me. I turned back toward the dark and kept forward.

My flashlight fell upon something there, sticking out from behind a stack of crates in the far back of the alley. I could see, yes, it stood filled, a white plastic bag. I moved toward the crates, stepping through the fog of my own breath with each step. A tarp hung from the top of the crates. It was secured at the other end with a cinder block on a ledge maybe shoulder length high. The blue plastic covering sagged under a mound of snow. As I rounded the crates I saw two legs in a pair of sweatpants, the sweats stretched and tucked up over two feet.

I clasped my glove over my mouth, leaned down, and peered below the tarp where his body lay sprawled across a bed of newspaper, his bulbous chest tucked beneath what looked like an airplane blanket, stretching only far enough to cover his crotch. Then I saw his face. His face appeared blue-bloated, the circular glass lenses frozen over so that I could not see his eyes. His mouth half open, nostrils pointed toward the sky, his red-gold beard covered in a froth of white, stiff tangles that resembled less human hair than a web of sticks and tree wire like a bird's nest. His vegetable smell had rotted, replaced by the repugnant odor of the innards of a dumpster and the unmistakable stench of body fluids.

I gazed back toward the boys to see their silhouettes scurry off, leaving behind a white blanket atop a destitute scape of concrete and steal that bent toward tomorrow.

I fell to my knees and shook him with one arm. Both arms. Nothing.

Under his rubbery skin was a pillow of bloated puss but I could feel beneath it a stiff core. "Renton, Renton," I pleaded. But no response came back to me through the empty air. I reached down to remove his glasses and it was then that I could see that part of his outward ear and the flesh around it had been torn away, nibbled off by rodents. I was happy it was winter – at least there were no flies buzzing about, landing on his open lips. I removed the frames from his head and looked into his eyes, two terrene-grey ballooned pupils staring up through the tarp toward the heavens.

I threw my arm around him, tucked my head beside his missing ear – the frozen tears of flesh against my cap- and wept. I opened up and let go a procession of choking sobs and for some while I lay there, my cheek on the newspaper, crying and crying.

In the morning, when the light finally came up on New Year's Day, I called Marr using the cell phone The Agency had given me. I could hear the TV and his family in the background cheerful of their new beginning as I asked him to come meet me. When I took him in the alley and showed him the body he stared a while with nothing to say. I buried my face in his chest and wept a while, his stubby arms wrapped around me as best they could.

He called Cheggins on the phone and in a half hour or so Cheggins was there too. Cheggins got sick and threw up against the brick wall. Then the three of us waited for someone Cheggins called on the phone.

Two men arrived dressed in khakis and blue winter jackets. They strapped on white gloves and with a lunge and grunts got the body onto a gurney which they pushed through the snow with a good deal of trouble. They said nothing; just loaded the body into some type of ambulance van. I watched them drive off atop the ripped up blanket of snow, muddied by sand and dirt and packed down by plows, with a friend of mine, his discarded body across a gurney in the back.

The Favorability clause stipulated that I was to be let go, avowed of any association with The Agency. There was paperwork that took a few days to complete. In that time I got to stay in some kind of hotel-like apartment that was to be used for Agency agents who were spending the night at work and such. It was warm and nice and I slept through the night.

At the end of it, there was no ledger. No debts or further obligations. All documents would be locked away with no memory of anything that had happened or any association had between them and I.

The Agency would not help or hide me. They were not in the business of abetting their 'clients.' They simply erased the books, forgave and forgot. One was to be on his or her own, to make it or not. Abetting clients? Those were things done by lesser agencies such as the FBI, I was told. It was as if the Agency had no time or memory. A client went in. A client went out. And there should be no difference in the life of the client upon emerging at the other end. Were there any difference, were clients protected or assimilated back into society, then the Agency would exist outside its own walls. And that, I was told, was dangerous.

"We like what we do," said Marr. "But there are some

things about how we operate I wish were a bit different."

"Agreed," nodded Cheggins.

We stood in the edge of the underground parking garage saying our goodbyes.

"We're not supposed to do this," said Marr, leaning far in toward me. He whispered into my ear, "We're sorry for what you had to go through. All of it." He put his arm around me and gave me a hug. Cheggins, with his lips thin, nodded his agreement with Marr's sentiments and the two of us shook hands.

"There's so much I don't understand," I said, smiling.

"Be careful," said Marr. "We don't know what you're up against out there."

EPILOGUE

THEY CAME FROM AFAR: down a ways from the direction of the Lincoln Memorial, perhaps further west. Their feet stomping in the slushy streets. I walked toward the tens of thousands of them as I headed for the Roosevelt Bridge. As they marched past me I heard their chants, saw their dancers with wild-eyes, their signs jabbing upward – reading nothing of Emory Walden. Nothing of Liam Logan. Just signs of rage and accusation. Their puppets flailed high above, violent lurches, shoulders bent forward, bracing toward the Capitol.

Somewhere along the lawn we crossed paths. The ones in the front wore jackets over their "Fear the Art of Youth" t-shirts. Their banner read "Your Investments Belong to Us" and storms of them came following, row after row, as I paced west.

When they had finally all passed some ten or fifteen minutes later, I turned and stood with my feet beneath me and watched. I imagined Spivey in a hotel suite somewhere, watching from his wheelchair, his gaunt remains sagging, legs stuck to the vinyl; smiling as he watched the puppet show. But this was happening only in my head and I no longer knew who was pulling the strings.

Down a ways in front of the old building of brick clad marble and iron, stood a barrier of riot police, perhaps Brock

Grismore among them.

On a rooftop near 2nd street, behind a gas station where Congressmen's aids fill up cars, is a black garbage bag twisted-sealed, buried under a mound of snow. Inside the bag is my rucksack. Inside it is a black case with my passport inside and twelve or thirteen envelopes pressed with Fletcher Spivey's pen. Maybe I will come back tomorrow and get them. If I can get to northern Idaho and trickle across the border through the wilderness maybe it would be worth it.

Right now, as I cross the bridge, I'm recalling not the words of past idols whom I turned to in those days when you first came to know me. I see now those were false. Not Chomsky, not Gramsci, not Marx, or any of them.

I'm remembering the words of someone obscure to me, Christian Dietrich Grabbe. I'm remembering Hannibal, a piece I read while in Europe to which I then held no interest and picked up only to pass the time. I'm remembering this:

"Indeed, we shall not fall out of this world. We are in it once and for all."

And I guess it is time to grow in another direction.

As we age we live our lives with a profound and subtle sadness that lingers over us like drizzle on a day when the sky looms on our shoulders. With time our sadness is less for the fate of the masses, the political, the condition of humankind. Our sadness is for the distance that grows between us and those we shared childhood afternoons with, those who struggled to help us understand ourselves, and those whose arms we found respite in in times of fear and confusion. We miss them. We miss who we could have been when they loved us.

And perhaps Fletcher Spivey and I had a lot in common. Perhaps Ella Alice and I were the same. Perhaps the moon was the only thing that changed. Perhaps it was as Marr and Cheggins had said, a formula predicts the future from the past. And we live our lives that perhaps we could do as Renton had done – to not become someone else but to become someone different. Somewhere someone sits alone gazing back on their life with a telescope and they see the things the Agency cannot understand. I like to think we have a name for that. I feel the emptiness longing for something far away and I wonder, who should try to remember me?

THE ORIGINAL LETTER

Below is a scan of the original letter Emory Walden sent James Wallace Birch in the summer of 2011.

James,

It's Emory from high school. Don't throw this letter away. Please read it.

I need your help. This is serious. You're the only one I can go to. I'd like to think you're over all that. I hope you've forgiven me. I've forgiven you. So much has changed. Please do this for me as I know you would've done before all that happened.

If all cannot be forgiven then here is a tangible incentive: there's money. It's enough to make it worth it. Trust me. When you've done what I'm asking for in this letter, the location of the cash will be clear to you. This is no joke. I promise you that. If you're still reading - thank you, thank you!

There's something I want you to publish for me. It's to clear up what happened to me. The only way people know things is through the slanted news reports and a corrupt half picture. I wrote my story out - just as it happened. By now it's been months. I want whoever will listen to know about some people and things that happened. Then, maybe they'll think differently about me and know the truth about what became of me. I hope you understand. Please read it. Another envelope will arrive in about a week with further instructions.

There's something called a data drop. Have you heard of this? It's these flash drives in public places plastered in the wall or under a chair. You can plug in your computer and add and copy files. Do you remember the bar we'd get served at in high school and SHE threw up in the men's bathroom stall while you held her hair? And do you remember under the bench where Reed used to hide cigars by the lake? Go to those places. Take your laptop and there's going to be a file on each flash drive named JAMES.emy. When you have both files on your computer in the same folder you can click on one and it'll open with the password. The password is the title of her favorite song (no spaces, no caps). That's my story. That's what really happened. People need to know.

I don't know how to say thanks. But I know I'll never see you again.

Emory Walden

HELP SPREAD EMORY'S STORY

Thank you so, so much for reading Discontents! Without your support, this book wouldn't exist. You're the only people I can count on. Can you please help me spread the word about what happened to Emory? I've got no big marketing budget and I don't know much of what I'm doing. If you can do 1 of these things, I'd really appreciate it. It will help me help Emory:

- Giving a positive review on Amazon or GoodReads. This helps immensely!
- Sharing your copy with a friend.
- Posting a photo of the book in paperback or on your Kindle with #WheresEmoryWalden on Instagram and tagging me: @jameswallacebirch.
- Sharing the book on social media. #WheresEmoryWalden
- Sharing your theories and thoughts about Emory Walden online or emailing them to me.
- I don't use Reddit, but if someone could help spread the book on there that would be amazing.

Starting with the 2018 publication of this book, if you have theories, clues, or tips about what happened to Emory after New Year's 2011, email them to me with the subject line "Thoughts and Theories" to JamesWallaceBirch@gmail.com and I will share them on social media. I love hearing from you.

All profit from the sales of this book go back into promoting it so more people can hear Emory's story.

Thank you so much for your help!
– James Wallace Birch

ABOUT EMORY WALDEN

Once a well-known activist and graffiti artist, Emory Walden mysteriously disappeared circa New Year's Day 2011. He claims to have played a little-known but instrumental behind-the-scenes role in sparking the political unrest in the United States that began in the early 2010s and which has defined much of that decade. His claims remain unconfirmed to this day. For reasons unknown, little can be found today of his existence.

ABOUT JAMES WALLACE BIRCH

Discontents is published by James Wallace Birch. James is from outside of Washington, D.C. He never heard from Emory again. He was married a few years back and together he and his wife live happily in the suburbs.

JamesWallaceBirch@gmail.com